DESTINATION YOU

AN AGE-GAP LESBIAN ROMANCE

J.J. ARIAS

For my wife.

CHAPTER 1

TAYLOR LOPEZ SHOULD'VE USED a suitcase with wheels instead of stuffing three days' worth of clothes into a duffle bag she hoped to fit in an overhead compartment.

Usually, she'd have no trouble packing light. Half the reason she'd moved to New York after high school was to live at the center of the universe while having her pick of airports; gateways waiting to be explored.

But a ten-year high school reunion, one spanning a long weekend, required more than a couple of flexible outfits. She was so excited about the trip, she hadn't realized how heavy the duffle and backpack had gotten while stuffing clothes into it.

It was only that morning, when she had already squeezed into the hot, muggy, urine-scented D-train taking her from the Bronx apartment she shared with her ex-girlfriend, who was now mostly staying at her *new* girlfriend's place, that she realized she should have called a shuttle, or an Uber, or freaking walked the eleven miles to LaGuardia.

In early July, the city was already sweltering before noon. If she missed anything about Miami, it was the ubiquitous and almost wanton presence of air conditioning.

When she first moved to the city, she was shocked that her three-hundred-square foot Chelsea studio had neither a full-sized fridge nor an AC. The window unit it had rattled like an injured 747 trying to take flight. As soon as her lease ended, she took off for a more cost-effective borough. Her Fordham building was nothing to look at from the outside, but at least it had a brand-new split that turned her bedroom into a meat locker.

Trading looks for comfort, Taylor tossed her long, brown hair into a messy bun and waited for the reflective train doors to open. Even her loose tank top and light joggers were stifling. She was eager to get out of the suffocating subway car packed with people returning to work, or going to the airport, or judging by the smell, attending a sauteed onion convention.

"Delayed," Taylor grumbled, her attention on her phone as she followed the throng snaking its way through security.

Taylor closed her eyes and accepted that her flight was taking off two hours later than expected. She decided to be grateful. At least hers wasn't one of a hundred flights canceled outright thanks to some computer glitch crippling an air traffic control tower.

In the middle of the terminal, people were arguing and yelling into phones. Phones on speaker.

Once through security, Taylor popped her earbuds back in her ears, let the soothing dream pop wash over her, and adjusted the pack on her back. Hanging the increasingly heavy duffle across her modest chest, she set out for somewhere to eat lunch.

Taylor wasn't a big bar food person, and she'd never acquired a taste for beer. Normally, she would have checked the bar off her list of possibilities as she passed it, her eyes scanning the other food court offerings instead, but her attention snagged on a woman nursing a full pint. The woman wore glasses now, oversized ones with thin tortoise-shell frames.

She was older, too. She was ten years older than the last time she saw her. Dark hair fell in soft waves like crumpled silk, stopping at her jaw as she scrolled through her phone.

Mrs. Alonso.

Taylor's high school history teacher.

She had been Taylor's crush for three years—opened her mind and made her curious about the world... Infected her with insatiable wanderlust... and regular lust, too.

In tight jeans that hugged the curves Taylor spent years dreaming about, and a light cotton blouse, Mrs. Alonso was like a superhero in disguise. Or maybe without her disguise, Taylor couldn't think.

Even without her formerly long hair in a tight bun, or a severe black blazer making the sharp edges of her high cheekbones and strong jaw sharper, an intimidating air swirled around Mrs. Alonso. She wore it like a perfume. *Eau de back-off.*

Taylor knew she was standing in the middle of the walkway and blocking traffic. Knew she was staring. Knew that an odd freeze or flight thing was happening to her, but it wasn't until someone slammed into her and called her an idiot that she moved toward the airport bar.

As she walked, Taylor pulled the hair tie off and shook out her hair. Hoping she was giving sexy bedhead rather than hot mess, she tossed her long hair to one side. She moved the duffle bag strap to her shoulder so it didn't sit awkwardly and unflatteringly between her boobs. Digging into the side of the duffle where she'd stashed her toiletries, she spritzed herself with perfume to cover the scent of the subway.

"Jeez, lady. You got that all over me!" A man walking behind her made a show of wiping his shoulder like Taylor had tagged him with mace.

In Miami, she would've apologized. In New York, she couldn't show weakness. "Don't worry, it's unisex." She sniffed the air. "And an improvement. You're welcome."

"Hilarious," he grumbled.

As she stepped out of the busy walkway and into the slower paced food court, Taylor let her city armor slip away. With her eyes on Mrs. Alonso, she drifted back in time.

Adrenaline blasted through Taylor. Every step she took unleashed havoc on her nervous system, her brain, her pulse. She'd imagined scenarios like this as a teenager. Thought up all the ways she might casually meet Mrs. Alonso outside school and charm the pencil skirt right off of her. She imagined Raquel being swept away and saying something like, 'You're not like other girls your age.' Taylor would have cringed if she had time.

Taylor wasn't enamored with her because she was one of the few teachers at Our Lady of Solitude High School who wasn't a nun, or because she was the only one under forty, or because Taylor had an unhealthy obsession with *Saving Annabel* and *Bloomington* at the time, or because Mrs. Alonso was the most objectively attractive person she'd ever seen—although that was a big part of it.

The way the woman made her feel is what had enthralled her. Mrs. Alonso woke something up in her. Activated her. Made her feel alive. Made her aware of everything that existed outside her tiny Miami bubble.

Considering it to be divine providence, Taylor suppressed her racing heart and heaved her bag onto an empty stool two seats down from Mrs. Alonso.

Mrs. Alonso didn't look away from her phone. She kept her face neutral. Some people would call her demeanor icy, but Taylor knew better. Mrs. Alonso was the first woman who'd ever told her class full of Catholic school girls they never had to smile or be pathologically polite if they didn't want to. A radical notion.

Mrs. Alonso almost never smiled. It was something to earn.

When Taylor slid into the seat next to her, Mrs. Alonso looked up from her phone. Her dark eyebrows, expertly arched and penciled in against her perennially tanned skin, twitched. Mrs. Alonso obviously recognized her, but she couldn't place her.

Bronzed honey eyes, still as big and deep and mesmerizing as she remembered, searched her. Scouring her face for familiar markers.

Mrs. Alonso's expression was serious. Unreadable. The reason for her undeserved *RBF* designation was still delightfully apparent.

Her lips—full and pale pink—parted, but didn't curve into a smile. They teleported Taylor back ten years. She was a seventeen-year-old with an unbearable crush.

"Mrs. Alonso," she managed, her hammering heart making her

voice sound alien to her own ears. "I don't know if you remember me." Taylor waited a few seconds to see if her expression changed. When it didn't, she added, "Solitude. Class of 2012. I'm—"

"Miss Lopez," she finished the sentence, her voice richer and huskier and even more likely to drop a panty than Taylor recalled. "I remember you."

CHAPTER 2

WHEN RAQUEL BOOKED her travel from Vermont to Miami, she'd groaned at having to take a connecting flight in New York. When she learned her flight had been delayed, she wished she'd picked the Atlanta connector instead.

She didn't complain for long. The school had been gracious enough to comp her expenses, and she'd been the one to select the cheapest flight. Plus, if she was taking three guilt-ridden days away from her responsibilities, she wasn't going to allow herself to be in a bad mood.

The last thing she expected to happen while killing time in an airport bar was to have a former student saunter up to her. She turned her phone face down on the bar, hiding the live-streaming video from the cameras in her house.

Taylor Lopez didn't look like the gangly girl she remembered. The person sitting across from her with an expectant smile had undeniably grown up since the last time she'd seen her.

Raquel stopped her gaze from dropping below her fresh, pretty face, cheeks bright from the obvious exertion of hauling her bags.

What she could see in her peripheral vision was dangerous enough. Unblemished olive skin. A smooth, slender neck. Visible collarbones. The suggestion of cleavage exposed by her tank top. A thin, abstract wave tattoo on her tanned forearm.

"Do you mind if I join you?" Taylor's question came after she'd already made herself comfortable. Before Raquel responded, Taylor was already talking. "It's so crazy to run into you today, of all days. I'm on my way to Miami for my ten-year reunion."

Raquel ran her thumb back and forth over the bottom of the glass, picking up the condensation created by her warming, low-carb beer. "Then it's not a coincidence."

Taylor's doe eyes sparkled with excitement. "Shut up! You're going too?"

With a lip twitch, Raquel tipped her head. "Receiving an award from your class."

Dimples bloomed on Taylor's slim cheeks. Her ever-broadening smile had a contagious quality. Raquel found her lips tingling and eager to return the expression.

"Well..." Taylor rested her chin in her hand, her eyes still fixed so securely on Raquel it sent a warmth spreading over her skin. "You were my favorite teacher, so that makes sense. It was too late for me to vote when I found the email in my spam." Her nose wrinkled when she winced, but her smile didn't falter. "My vote was going to you."

Raquel took a sip of her flat beer, needing a break from Taylor's solar flare gaze. "Thank you."

"Can I get you something?" The bartender, dressed in black and flashing shockingly white, equine teeth, leaned against the bar.

Taylor accepted the menu he offered and glanced over at her. "Did you order something to eat?"

Raquel nodded. "Cobb salad." She didn't add that while airport lettuce sounded gross, it was the only thing she could eat on her new low-carb diet.

"Okay," Taylor said, turning to the bartender, "I'll have that too. And an iced tea, please. Thanks."

He nodded and disappeared.

"When did you move to New York?" Taylor asked, folding a leg beneath herself while she rested her arm on the backrest.

"I didn't. I live in western Vermont."

"Vermont," she repeated, her eyes bright. "I love it there. I went skiing in Stowe a couple of years ago. Are you still teaching history?"

Raquel nodded. "I've graduated to college professor."

Taylor moistened her pink lips. "Should I call you Prof. Alonso then?" She quirked her eyebrow in a way that was almost flirtatious.

"Or Dr. Alonso." She exaggerated her serious tone.

Taylor laughed, her throat bobbing as she did. The sound caused an unexpected pang of excitement in Raquel's chest.

"Congratulations, Dr. Alonso. What did you get your doctorate in? I mean, history, obviously. What was your dissertation about?"

Without getting into the extremely granular topic, Raquel provided the same general answer she usually did. "How female spies were crucial to the allied forces in World War II."

"I just read the best book about Virginia Hall! She had to be part of your research, right?"

Raquel leaned back. She wasn't expecting that response.

Until their lunch arrived, they discussed the American spy who didn't let her gender, or disability, stop her incredible efforts in occupied France.

"Do you teach at an all-women's college?" Taylor asked while shaking pepper over her sliced avocado.

Raquel moved a halved boiled egg to the side of her plate. "It became co-ed in the late sixties."

Taylor smirked, looking like she was debating whether to say what she was thinking. "I guess that's good for you."

Raquel cocked her head to the side.

"Actually, I bet you inspire crushes in all genders." She speared a piece of avocado and popped it in her mouth. "So it probably doesn't matter."

Before Raquel could process what she'd implied, Taylor barreled forward with her conversation.

"I can't believe I haven't seen most of these girls in ten years." She said it like it was an immeasurable amount of time. "It's weird to spend your whole life with people and then scatter. Why am I nervous about seeing them? I've known them since first grade."

A year away from her *thirtieth* high school reunion, Raquel had to resist the urge to laugh. *You think ten years is weird? Wait until half the girls you went to school with have become grandmothers.* Raquel shuddered at the thought.

"What do you do in New York?" Raquel indulged her curiosity while picking at her unappetizing, thirty-dollar salad.

She straightened, jutting out her chin. "I like to call myself a scribe." After a beat, she shrugged. "It sounds more exciting than transcriptionist, right?"

"Like a court reporter?" Raquel couldn't imagine Taylor—and the swagger she'd seemed to have acquired—sitting at the base of a judge's bench, typing away on one of those blank keyboards like a fifties girl Friday.

"Yup." She held her straw between her front teeth, drawing Raquel's attention to her mouth. "But I don't go to court. It's all recorded by a computer. If the lawyers or judge want a transcript, they call my office and identify the date and case. Then my boss sends me the recording and I type it up." She chuckled. "Sexy, I know. But I can work from anywhere and make thirty bucks an hour. Not bad for someone who didn't finish her college history degree."

Raquel's lip twitched into a momentary smile. She didn't remember every student from her ten years of teaching at her alma mater, but she remembered most of them. She remembered Taylor always sat at the front of the class. Always had interesting questions, but struggled to turn assignments in on time. It didn't surprise her that she didn't continue her studies. There was such a restlessness in her. A need to move. To explore. To see things for herself. After a lifetime in academia, Raquel understood how paradoxically stifling it could be; how limiting and sterile.

"And working from anywhere is important to you?"

"I needed a new passport last year because I ran out of pages." She chuckled and picked up her fork again. "I've transcribed child custody fights while sitting on the beach in India, murder trials while cruising the Brisbane River." She smiled again. "Beats sitting in an office, right?"

Curious about a life so alien to her own, Raquel leaned in. "What has been your favorite destination?"

Taylor replied without hesitation and told her about the Oasis she stayed in while visiting Namibia. While she talked about hot air balloons and biking across the highest red sand dunes in the world, Raquel was transfixed. She couldn't imagine that kind of freedom. Of adventure. Of choice.

An unstoppable burst of curiosity formed a question before she had time to moderate it. "And your... traveling companion doesn't mind that you work while on these trips?"

Taylor laughed. "I had a designated travel companion for three years." She pulled her phone out of the backpack hanging from a hook under the bar. With a few flicks, she pulled up something on her screen. "Now we're roommates and share custody of a Papillon named Phillip."

Accepting the phone being handed to her, Raquel suppressed any visible reaction. Three women were lined up in front of a Christmas tree and all wearing matching red and green flannel pajamas. At one end, Taylor was holding a cute, white and black dog who had not been spared the matching outfit. At Taylor's side was a very attractive blonde. A tall woman with a piercing and half of her head shaved stood behind her.

"The tall one with a mohawk, that's her *new* girlfriend." Taylor took her phone back, her gaze lingering on Raquel, investigating. Her energy dropped as she shifted in her seat. "Sorry, I mean. I'm not *sorry*, sorry. I just didn't think you'd be uncomfortable with me being gay."

Heat rushed over Raquel's skin like boiling water had been dropped on her *Carrie* style. "Oh, God. No. I'm not. Not at all."

If they'd been talking a while longer, if she didn't still feel like her teacher, Raquel would've told her she had her own ex-girlfriend, but it seemed too personal. Too intimate. It might require too much explanation. When she was Taylor's teacher, she'd been married to a man. Not that being pansexual was hard to understand, but she'd have to explain her name. Despite the divorce eight years ago, she'd kept his last name, but only because the name Raquel Miguel was so awful. She still didn't understand what her parents were thinking.

"Yeah?" Taylor's dark eyebrows shot up her face. "I mean, I know you worked at a Catholic school, so…"

"The same all-girls' school we both attended," she replied, wondering if Taylor would pick up what she was putting down. "I think Our Lady of Solitude High School has always broken the mold by welcoming everyone."

Taylor relaxed her shoulders, but didn't seem to catch her hidden meaning. "As long as you're Catholic, maybe. I remember when Maritza Sedillo brought in a book on natural remedies and was nearly branded a green witch. I'm pretty sure we could hear Sister Gloria losing her mind on the other side of campus."

"Sister Gloria," Raquel repeated. "That woman is an institution." She pictured the imposing nun. Six feet tall and made of steel. Even dressed in her all-white habit, she looked severe. She'd been Raquel's first mentor; taught her so much as a young teacher.

"I can't believe they finally made her retire after she turned ninety. You know she once caught me and my friends smoking under the bleachers on the soccer field, and after she called all of our parents, she made us each go into a different empty classroom and write on a whiteboard, '*I swear I will not debase myself with cigarettes*' about a thousand times." She smirked. "That was also the day I learned the word *debase*, so way to pull double duty, Sister."

Raquel recalled the formidable woman fondly. Sister Gloria had a way of rooting out rule-breakers. "Did it work?"

"Heck yeah!" She laughed. "I'm pretty sure it's a contributing factor to my carpel tunnel, but I never smoked again."

"I only had a couple years of experience when I started at Solitude. She used to sit at the back of my classroom every day and give me notes. Do you know how intimidating it is to have her judgmental eyes on you while teaching ninth graders about migration patterns?"

"Oh, come on. Nothing intimidates you. You're like Miranda Priestly, Cersei Lannister, and Claire Underwood levels of IDGAF."

It took Raquel a beat to match the pop culture references. "Aren't those all villains?" She raised a single brow.

Taylor's face flushed with color, but she didn't back down. "It depends on who you ask. If you ask the weak and unworthy, perhaps. If you ask me, then I would say they're all bosses our misogynistic culture doesn't know how to appreciate."

Allowing herself to feel flattered, Raquel couldn't suppress her smile. "It looks like you're ready to start a dissertation on the topic."

Taylor laughed. The sound rushed over Raquel and seeped into her skin, warming her. "I bet if I strung together all my late-night social media musings, I'd be halfway there. You definitely don't want to get me started on why all the female villains in Disney movies are really the heroes, but you know, misogyny."

Raquel couldn't be more interested.

"You know you're intimidating, right?" Taylor asked after ordering a glass of water once their plates were cleared away.

Raquel leaned back, crossing one leg over the other for effect and instantly regretting the uncomfortable position. "Am I?"

"It's that look!" Taylor pointed at her. "You can melt bones with that thing."

Pretending not to know what she meant, Raquel slipped her hand beneath her thigh to hold her leg. She'd been told she was too intense. Too unapproachable. Too cold.

It was Sister Gloria who'd reassured her. Who insisted she should never break off pieces of herself to fit in anyone's box. A lesson she hadn't seemed to learn in her personal life, but that she'd taken to heart in a professional context.

"You wouldn't have come over here if you found me intimidating."

Taylor moistened her lips again, her teeth dragging over her bottom lip. "Well…" She held Raquel's gaze before dropping her attention to her mouth. When her gaze shot back up to Raquel's eyes, she felt it rush over her like hands and lips and teeth. "I did say that I have a soft spot for misunderstood women."

"Can I get you anything else, ladies?"

The bartender was a sheet of ice reacting to her body with a sizzle.

Raquel sat up, clearing the haze that had fallen over her. "I should get going." She checked the time on her phone. "My flight is boarding soon. The check, please."

"Just one check." Taylor winked at her. "I'd like to treat my favorite teacher to lunch."

"That's not necessary—"

"Please." Taylor's hand was warm and soft when it slid over hers. "I insist."

"That's going to cost nearly three hours of transcribing."

Taylor laughed. She did it so often. So freely. "I guess I'll have you to think about when I'm typing up three hours of jury selection." Her eyes brightened.

Raquel slid off the stool, taking her time collecting her things to give her circulation a chance to return the feeling to her left leg. "I suppose I'll owe you one."

She opened her phone, quickly closing her home security system and opening her electronic boarding pass. She double checked her gate number.

Taylor abruptly looked away from Raquel's phone and checked her smart watch. "I have an hour before takeoff. Guess I'll be seeing you at the welcome happy hour later."

In an act of recklessness, Raquel let her gaze roll over Taylor's lean form. "Maybe," she said. "Safe travels, Miss Lopez. Thank you for lunch."

She walked away, adding a sway to her curvy hips, knowing Taylor was watching her. Hoping she was.

CHAPTER 3

SETTLED INTO HER WINDOW SEAT, Raquel closed her eyes, crossed her arms, and tried to get comfortable; an arduous task given the tiny space.

They delayed her flight three more times before it boarded. She should've been tired enough to knock out as soon as they hit cruising altitude, but she couldn't doze off.

While she'd waited at the gate, she considered looking for Taylor. She wondered if she was still at the airport.

Raquel didn't give in to temptation, even if she'd had a better time chatting with Taylor over abysmal salads than she had on her last five dates combined.

Without her permission, Raquel's mind drifted to lunch. To Taylor's face. To the dimples seared into her corneas.

She bumped into the man sitting next to her, looking for a better position. She glanced over to apologize, but he apologized to her instead and then leaned his body toward the person sitting in the aisle seat to give her more room.

It shouldn't have surprised her that Taylor dated women. She could tell who was dating at Solitude. She recalled more than one young lady looking at Taylor longingly across the room. Taylor never looked back. Her attention was always laser-focused on the lesson.

Their lunch conversation returned to her mind. What had she said about crushes? Was Taylor impliedly confessing her own?

A trickle of excitement dripped into Raquel's stomach. She wasn't ignorant. She knew some of her students had developed minor infatuations over the years. It was normal and usually harmless.

It happened more often with her college students than it had in high school. She could usually see them coming a mile away. The ones who sat in the front and stayed after class to talk. Who watched her too closely. Who never missed class and signed up for office hours even if they didn't need extra help.

Raquel found herself smirking. She'd had her own crushes as a student. Even in her doctoral program, she'd developed a serious fondness for her department chair. An impossible to please woman with slicked back white hair and a penchant for finding something to criticize. With a chuckle to herself, she realized Taylor might be on to something with her villain theory.

How had they talked for so long? There were no obvious gaps or silences. No hiccups. Raquel could've listened to Taylor recount her travels for hours. She relayed everything with such enthusiasm. Such wonder. Like she'd visited places to truly see them, not just check them off a list. She really appreciated their essence, their uniqueness.

Was it strange to notice how attractive Taylor had become? To so easily recall the way her throat bobbed when she laughed? To feel the early roil of something in her chest, like a pot on the verge of simmering?

Objectively, there was nothing wrong with enjoying the company of a former student. She knew that. But Taylor had been a teenager the last time she'd seen her. There was something unsettling about that.

Raquel closed her eyes again and forced the thoughts of Taylor from her mind.

It had been eight years since she'd last been in Miami. She couldn't imagine that the place where she'd lived for over thirty years could feel so foreign.

There was nothing left for her there. Soon after she moved to Vermont to pursue her PhD, her mother died unexpectedly. Not long after that, her father suffered a stroke. When he started showing signs of dementia, she could no longer abide his wishes to continue living alone in Miami.

It had broken her heart to sell her parents' house. The one they had purchased after years of backbreaking work; her mother sweating in a garment factory and her father on his hands and knees in the dirt installing sprinkler systems. He'd been a professor of electrical engineering before they joined the mass Cuban exodus of the Mariel Boatlift in the summer of 1980. Her mother had been a celebrated ballerina.

Raquel was only four when they crammed into a rusty boat, stuffed so full that the barely seaworthy craft heaved with the combined weight of a hundred desperate souls. She only had fragments of memories, but she heard the stories her parents whispered when they arrived at their relative's Hialeah home. Despite their hushed tones, she heard them talking about people drowning in sabotaged vessels. Boats with holes cut in the hulls or deliberately destroyed in other ways.

All she could remember clearly was clinging to her mother and burying her head in the crook of her neck. She remembered the noise and chaos and the wet tears on her face. She remembered her mother telling her not to cry. Telling her to be brave. Not to let them see her fear.

Ten years it took them to buy their little house in the space between Coconut Grove and Downtown. The little undesirable tract that was worth millions now. Owning a home was as important to them as sacrificing every penny to afford Raquel's Catholic school tuition.

She would have loved to keep the house in their family, to entertain the idea of moving back to it someday, but her father's care was too expensive.

Raquel wished she could shut her eyes tightly enough to banish the worry. In the six years her dad had been living with her, she'd never left him. Not once. Not even for the night.

When she mentioned the award and all-expenses-paid trip to Miami to Nadia, her dad's primary home health aide, she convinced Raquel to accept. Nadia promised to arrange twenty-four-hour care and make sure the additional aides knew his routine and understood his needs. Knowing how hard it had been to find a single Spanish-speaking aide who also got along with her dad, she was skeptical. She was so tired that she allowed herself to believe it was a good idea.

It felt wrong to be flying away from him. She should be home taking care of her father. She should be grading assignments from the Sex and Gender in Antiquity seminar, or the freshman Western Civilization class she was teaching that summer, or working on drafting her next book. *Publish or perish* was so much realer than she imagined as a young TA complaining about checked-out professors.

Raquel forced herself to take a deep breath. She'd already committed to the trip, and she'd gotten regular updates from Nadia that her dad was doing just fine. Her therapist had also agreed that caregiver fatigue was real and she wouldn't be any good to anyone if she burned out. A break was long overdue.

She clenched every muscle in her body and then relaxed it one section at a time. Her hands. Her shoulders. Her jaw.

After taking several deep, cleansing breaths, Raquel relaxed into her headrest. She let herself remember lunch again. Let herself feel something other than crippling worry.

Her life was too complicated for romance. Plus, she couldn't flirt with a woman she'd known as a teenager. A woman half her age.

Those were objective facts she knew to be true. But with two hours left on her flight to Miami, she decided there was no harm in a little daydreaming.

CHAPTER 4

WHILE TAYLOR WAITED for Mrs. Alonso's flight to land in Miami, she debated whether waiting for her was creepy or cute. It all depended on whether she wanted to see her or not, she supposed. For sure, it was less weird than her original plan, which was to try to switch her ticket from her flight to Mrs. Alonso's.

The waiting for her wasn't the strange part, she realized. It was knowing her flight number to figure out that her flight was both arriving after hers and at what gate.

Taylor hadn't planned to memorize Mrs. Alonso's flight number, it just kind of happened. When she noticed it was still marked delayed on the arrivals board when she landed in Miami, she found herself sticking around.

Maybe she'll think it's sweet that I waited so we could ride to the hotel together.

She dropped her bags in an empty chair next to the gate. There was no flight leaving from that gate after the one from LaGuardia arrived, so she had the space to herself. She felt strangely alone in a sea of empty blue chairs.

Unless she's not staying at the hotel, you dummy.

The school had gotten them a great group rate at the hotel where the reunion was happening, but Mrs. Alonso didn't have to stay there. Maybe she wanted to stay in the comfort of her parents' house, or with friends, or maybe her husband was coming to meet her later in the weekend and they were going to—

Taylor shook her head while she paced. No adult was going to want to stay at someone else's house for three days. And even if she wasn't staying at the hotel, she would still be touched that Taylor cared enough to wait.

Or she's going to think you're clingy and desperate.

Dropping her shoulders, Taylor groaned. There was no way to know how her gesture would be received.

By the time Mrs. Alonso's flight touched down, the afternoon was starting to burn away into early evening. The sun wouldn't actually set until after eight, but at least the heat would be more manageable when they emerged from the airport.

As soon as the gate opened and the first passengers began filing out, Taylor realized she had no idea what to do with herself. She didn't want to look like a puppy waiting for its humans to come home, but she didn't want to play it so cool that she missed her walking out.

Thanks to a last-minute possession by the ghost of James Dean, Taylor pulled on her sunglasses, jammed her hands in her joggers, and leaned against the column where she'd been charging her phone.

Behind a pair of women in orange and red saris, Mrs. Alonso rolled out like she was walking in slow motion. Sunglasses on, expression set to kill—there should be a smoke machine filling the surrounding floor. Slow, bass-heavy, music punctuating every deliberate step of her ballet-flat covered feet. The carry-on she was rolling, disappearing somewhere behind her.

Hammering in her chest, Taylor's heart was a prisoner making a daring escape. Perhaps two black teas while she waited had been a bad idea. Dropping dead at Mrs. Alonso's feet wasn't exactly the smooth move she was plotting.

Before Taylor had to come up with a way to get Mrs. Alonso's attention, the woman turned her attention toward her.

With every fiber of self-control, Taylor continued to hold up the column, desperately trying to put out chill vibes. Her presence there was overeager enough. She had to play the moment right.

"Miss Lopez." She stopped in front of Taylor, her hand on the handle of her bag. "What are you doing here?" Her tone didn't give away that she was surprised, either happily or otherwise.

Despite the excitement of a colony of bees drunk on Red Bull, Taylor responded with an intentionally slow smirk. "My flight just landed," she lied, but it was so white it barely counted. "It was taxiing so long, I thought we might just drive the whole way here." She pointed at the board above the gate. "I noticed yours was just arriving. If you're going to the hotel, we can share a ride." She delivered her lines as coolly as she could manage.

Mrs. Alonso perched her sunglasses on top of her head, blasting Taylor with her dark, sultry gaze. If she hadn't been leaning against something, she might have fallen over like a tree chopped at the ankles.

It was obvious, almost instantly, that Mrs. Alonso didn't believe her, but she didn't ask anymore questions. She moistened her lips with the very tip of her tongue and leveled her with a look that swept over her face.

"How thoughtful," Mrs. Alonso said before turning away.

Throwing on her backpack and grabbing her leaden duffel bag, Taylor scrambled to catch up. She tried not to check out Mrs. Alonso's hourglass-shaped body, or imagine a Coke bottle crying with envy. She forgave herself for failing.

"I suppose this means you did not arrange for the hotel shuttle to pick you up, Miss Lopez?" she asked casually when Taylor caught up with her a few seconds later.

Being low-key chastised by Mrs. Alonso, Taylor realized, was her new kink. She didn't mention that she forgot hotel shuttles existed. When she traveled, she liked to live like a local as much as possible and avoided hotels and tourist zones.

"I guess it's a good thing I waited for you then." Taylor adjusted the bag digging into her shoulder and wished she'd made ten different choices that morning. A shirt that wasn't gauzy thin, or maybe borrowing a carry-on with wheels. Definitely should have worn make up and maybe done something with her hair. "Also, you know you can call me Taylor, right?"

Mrs. Alonso gave her a quick glance before getting on a descending escalator. Her expression was unreadable, sending a confusing spike of heat pulsing over Taylor's skin.

She didn't say anything until they stepped off the escalator and followed the signs for shuttles and other ground transportation.

"I suppose you know my name is Raquel," she said so dismissively, Taylor wasn't sure whether it was an invitation or a statement of fact.

Taking a plunge slightly more exhilarating and death-defying than the time she jumped out of a plane, Taylor tested out the shape of the name before speaking it.

When they stopped under one of the many designated bus zones Mrs. Alonso had obviously looked up beforehand, she went for it.

"Raquel." She extended her hand. "I'm Taylor. It's nice to meet you. Again."

A dark gaze slid down Taylor's body and landed on her open palm. Before Taylor could pull her hand back and abandon her attempt to be cute, Mrs. Alonso gave it a quick squeeze.

Taylor bit the inside of her cheek to keep from grinning.

Play it cool, she reminded herself. *Play it cool.*

They only had to wait a few minutes in the thick humidity of the covered arrivals area before a small white shuttle bus pulled up. It took another minute to show the driver her hotel confirmation and convince the woman to let her on, even though she was only expecting five passengers and not six.

After storing her bag in the rack at the back and then Mrs. Alonso's—no, Raquel's—Taylor took the seat next to her.

"Do you do that often?" Raquel asked, pulling her sunglasses back on while the shuttle driver waited for the bus blocking her in to move.

"Do what?"

"Talk your way into things."

Taylor smiled. "Sometimes," she admitted. "But I only use my superhuman power of persuasion for good and only when absolutely necessary."

Raquel's lip twitched in amusement, the subtle shift sending a rush through Taylor's system.

Taylor relaxed into her seat. Her gamble had paid off.

As soon as they pulled out from the covered area, Taylor's eyes were assaulted by the sun. She pulled on her sunglasses. "It's almost sunset. How the hell is it so bright? I swear the sun is so much brighter here. By the time I adjust, it's going to be time to go back to the hazy Bronx. Before my parents moved to Portugal a few years ago so my dad could be a digital nomad, I used to visit Miami more, but now I can't see the point."

Raquel nodded, her attention out the window as the palm tree-lined streets and bumper-to-bumper traffic were the first to welcome them back.

"When was the last time you were in Miami?" Taylor asked.

"A long time ago," she replied, her voice heavy, like it was weighed down with unhappy memories. She picked at the cuticles of her manicured nails painted a deep plum.

Picking up that Raquel needed a little time to acclimate, Taylor didn't ask any more questions. She did, however, notice that Dr. Alonso no longer wore a wedding ring.

CHAPTER 5

THE HOTEL WAS an uninspiring chain at the furthest edge of Downtown Miami. Nestled between the I-95 overpass and a construction site for a forthcoming high-rise, the place was close enough for a view of Biscayne Bay, if it wasn't for the line of skyscrapers standing in the way.

Taylor opened the door to her room with her foot and happily dropped her heavy bags in the closet. Relishing the freezing cold room, Taylor collapsed onto the enormous king-sized bed face first and sighed.

She was being lulled into a nap when her phone buzzed. And then again. And again. The telltale sign of a group text burning up.

Flipping onto her back, Taylor pulled her phone out of her pocket. As she suspected, the group chat named STATE CHAMPS '12 followed by a bat and softball emoji was alive with white chat bubbles.

Jessica: *Tay, did you land already?!! I just got to the hotel. Where is everybody??*

Alexis: *I'm stuck at the freaking off-ramp. Why is there still so much traffic?? Where is everyone going at 7:30 on a Friday??*

Brianna: *Is Taylor's flight still delayed? I'm dropping the baby off with my mom and I'll be there in twenty. I have a mini-bar in my trunk, so you bitches better not start pre-gaming without me. I've been looking forward to this for a month! I pumped so much in advance the kid is going to have enough for a week!*

Jessica: *Jesus, Bri! TMI*

Brianna: *Oh, okay... Because when I helped you weed whack your vag the first time, that was TOTALLY NOT TMI.*

Jessica: *That's not the same thing! We were dating then!*

Laughing, Taylor responded before the conversation took a header off a cliff.

Taylor: *I just got to my room. I'm jumping in the shower real quick. My room is 801. I'll ask the front desk to give you guys keys when you get here. Come up and let yourself in!*

By the time Taylor emerged from the bathroom with her wet hair wrapped in a towel and wearing jeans and a cute crop top she cut from an old Heart concert T-shirt, Jessica was sitting in the armchair by the window looking down at her phone.

The former all-American pitcher was by far the tallest in their friend group. At over six-feet tall, she towered over all the other students and most of the teachers. Being the only Bahamian-American in a sea of Hispanic girls didn't trip her up though. When she opened her mouth, she spouted Cuban slang in the streets and enviable, proper Spanish in front of everybody's *abuela.*

"Tay!" Jessica unfurled her long legs as she stood.

"Jess! I've missed you!" Wrapping her arms around Jessica's body, the one that had grown softer since she graduated college and stopped playing D1 softball, Taylor squeezed her tight. "Sorry, I didn't mean to motorboat you."

Jessica laughed. "Girl, it's been a minute since anyone has, so I don't mind."

"God, don't tell Brianna that. She'll ask you to be her third again."

With a pained expression, Jessica agreed. "Despite everything her husband and I tell her, she won't let that dream go."

Taylor laughed. "Danny has the patience of the saint."

"Right?" She chuckled. "We play golf together a few times a month.

We've been contemplating making up a girlfriend for me so Bri will stop wiggling her eyebrows at us every time we go."

While they talked about Jessica's new job teaching health and coaching softball at a local public high school, someone knocked on the door a second before opening it.

"Sup, bitches!" Alexis burst through the door, her prematurely salt-and-pepper hair in her trademark tight bun with the bottom half shaved. All her life, Alexis was asked whether anyone had told her that she looked like a younger, Cuban Rosie O'Donnell. Yes, they had. And yes, she took it as the highest compliment, as evidenced by her Rockford Peaches tattoo sleeve.

"Alexis!" Taylor sprang forward and tackled her in a full-contact hug. "I'm so glad you made it!"

"And all I had to do was trade two primo day shifts for three nights," she replied, giving Taylor a tight squeeze.

"Aren't you queen of the nurses?" Jessica asked, waiting to give Alexis a kiss on the cheek.

"Charge nurse," she corrected. "And we work overnights too."

The front door burst open again. In the doorway, Brianna stood with a huge brown paper bag in each arm. "Are you all going to help me, or are you just going to stare at me?"

At barely five-feet tall, Brianna was an imposing, pushy little dynamo. From the time she and Taylor had been in kindergarten together, she'd been unapologetically bossy, and Taylor couldn't love her more.

Dutifully, the three of them rushed to relieve Brianna of her bags.

"Jesus, Bri." Taylor took a bag. "What do you have in here?" She gave her a crushing side hug while juggling the bottles threatening to rip through the paper.

"I haven't had a drop of alcohol in a year. If I'm doing it, I'm doing it big."

"As if you ever do anything *small*," Alexis joked before kissing her on the cheek.

From the casual way they all greeted each other, it was obvious

Taylor was the only one missing from the group. The one no one had seen in a few years.

"I can't believe you were delayed so long," Brianna said after sending Jessica and Alexis to get enough ice to fill the bathroom's double sinks. The exaggerated haul of booze wasn't going to fit in the room's small refrigerator.

"You'll never guess who I ran into at the airport." Taylor sat on the edge of the bed, a grin on her lips. "And had lunch with."

Brianna kicked off her flats and sat in the armchair by the window. "Who?"

"Mrs. Alonso." She cleared her throat. "I'm sorry, I mean… Raquel."

Brianna's artificially green eyes widened. "The praying mantis?"

"Don't call her that," Taylor snapped. She hated the nickname when they were in high school, and she really hated it now.

"Don't call who what?" Jessica asked when she walked in with two buckets of ice. Alexis followed her in with two more.

"She doesn't want me to call the love of her life the praying mantis."

"Alonso? Why are we talking about her?" Alexis asked before dumping ice into the sink with a satisfying rattle. "Did she win that teacher appreciation award?"

"Because Taylor found one of those monkey paw things and made a wish." Brianna laughed. "Apparently, she had lunch with her at the airport."

Heat flooded Taylor's face, but there was nothing she could do about it.

Alexis slid onto the dresser in front of the wall-mounted TV. Her heels banged against the faux wood grain as she excitedly sought clarification. "Wait, what?"

Jessica sat on the edge of the bed next to Taylor. "Yeah… What?"

With a strange mix of excitement and apprehension over being ragged on by her friends, Taylor recounted her afternoon adventure.

"Wait a second." Brianna held up a hand. "So you and Alonso were like… vibing?"

"It sounds like they were vibing," Alexis agreed as if offering a second medical opinion.

"Alonso, though? No way." Jessica rested her weight on her open palms spread out on the bed behind her. "Doesn't she have a whole husband?"

Taylor shrugged. "She doesn't wear a ring anymore. And I don't know... there were eyes."

"Eyes?" Brianna tipped her head to the side. "What eyes? Describe the eyes."

"You know." Taylor tried to imitate Raquel's bedroom eyes while casually moistening her lips. "That look."

"Constipated?" Alexis guessed before dodging the pillow Taylor launched at her.

"I'm not saying I'm a hundred percent sure, you guys. But I think we were flirting." Worry tugged at her edges, keeping her excitement in check. "I may have come in a little hot. I talked too much. I was too excited. I should've played it cooler."

"There's still time for that, girl. Is she going to the welcome drinks thing tonight?" Brianna asked.

"She didn't say for sure, but I would guess so."

Brianna stood. "Well then, we have to do better than this." She pointed at Taylor's damp, wavy hair. "And that." She pointed at her shirt.

Taylor looked down at herself. "What? This one of my cutest looks."

Brianna made the sign of the cross over herself and put her hands together in prayer while looking up at the ceiling. "*Diosito*, help me."

"Don't listen to her. If I didn't look at you like a sister, I would totally hit on you," Alexis said in her defense.

"Thanks, Alex."

"Okay, but like, you've been rocking that bun for twelve years, babe. Maybe you're not Vidal Sassoon." Brianna made a face like speaking the truth was physically painful.

"Don't hate what you don't understand." She smoothed down her slicked back hair and super tight bun. "This is a certified femme magnet."

Jessica and Taylor murmured their agreement.

Brianna waved her away. "I'm the one who knows how to snag somebody, okay? Let's not forget I'm the only married one among you." She puffed out her chest and jabbed her small, round chin in the air.

"Yeah, because you bullied poor Danny into your first date." Jessica poured herself a drink.

"And the second, third, and fourth," Alexis added.

Taylor couldn't resist. "And sent him a detailed memo on how, where, and when to propose."

"Complete with pictures and how much to pay for the ring she pre-haggled with the jeweler," Jessica muttered into her cup and pretended she hadn't spoken.

"What are you people telling me that I don't know?" She put her hand on her hip. "I got what I wanted, right? That's the point here. Now sit down and bring me that shitty little blow dryer in the bathroom. If I'd known you were going to need me, I would've brought my ionic, ceramic *plancha*. I got it at the beauty supply when I still had my license. It's worth more than your life—"

"I don't need to iron my hair—"

"*Sientate*," Bri snapped, her mom voice and menacing eyes ready for action even though her kid was only three months old. "Someone make momma a vodka tonic so I can work."

No one disobeyed.

Before Taylor appreciated what was going on, she had a drink in her hand and Brianna was blow-drying her hair straight. As if they hadn't missed a day together since high school, they talked nonstop until Brianna had done her hair and makeup and picked out a slinky, white, V-neck shirt and black jeans for Taylor to wear.

Checking herself out in the mirror, Taylor had to admit Brianna was right. If Raquel was even a little into her, she wouldn't be able to resist her smokey eye and bold, red lip.

A little tipsy, and buzzing from her friends' encouragement, Taylor slipped her room key in her back pocket and set out to conquer.

CHAPTER 6

"THANK YOU, NADIA," Raquel said to the woman on the video chat. "I'm so glad it was a smooth day."

Nadia pushed a dark curl off her forehead. "I wanted you to see for yourself that he's doing great." She aimed her phone at Raquel's father, happily napping in his armchair by the picture window overlooking the front porch.

They spent a while longer on the phone until Raquel was sure she could rest easy for the night. She thanked Nadia about a thousand times and then prepared for the awkwardness of attending a social event alone.

Trading her soft robe for the tight Spanx she pulled up high enough to cut into her ribs, Raquel considered skipping the festivities. It's not like the welcome drinks were mandatory, more like a complimentary meet and greet.

She pushed away her doubt and trepidation. If she was sacrificing time with her dad, she wouldn't waste it by staying in.

She pulled out the outfit she'd steam-cleaned and hung up in the closet. It was a simple plum wrap dress, but it flattered her curves without flaunting them. Stuffing herself into a push-up bra, she heaved her girls up to where they'd been twenty years ago.

When she finished putting some product in her hair to accentuate the waves in her new bob, she threw on a little make-up too. Figuring *what the hell*, she even traded her comfortable glasses for contact lenses.

"Not bad," she said, checking out her reflection in the bathroom mirror. "You look damn good for forty-six." She didn't remind herself about the thirty pounds she could stand to lose and slipped on a pair of nude pumps.

Her confidence lasted as long as it took her to ride the shuttle from the hotel to the school a couple of miles away. There, she was assaulted by the sight of twenty-somethings congregating at the entrance of the small assembly hall at the corner of the school's Spanish-style courtyard.

Grown women she used to teach now showed off pictures of their own children. How much time had whizzed past her?

By the time she made it through the first crowd, she was desperate for a drink. Being back in the place she'd been both a student and a teacher was disorienting and surreal.

The assembly room hadn't changed since the nineties. Thick, brown and tan Berber carpet covered the floor, and the walls were still painted a pinkish tan.

A faint musty smell in the air transported her to her eleventh-grade ring ceremony. Receiving her class ring had felt like such a rite of passage. Such a moment in time. She wasn't sure where the ring was anymore.

Most of the chairs used to seat two hundred people at a time were removed from the room. A few dozen people were mingling in the altered space.

She got a glass of supermarket merlot in her hand as a woman Raquel didn't recognize shouted over the ambient noise.

"Welcome, class of 2012!"

The crowd cheered. Raquel judged that half the former students were in attendance. She only saw a handful of teachers, including Brother Peter, who'd taught trigonometry since before Raquel was born. No one exciting.

When the crowd settled, the woman continued. "Thank you all for coming tonight to kick off the best reunion weekend ever!" she screeched like she was practicing to be a garage band's new hype-man.

While she continued her remarks, a commotion yanked Raquel's attention to the entrance. She recognized the tall woman first. One of Taylor's best friends, if she remembered correctly. The one who'd won a full ride at a very prestigious university to play softball. The way they stumbled in joking with each other, she guessed they'd done some partying before the night's festivities.

Raquel held her breath until she saw her. Glossy brown hair long and loose around her shoulders. Perfect red lips. And her laugh. It wrapped itself around Raquel, filling her.

When Taylor and the group she'd been glued to in high school realized they'd walked in on something, they quieted down immediately.

Raquel tried to focus on what the woman was shouting.

"You'll all get bingo cards with bits of trivia on them. Not everyone provided a little factoid and all the cards are different, but the idea is to get around the room and talk to each other. First person to fill up their card wins a free spa treatment!" She held a gift card above her head.

As she explained the ice breaker game, Raquel knocked back her wine and retreated to the makeshift bar for another. While she waited in a short line, someone handed her a blank card with things like: *has been to Antarctica, had dinner with Aretha Franklin,* and *has a collection of 1,700 stamps.*

Raquel hadn't replied to the email asking for *fun facts.* All ice breaker games were anathema to her.

While she was accepting her drink and chatting with a pair of former students, Brother Peter sidled up to her. The young women scattered.

"Raquel, I wasn't sure that was you," he said over the scores of simultaneous conversations. "It's so nice to see you."

She accepted his pat on her arm.

"Brother Peter, I didn't know you were still around Solitude."

The sweet, extremely talkative, elderly man plunged her into a one-sided conversation about what he'd been doing in the eight years since she last saw him. She nodded and tried to listen.

Despite her best efforts, Raquel's attention drifted to the other side of the room.

At the center of the mixing groups, Taylor and her friends were excitedly meeting old friends. Raquel didn't belong there. She was on the periphery. Even if she attended her own thirty-year reunion, she was sure she wouldn't fit in. She just didn't have that readily accessible effervescence everyone else seemed to have. There was too much noise. Too much newness covering the old.

While Brother Peter droned, they picked up another former teacher. A crone named Mrs. Fraga who taught English and had given Raquel her only C in all of her academic life.

The woman pretended not to recognize Raquel. To make her uncomfortable, no doubt. They'd worked together for years and Raquel had changed little. She'd never been sure what she'd done to offend her other than ask questions. Being pushed to teach was offensive to some.

"Dr. Alonso," Taylor said while tapping her on the shoulder.

Raquel turned, not expecting the interruption, but welcoming the blast of energy in a stagnant interaction.

"I'm so sorry to interrupt." Taylor unleashed her dimpled smile on the others. "You left the lights on in your car. I don't want you to find a dead battery when you leave." With her doe eyes and her genuine smile, no one would guess Taylor was lying through her straight, white teeth.

For a moment, Raquel wasn't sure how to respond.

"Miss Lopez." Brother Peter gave her hand a squeeze. "You've always been thoughtful." He turned to Raquel. "You better take care of that, Raquel. You don't want to get into trouble later."

"Trouble," Raquel agreed, her eyes on Taylor. "I definitely want to avoid that."

CHAPTER 7

THEIR FOOTFALLS ECHOED as Taylor and Raquel strolled through the empty hall lined with blue lockers and closed doors leading to dark classrooms. Our Lady of Solitude High School hadn't changed a bit in ten years.

"Lying is a sin, Miss Lopez." Raquel's tone was sharp and disapproving, but it didn't fool Taylor. She'd not only followed Taylor out of the assembly room knowing full well there was no car, she'd led them out of the courtyard and into the main building.

"So is torture," Taylor countered, "and you looked pretty miserable being cornered by the *Dementor*. I think Jesus will forgive me for choosing the lesser of two evils."

"Dementor?" Raquel glanced over at her, her confusion apparent. "Brother Peter?"

"No, he's Cecil. You know… because he looks like a goofy little turtle." She slid her hands into her back pockets. "Mrs. Fraga is the Dementor because she sucks the fun out of everything."

When Raquel didn't appear to get the reference, Taylor felt childish for talking about a book series written for kids.

"Do you have nicknames for all your former teachers?"

Taylor instantly regretted not having called Fraga by her name. "We did for some."

Raquel's dark eyes glinted. "Did you and your friends have one for me?"

Laughing too loudly, Taylor shook her head. She didn't want to lie, so she changed topics.

"Who do you think is in your old classroom?" Taylor nodded toward the door at the end of the corridor.

Something unreadable crossed Raquel's face. "There's only one way to find out," she said, making it sound like a dare.

Following Raquel into the classroom, Taylor flipped on the lights. The posters on the walls were different, but the basics were the same. The same thirty desks faced the same wall-sized whiteboard. Angled in the corner was the same metallic brown desk, the one Raquel used to lean against when she talked.

"How does it feel being back here?" Taylor slid into her old desk. The one nearest Raquel's. She could almost feel the scratchy material of her old uniform. The over-starched white oxford shirt, the plaid skirt, the polished brown penny loafers.

Raquel glanced around the classroom. The distant look on her face made Taylor wonder whether she was also imagining how it used to look. "Strange."

Taylor leaned back in the hard seat, letting the buzz of too much vodka and being close to Raquel wash over her. She never imagined running into Raquel again and certainly never thought she'd be back in that classroom with her. It had been the setting for so many fantasies.

"I always loved watching you teach," Taylor confessed before she could think about what she was saying. What she was revealing.

Raquel slid onto the top of her desk, crossing her smooth, shapely legs and pushing Taylor closer to a coronary.

Taylor knew she shouldn't follow the curve of her calves. Shouldn't focus on the sliver of thigh exposed by her dress. Shouldn't strain her sight over the hint of cleavage. Shouldn't linger on her mouth, imagining the taste of her kiss.

"Yeah?" Raquel's lip twitched, but didn't go as far as curving into a smile. "Is that why you and your friends called me the praying mantis?" She quirked a brow.

Shock and shame had Taylor on her feet before Raquel finished her question. "I've never called you that." She stopped a foot away from Raquel. "I would never."

"No?" Raquel's full, plum lips eased into a smirk, her dark eyes shimmering in amusement, putting Taylor at ease. She was playing a game. "Why not?"

Taylor held her gaze, unsure of how much truth Raquel was expecting. How much could she handle? An hour of drinking and being egged on by her friends had interrupted the normal functioning of her brain. She couldn't tell the difference between mutual interest and wishful thinking.

"Didn't I tell you I'm a great defender of misunderstood, powerful women?" Taylor stepped in close enough to drown in Raquel's perfume.

While Taylor watched, Raquel moistened her lips. The tip of her tongue flashing for just a second, but it was long enough to snatch the air from Taylor's lungs. "And that's who you think I am, Miss Lopez? A *misunderstood* woman who needs defending?"

Taylor's heart crawled out of her chest and vibrated like a caged humming bird in her neck. There was no way she was reading this wrong. She couldn't be. The energy between them was unmistakable.

"I used to hang on your every word when you stood up here," Taylor confessed, inching closer until there was barely any space left between them. Until it was obvious that Raquel wasn't moving away. That she wanted to be within a breath of Taylor's lips.

Raquel's eyes moved slowly, deliberately. She dropped her gaze to Taylor's mouth and back up. "Is that what you were doing when you were watching me?" She bit her bottom lip, letting her teeth drag over her full flesh.

Heat thumped over Taylor's skin, electrifying her. "Mostly." She hadn't meant to whisper, but she was too transfixed to speak any louder.

Raquel's lip twitched into a knowing smirk, leaving no doubt she absolutely knew what she was doing. That she was trying to obliterate Taylor's self-control. Trying and succeeding. "And the other times?"

"I had such a wild imagination back then." Taylor didn't look away from the lips silently screaming her name. The ones she wanted so desperately to kiss. "It's your fault I have such a specific blazer and pencil skirt fetish." She forced her attention back to Raquel's eyes. "When my mind would drift, I'd imagine you asking me to stay after class... needing my help with something."

Raquel tipped her head to one side, intentionally exposing a mouthwatering length of neck as if testing her. "Help with what?"

Resisting the urge to put the games aside and lunge for what she wanted, Taylor pretended to think about it. Pretended the decade old fantasies hadn't come rushing back the moment she saw Raquel sitting at the airport bar.

"Help with all kinds of things." She couldn't tear her attention away from Raquel's neck. "But it always ended the same way." With lust clouding her judgment, she pirouetted over the point of no return. "You pressed against this desk and my hand sliding up your skirt."

For a full second, Raquel said nothing. She didn't back away. She didn't breathe. "How inappropriate," she said, her voice low and husky and thick with the same desire pulsing through Taylor's body. "That's incredibly illegal, not to mention completely unethical."

Taylor grinned, adrenaline heightening her senses. "Am I in trouble, Mrs. Alonso?"

"If you were my student, I would have to reprimand you." Her voice was just above a whisper.

There was no reason something so soft should be so shattering. Taylor imagined all the ways she wanted Raquel to punish her, but that wasn't a game she wanted to play. Not yet.

"I guess it's a good thing I'm not your student anymore." She leaned in, slipping effortlessly between Raquel's legs, parting them with her hips, sending her skirt sliding up her thighs. "You don't have to report me to the principal."

Raquel's mouth hovered warm and breathy over her lips. "I've always preferred to handle things myself," she whispered.

Taylor closed her eyes and pressed her lips to Raquel's waiting mouth.

Sweet and deep and complex and intoxicating, Raquel tasted like the red wine she'd been drinking. Fighting for dominance, Taylor tried to control the kiss, but she didn't stand a chance.

Raquel set the pace, forcing Taylor to slow down. To be less eager. Taking Taylor's bottom lip between her teeth, Raquel pulled.

Fuck.

Pain synthesized immediately into desire.

Wrapping her arms around Raquel's waist, Taylor deepened the kiss. When Raquel slipped her fingers through her hair, her nails scraping the nape of her neck as she pulled her closer, Taylor groaned.

Her entire body hummed like a Las Vegas neon sign. The act of kissing Raquel was both unbelievable and the realest thing she'd ever experienced. Hot and sensual and all-consuming, she lost herself in the kiss.

Dropping her hands down, Taylor slid her palms over her ass. The one she'd spent years staring at. The one that would make J.Lo jealous. When she squeezed her hard, Raquel tipped her head back and gasped.

Seizing the opportunity, Taylor slid her mouth over Raquel's neck. Gripping her harder, Taylor pulled Raquel closer, wishing she wasn't wearing jeans so she could feel her through the fabric when she pressed against her.

In retaliation, Raquel made a fist in her hair and pulled. The pain was a thousand little currents rushing to where she was already soaked and aching.

It spurred Taylor on. Running her teeth over Raquel's collarbone, she moved her hands to Raquel's outer thighs. Digging her fingers into soft flesh, she yanked her hard.

Without resistance, Raquel slid over the desk and slammed against Taylor's pelvis. At the hard contact, Raquel groaned.

"Don't leave a mark," she warned, jerking Taylor's head back.

Her unquestionable authority made Taylor's legs weaken. The sight of her lips, swollen and smeared, made her body turn to jelly.

"You're so fucking hot," Taylor confessed, breathless and possessed so completely by desire that she feared she might die before she found release.

Raquel's smile was mischievous, like she wanted nothing more than to watch her squirm. "Language," she warned, but her tone was too heavy with lust to sound serious.

As soon as Raquel released her hair, she leaned in again. Kissing her even more fiercely, all Taylor wanted to do was tear off her clothes and taste every inch of Raquel's body.

Sinking her nails into Taylor's upper back, Raquel kissed her hard before pushing her away. "We should go before anyone comes looking for us."

Through the thick haze impeding her thoughts, Taylor shook her head. "Why would anyone come here?"

Kissing her again, Taylor was convinced she'd never want to stop. Raquel's lips were every drug she'd ever been warned about. Instantly addictive and impossible to quit.

Raquel indulged her, moaning against her lips before pulling away again. "*We* came here." She leaned back on her open palms.

Taylor's gaze clung to Raquel's perfect body, dangerous curves on mouthwatering display. "This is not the way to convince me we should go," she groaned, eyeing her hungrily. She leaned over the desk, capturing Raquel's lips again.

For a moment, Raquel's high heels dug into the back of her thighs while she hooked her legs around her.

Fuck, yes.

Abruptly, Raquel unhooked her legs and slid off the desk. "We need to go." She wiped the smudged lipstick around her mouth as if that could erase the very obvious fact they'd been making out like teenagers.

"Let's go to your room," Taylor suggested, reaching out for Raquel's hand.

Allowing the intimate touch, Raquel used her free hand to clean the lipstick that was no doubt smeared all over Taylor's face. "Don't you think we've broken enough rules for one night?"

Taylor responded with double-barreled dimples. "There isn't a single rule against what we've done. What I hope we can keep doing." She cocked her head to the side, knowing she looked cute. "But if we try hard enough, I'm sure we can find some rules to break."

Raquel's dark eyes reflected her amusement, but she wasn't budging. "Goodnight, Miss Lopez. I'm sure you'll have a wonderful time with your friends where you belong." She squeezed Taylor's hand before letting it go. "Give me a few minutes before you walk out."

With a kiss on the cheek, Raquel was gone.

Taylor dropped into her old desk, dazed and shocked.

She closed her eyes and touched her lips.

"Holy shit."

CHAPTER 8

SITTING around a table in the old 24-hour diner they used to stumble into after parties, everyone but Jessica was nursing a serious hangover. After having passed out in Taylor's hotel room, they were all still in yesterday's clothes.

"I knew I shouldn't have drunk your trash vodka," Alexis said while looking down at her coffee, even though they all knew she was talking to Brianna.

Brianna, whose fair skin had taken on a greenish tint like she'd been encased in fake jewelry, didn't have the energy to argue. A first for her.

"It was all the sugary crap y'all mixed it with," Jessica said, her eyes bright and focused.

"We'll be fine after some greasy food," Taylor said, praying she was right. When she returned to the happy hour thing, she'd had way too much of the Hunch Punch Brianna made and smuggled in her enormous mom purse.

"Who knew Hawaiian Punch could do me so dirty? I used to love that stuff." Alexis rested her head in her hand and audibly groaned. "Now I'm not sure I can ever look at fruit punch again without wanting to hurl."

"Yeah, you liked it when you were twelve," Jessica joked. "I hope your palate has matured in the intervening fifteen years."

"I've taken, like, four Tylenol," Taylor complained. "Why won't this headache go away?"

"Drink more water," Jessica suggested for the third time.

Taylor tried, but almost immediately gagged. "God, why does everything taste like booze?"

"I think it's literally coming out of my pores," Brianna whined. "My kid might not breastfeed for a month."

"Oh, Jesus. You're not going to start talking about pumping again, are you? We already had to endure that production this morning." Jessica took a sip of coffee. "Whoever named it *pump and dump* is vile." She shuddered.

Taylor laughed. Brianna's pumping last night and this morning had caused Jessica an unwarranted amount of distress. Somewhere around the time Brianna was explaining the importance of maintaining a milk supply and Jessica compared her to the Panama Canal, Taylor and Alexis had fallen asleep on one side of the enormous bed.

"So where the hell did you disappear to last night?" Alexis asked, a glass of ice water pressed to her forehead.

Instead of an immediate and definite *what-do-you-mean* or *nowhere* or *ugh-I'm-going-to-puke-again*, Taylor hesitated. It was blood in the water and her old friends were gossip sharks.

Alexis put her glass down. "Taylor?"

Brianna's eyes shed some of their dull haze. "Bitch! Are you holding out on us?" She mulled over the possibility. "I didn't see Alonso, though." Her attention shot to Jessica. "Did you see her?"

With regret in her eyes, Jessica glanced at Taylor. "For a minute." She tried and failed to hide an amused grin. "Before Tay took her out somewhere and was gone for a solid hour," she muttered quickly into her coffee.

Alexis covered her mouth in disbelief. "You did not." She lowered her voice as if Sister Gloria was lying in wait to catch them doing something bad. "Did you and Alonso..." Using her coffee mug as a shield, she made a scissoring gesture. "At the school?"

"No! What's wrong with you?" Taylor whisper-shouted, also worried about ambush by nun considering how close they were to campus.

"You just turned eight shades of red, girlfriend." Brianna looked significantly less ill, like gossip had medicinal, restorative properties. "Spill."

Saved by the grits, Taylor had until the server finished unloading a million plates onto the table to come up with her story.

She wished Alexis hadn't asked her where she'd been. They hadn't made a big deal about it the night before, and Taylor had been grateful for whatever assumptions they'd made. She'd hoped she hadn't been gone long enough for them to notice she wasn't in the room.

It's not that she wanted to keep Raquel a secret, but she wasn't sure what happened, or more critically, what would happen next. The memories were a blur, like she was confusing a dream with reality.

Taylor's lips tingled like the time she discovered she was allergic to penicillin and her mouth swelled up like a botched filler job. All she knew for sure was that she wanted to kiss Raquel again. That she wanted to do a hell of a lot more than kiss her.

Raquel wanted that too, right? It wasn't like she was sitting in her hotel room regretting what they did. Taylor's nausea intensified at the possibility. She both dreaded learning what Raquel thought about things in the light of day and desperately needed to know what she was thinking.

What if she's hung up on the former-student thing? That can't really matter all that much, right? I'm like halfway to twenty-eight. That's a whole ass adult.

"Reprieve over," Brianna announced when the server left. "What's the tea? You're killing me!"

Taylor winced, a strange combination of pride and shyness coursing through her along with the lingering intoxication. "We may have kissed."

"Shut up!" Alexis shoved her, making no attempt to hide her giddiness. "No!"

"Where?" Brianna pressed.

Taylor thought about lying, but her alcohol-soaked brain wasn't cooperating. "Her old classroom."

Jessica stood and clapped like she was giving a standing ovation at the Oscars.

With a laugh and a fierce flush on her face, Taylor reached out and pulled her back down to her seat. "Be cool, guys. Don't make a big deal."

"You freaking got busy with our former history teacher at the freaking high school reunion, and you think that's not a big deal?" Brianna was unhinged. "That's like one of those *Letters to Penthouse* things."

"Remember when we stole those from your brother?" Jessica chimed in with a chuckle.

Taylor tried to protest. "We didn't *get busy*—"

"What base did you get to?" Alexis wiggled her eyebrows.

"Do lesbians have bases?" Brianna asked as though it were a teachable moment. With her head to one side, she seemed to run through the options. "What the hell is the difference between third base and home plate?"

"Okay." Taylor held out her hands. "We're not having this conversation. We just kissed, okay? No one was rounding the bases."

"Jess, you're a softball lesbian. You gotta know what bases—"

Jessica didn't let Brianna finish. "Let's focus on the task at hand, yeah?"

Brianna giggled. "Pun intended?"

"How was it?" Alexis cut a slice of pancake and stuffed it into her mouth. "Is she a good kisser?"

Leaning back in her chair, Taylor took an intentionally long drink of her burned coffee. "It wasn't bad."

"Ha!" Jessica pierced a wedge of cantaloupe. "Wasn't bad? Either you're lying and you didn't kiss her, or—"

"Or you creamed your pants the second she got close to your face," Brianna finished.

"You know just because you pushed a baby out of your body

doesn't give you license to just be crude now," Taylor objected, without satisfying their curiosity.

"Doesn't it?" Brianna replied seriously. "The things I've seen." Her eyes went wide and her expression distant.

"Okay, back to the point," Alexis insisted. "Tell us everything."

After a cleansing breath, Taylor sang like a gay canary. She stopped short of telling them how suddenly it had all ended. She was still trying to sort that out herself.

"So, what now? Are you going to see her again?" Brianna asked.

"I mean, we're here all weekend." Taylor laughed.

Brianna rolled her eyes. "You know what I mean. Did you, like, plan to spend time together?" She mimicked Alexis' scissor fingers but with significantly less subtlety.

Taylor shook her head. "We didn't discuss it. It ended kind of abruptly." She let the worry she'd been suppressing seep through. "I hope she's not in her head about it or freaked out." The Catholic in her couldn't stop confessing.

"She is like twenty years older than us, babe," Brianna said with a mouthful of pancake. "And she was your teacher. That's gotta be weird for her. That's like, a full metric ton of internalized Catholic guilt."

"Alonso couldn't have found it all that weird if she was all over our girl," Alexis pointed at her with her fork. "And who cares if she is forty-something? She's still hot as hell. Oof. Have you seen that ass, though?" Alexis made a pained expression as she bit her lip.

"Appearance isn't all that matters," Jessica interrupted. "She's a mature woman. There's no way she's in the same place in life as us. And if she is"—she raised her eyebrows—"that might be a red flag."

"Hey, I have a lot to offer. I've got a good job. Dental insurance. A 401(k) that I almost understand."

Brianna laughed. "And where are you going to bring her back to? The shoebox you share with Robbie?"

"She doesn't live in New York."

"I thought y'all had lunch at the airport." Jessica rested her chin on her hand and nibbled on a piece of toast.

"She had a connecting flight. She's a professor in Vermont."

"Oh!" Brianna threw her hands up in relief as if that fact solved everything. "Good! So this is a fling."

"I didn't say that," Taylor snapped, not liking the dismissive tone of *fling*. "I just don't know what it is yet. We haven't even talked."

"It's a long weekend with a hot, young *thang*," Brianna said. "This is the stuff of the best romances. You'll have some super steamy, forbidden sex and say goodbye. Everybody wins."

"Why is it forbidden?" Alexis asked before Taylor could. "They're consenting adults."

"Yeah, yeah. I meant that in a hot way. They're always going to have this underlying prior relationship. Alonso is always going to have known her as a braces-wearing teenager. That's what gives it all an added layer of spice," Brianna said.

While her friends discussed the hypothetical sex she would have with Raquel, and whether it would be hot or creepy if she got her hands on an old school uniform, Taylor's mind wandered. She didn't know what she wanted or what this could be. All she knew was that she wanted to see her again.

After breakfast, Taylor went back to the hotel for a shower and a nap while the others scattered to do the same in their own homes. They agreed to meet back at the school for the flag football game that afternoon.

Until the moment Taylor passed out, she couldn't stop thinking about Raquel. Of her soft skin. Her full lips. Her incredible kiss.

CHAPTER 9

WEARING DARK SUNGLASSES AND A WIDE-BRIMMED, cream-colored hat, Raquel crossed the soccer field to where groups were already forming near the metal bleachers. After a nice, but dull, lunch with former colleagues, she was looking forward to the excitement of outdoor activities.

She wasn't looking for Taylor, that's what she told herself, when she spotted her in her periphery. Standing in a group near the edge of the field, Taylor was strapping on a belt with three red strips hanging off of it. The same flag football belt her friends were clipping on while they chatted and laughed.

Raquel didn't want to notice Taylor's legs in short shorts, or the smooth skin exposed by her racerback tank top. The lean muscles of her upper back flexing when she picked her hair up into a messy bun.

She had no intention of thinking about last night. Of remembering that kiss. Those kisses. The ones that ignited something wild and dangerous and long subdued.

There was no controlling the heat that surged over her skin. No way to tame the desire that pounded so hard it was desperate to break free. But she could control what she did about it.

Taking great pains to avoid looking at Taylor again, Raquel

focused on the people her own age clumping together near a line of coolers being filled with ice and water bottles.

Raquel made it as far as shouting distance to the others when Taylor noticed her. Her smile was wide and bright and instant. Without a word to her friends, she jogged toward Raquel.

Stopping short of joining the group for fear of what they might overhear, Raquel hung back and waited for Taylor. She could've justified stopping to herself. Could've reasoned that they probably should talk. That they should clear the air and establish what happened the night before would never be repeated, but Raquel had never been much of a liar. She stopped because she wanted to be near her again.

"Are you playing in that?" With her eyes, Taylor pointed at her pale blue sundress. "That's not optimal flag football gear." She grinned, her dimples and teeth and brown eyes all beaming.

Just her proximity was intoxicating. Raquel couldn't brush her off, couldn't tell herself that she didn't want to slip away with her again.

"Perfect for watching from the stands," she countered, her tone a little more sober than intended.

Taylor couldn't stop grinning, not even while she deliberately moistened her lips. "You didn't strike me as someone who just likes to watch. I expected you to get in on the action." She dropped her gaze down Raquel's body. "Maybe get a little dirty?"

Subtlety was obviously not in Taylor's arsenal, but the innuendo was so heavy-handed it was almost effective.

"I suppose that goes to show how little you know me, Miss Lopez."

At the formality, Taylor sparkled with excitement. "That's a matter of perspective. I see it as how much I get to uncover." Her eyes, a rich honeycomb of complex brown tones, brightened to bursting in the sunlight. "I really like getting inside of things, you know?"

Raquel couldn't stop the chuckle that vibrated in her throat.

Behind Taylor, her three friends had stopped talking with the others in the group and were openly gawking at them.

With a sigh, Raquel gave a slight shake of her head. "You told your friends."

Dropping her smile, Taylor looked over her shoulder. "No."

Raquel raised a questioning brow.

Taylor's nose wrinkled when she grimaced. "I didn't tell them," she insisted before deflating a little. "They figured it out on their own," she admitted sheepishly. "But don't worry, they're cool."

The three women elbowing each other and staring at them was a hair less obvious than gawking through newspapers with holes cut out. "Yes, very cool," she agreed. "Maybe next time they'll wear their plastic noses and mustaches."

Taylor's wince was entirely too cute. "They're good at getting information. Their ancestors would have been on the wrong side of the Salem witch trials." She chuckled at her own joke. "I guess it wasn't so hard to guess when they knew about the crush I used to have on you."

Unable to resist, Raquel tipped her head to the side. "Used to have?"

Taylor's smile returned in full force. "I'm almost thirty, Mrs. Alonso. I don't have crushes anymore."

"Almost thirty?" she pressed, knowing that couldn't be possible.

"I'll be twenty-eight on Valentine's Day. That's basically the same as thirty."

Raquel laughed at Taylor's tortured math. "Oh, yes. Of course. I mean, you're practically forty."

Her dimples bloomed. "See? You get it. There's no need to get weird about anything. We're all taxpaying adults here."

Crossing her arms over her chest, Raquel watched her expectantly. Staying quiet just long enough for Taylor to shift her weight between her feet.

"Is that what I'm doing, Miss Lopez? Getting weird?"

Taylor mimicked her stance. "Did they teach you that in your PhD program? How to cherry pick words and twist them into terrible sounding questions?"

Despite herself, Raquel laughed.

Two food trucks pulled up along the street at the far edge of the field, snagging Taylor's attention.

"Whaaat? We're getting *pastelitos*? I think that's what I've missed most about Miami. They just don't taste right anywhere else." Taylor gestured toward the trucks with a nod and Raquel silently agreed to go with her. "I think it's like San Fran and the sourdough. Something about the environment just makes it taste better."

Ahead of them, people divided themselves into equally long lines. Half lined up in front of the red and white King of Pastries truck, and the other half in front of the white and red Pastry King truck.

When Taylor slid into the Pastry King line, Raquel immediately judged her and stood in the other queue.

"Oh, no. Don't tell me you're one of those lunatics." Taylor covered her face before peeking at Raquel.

Raquel stared at her, waiting a long beat before responding. "King of Pastries is clearly the superior choice."

Taylor laughed with her entire being, sending a wave of contagious delight into Raquel's chest. "That's probably because that's the one you had closest to your house growing up, so that's what you got used to." She shook her head. "They literally taste exactly the same."

Taylor was close, but the bakery had been near the factory where her mother worked the night shift. She always brought home treats after getting paid on Saturday morning. It was Raquel's single favorite memory from childhood. A white box full of sweet treats meant she got to spend two full days with her mother. The woman who pretended she didn't need sleep, and dedicated the full forty-eight hours to her because her work schedule limited their weekday interaction to crossing paths in the morning.

"We should do a blind taste test," Taylor challenged. "I bet you absolutely anything you can't tell the difference between one pastry and the other."

"That's a terrible wager, and you're going to lose."

"Yeah? Then *you* have nothing to lose. I'll even let you choose the flavor you're most confident about."

Pretending to give in after arm-twisting, Raquel replied with a very serious, "Guava."

Taylor laughed. "I can't wait for you to admit they're identical."

Raquel resisted the urge to smile.

Two paper baskets in hand, Taylor led them away from the bustle of the crowd around the food trucks and to the shade of a sprawling Banyan tree a few yards away. The noise melted away and there was nothing but Taylor leaning against the massive trunk covered in thick aerial roots.

"Take your sunglasses off so I can make sure your eyes are completely closed," Taylor instructed very seriously.

Raquel feigned offense. "You think I'm going to cheat?"

"This has to pass scientific muster," she replied without a hint of jest. "When you fail, I don't want you poking holes in my test."

Instead of calling out Taylor's flawed reasoning, Raquel pulled off her sunglasses.

Taylor's smile returned as if looking in her eyes was like watching a sun rising over the Grand Canyon. "You're so beautiful," she whispered as if awestruck.

Raquel blamed the heat rushing over her skin on the terrible decision to have an outdoor activity during the afternoon in July.

"Distractions won't work on me, Miss Lopez. Let's get to your experiment." She kept her voice even despite the hammering in her chest.

Taylor shook the hearts out of her eyes and focused. "Alright. I'm going to give you a piece of one and then the other." She looked down at the small sections she'd cut from the rectangular puff pastry filled with sweet red guava paste. "Identify which is which."

If she was honest, she'd insist that she didn't need to close her eyes. She'd been so distracted by Taylor she'd already forgotten which pastry came from what truck and they looked exactly the same in their nondescript paper baskets, but she didn't want to ruin Taylor's game.

"Ready?"

Raquel nodded, glad no one could see them behind the tree, not even Taylor's friends, who hadn't stopped watching them. Unless someone came from the other side of the field, the enormous trunk would shield them.

Closing her eyes, Raquel parted her lips just wide enough for the small piece. When Taylor's thumb brushed her bottom lip as she fed her, Raquel felt it reverberate through her body.

She was back on the desk, pulling at the back of Taylor's shirt, desperate for her mouth to move further down her neck, starving for her hands to disappear beneath her dress.

Before Taylor could feed her the second piece, Raquel opened her eyes. "It's that one," she whispered, her husky words dripping with desire, her body eager to push Taylor against the tree and kiss her again. To taste her mixing with the sweet confection, to slide her hand inside her shorts and feel if Taylor wanted her as badly as Raquel did.

With a slow, lopsided grin creeping over her lips, Taylor shook her head. She stepped closer, eliminating her personal space. "I win, Dr. Alonso." Her gaze dropped to Raquel's hungry mouth.

Between Raquel's thighs, her body pulsed and pulled and ached. She opened her mouth, ready to ask Taylor to leave with her. To take her up on the offer to come back to her room. She wanted to taste her again. To consume her. To be consumed.

"Alright, everybody! Let's get this game going!" someone shouted, sending a stream of people back to the field.

Raquel took a step back before anyone saw them standing too close together. Needing to regain control, Raquel took the second piece waiting on the basket and popped it into her mouth.

As she let the sweet, delicious carbs melt on her tongue, she slid her glasses back on. Without a word, she walked away from Taylor again.

Damn, they really do taste exactly the same.

CHAPTER 10

IN THE FACULTY BATHROOM, Raquel leaned over the small pedestal sink and fixed her smudged black eyeliner. If there was anything she didn't miss about Florida, it was the humidity.

After spending the afternoon in the sun, she was a new level of drained. She hadn't noticed how hot it was, finding herself distracted by watching Taylor and her friends dominate the other teams at flag football. But after a shower and a quiet, early dinner in her hotel room, she was depleted.

It might not be so bad if the assembly room's air conditioner wasn't ancient. With a crowd larger than the evening before, the room was just this side of sweltering.

Raquel reapplied her pink lip gloss—the one she kept losing after switching from wine to water thanks to the stifling heat in the room.

She was grateful the actual reunion the following evening was being held in the hotel because she wasn't keen on sweating through another dress. At least the one she was wearing tonight was black and hid a plethora of sins.

Snapping her clutch closed and popping it under her arm, Raquel returned to the assembly room steam bath. She decided that as soon as she got back to the hotel, she was going to dive headfirst into the pool.

She was fantasizing about the relief of being submerged in cool water when she rejoined the group of alumni and faculty she'd been standing with. They were still chatting about the same inane topic and Raquel's attention wandered despite her best efforts.

Taylor and her friends hadn't arrived yet. She couldn't help but wonder if they'd skipped the event to do something on their own. Something other than play *Name That Tune* for silly prizes.

Disappointment crept over her spine like a daddy longlegs crawling lightly over her skin.

There was no point in pretending. She wanted to see Taylor again. Wanted a hit of her energy. To exist in that charged, intoxicating space that consumed her when they were together.

Something about Taylor made her feel reckless. Like she was stepping outside her suffocating skin and coloring outside the lines.

She smiled to herself, thinking about Taylor's *I'm-practically-thirty* logic. She wasn't, of course, but maybe that didn't matter.

It was just a long weekend. A hiatus from her normal life. Maybe all that mattered was that it felt dangerous. The artificial danger of a rollercoaster or a slasher film.

While chatting with one of her former students, and simultaneously justifying her completely selfish desire to give in to lust, Raquel felt a familiar gaze landing like soft fingertips over the nape of her neck. Raquel didn't immediately turn around. She forced herself to wait. To make Taylor wait.

Casually, she tossed her head to the side, making it seem like she was adjusting the hair falling over her jaw. As she moved, she confirmed Taylor's presence in her periphery. That she was watching her.

Dressed in jeans and a faded black concert T-shirt, Taylor's long hair fell in perfectly messy waves past her shoulders. It was the sort of style that took time to appear effortless.

Taylor reminded Raquel of the cool girls she was infatuated with as a kid in the eighties. Before she hit puberty and realized her friends didn't look at other girls the way she did.

With the kind of focus and determination that got her through her doctoral program, Raquel continued her meaningless conversation with a growing group of former students without looking back at Taylor.

The woman with the ice breaker game called for the room's attention again. Forced to break off her conversation and turn toward the woman shouting over the noise, Raquel couldn't avoid making eye contact with Taylor.

Leaning against the wall, a move she obviously intended to make her look smooth, Taylor was looking at her with bright brown eyes. The tanned skin on her cheeks and nose was pink from her day spent in the sun, and all Raquel wanted to do was cross the room and kiss her.

"Hi," Taylor mouthed, her lips looking so soft.

Raquel flashed a lopsided smile before she could stop herself.

"Alright everyone! Who's ready to play *Name That Tune* early aughts edition?"

While the woman explained the self-explanatory rules and various prizes, Raquel was unable to stop her attention from drifting to the other side of the room.

Laughing with her friends, her dimples on display and her energy light, Taylor was absolutely captivating.

"We will play in teams of five tonight." The woman at the front produced a red buzzer.

As she explained there would be roughly ten teams of five and how they would play in brackets, Taylor strode across the room and toward her.

"Raquel." She grinned like she was playing with a new toy. "Do you want to join my team?"

Over Taylor's shoulder, her three friends were pretending not to watch them. The short one, Brianna Alvarez, was doing the worst job of pretending to be on her phone, unless she always held it up to her face rather than bending her head to the screen.

"I can't say I will be an asset to your team." She screwed the top back on her water bottle. "This is not exactly my era of music."

Taylor's smile curved into something more mischievous. "I don't mind carrying you." She dropped her gaze as if Raquel might miss her meaning.

Raquel let her linger in a moment of silence.

"Plus, I did win that bet earlier." She slid her hands into her tight pockets. "So, you owe me one."

Raquel pretended to consider it. "You never set the terms of the wager, Miss Lopez. It wouldn't be fair to allow you to do so *ex post facto*, would it?"

Nothing was dampening Taylor's smile. "If I recall the conversation, Dr. Alonso, you were so over-confident in your abilities that you did not believe you'd lose." She moistened her lips. "The spirit, if not the letter, of our agreement was that I would get something I wanted if you were wrong. My cashing in my winnings is not *after-the-fact* under those circumstances."

Exhilarated by Taylor's unexpected response, Raquel bit the inside of her cheek to keep from grinning. She stepped into Taylor's space, whispering against the shell of her ear. "Are you sure this is what you want to spend your wish on, Miss Lopez?"

When she stepped back, Taylor's expression had changed to something pained.

After waiting a beat, Raquel smirked. "I didn't think so."

Raquel headed for the front of the room to volunteer as a judge. As she moved, she took great pains to saunter. Swaying what was universally agreed to be her best asset. She'd always understood what people wanted from her, and she was finding herself in the mood to give it.

It wasn't until she took her seat on the judge's panel that she hazarded a glance at Taylor. She was still standing where she'd left her, a combination of desire and surprise on her face.

CHAPTER 11

TAYLOR SAID goodnight to her friends and jumped onto the bus shuttling people from the school back to the nearby hotel. As soon as she saw Raquel among the dozen passengers, she grinned.

"Is this seat taken?" Taylor asked, hoping Raquel picked up that she was being intentionally corny.

Lifting a perfect, dark eyebrow, Raquel watched her for a beat. Without a verbal response, she moved her purse from the seat next to her.

Taylor fished the steakhouse gift card out of her back pocket before sitting down next to Raquel. "Who knew an encyclopedic knowledge of Shakira songs would ever win me a steak dinner?" She flipped the card over with her fingers. "My parents would be thrilled to know the hours I spent staring at her poster above my bed and listening to my iPod weren't wasted."

"I'm sure they'd be very proud."

Laughing, Taylor slipped it back into her pocket. "I think I would've preferred to win that massage." She rubbed her thighs, sore from playing flag football all afternoon. She hadn't intended to be so competitive, but there was no stopping herself when she was back with her old team.

Raquel's gaze fell to Taylor's hands over her jeans. Purposefully, Taylor moved in slow, methodical circles as she eased the pain in her quads.

Despite an obvious effort to conceal it, Raquel's expression darkened. Her lips parting as she watched Taylor's fingers with what she guessed was envy.

The shuttle stopped in front of the hotel lobby too soon, terminating Taylor's fun.

As soon as they stepped off the bus, Raquel's dark eyes fixed on Taylor's. "You should try the pool." Her voice was so low and husky that it alone could bring Taylor to her knees. "For your pain." She sauntered away in the excruciating way that made Taylor want to cry.

Convinced that Raquel was sending her a coded message, Taylor crossed the lobby, expecting to find Raquel waiting for her by the pool.

Despite the sign that said it was closed after sunset, Taylor's room key opened the gate to the poorly lit pool area. There was no doubt why she'd yet to see anyone out there. Thanks to the construction next door, the pool was surrounded by a tall fence of ugly black tarps and a huge, black screen acting as a canopy. She guessed it was to keep debris from getting in the water.

She imagined tourists hadn't been expecting that when they booked their sexy Miami vacation. With no sign of Raquel, Taylor dropped into one of the deck chairs dumped unceremoniously in the corner. The hotel had stopped pretending anyone was going to use the pool.

Taylor closed her eyes and rested her head on the chair. At nearly ten at night, the obstructed breeze off the bay was cool. She let it dry the perspiration on her skin.

Relaxed, she was sure she could've drifted off if she'd had another few minutes. If she hadn't heard the gate click open.

Despite the moonless night, and the only light outside coming from dim, yellow path lanterns half covered by the vegetation lining the pool area, Taylor recognized Raquel's shape in the dark. She could recognize her anywhere.

"Funny meeting you here," Taylor said, standing.

Raquel had changed into a black, gauzy coverup. On her arm, she carried a rolled-up white towel.

Taylor's heart raced at the mere prospect of seeing Raquel in a bathing suit.

As she neared, Raquel dropped her gaze over Taylor's body. She didn't need to speak to convey her disappointment that Taylor hadn't understood the assignment.

Taylor kicked off her shoes, hoping to show her that nothing was going to keep her from getting into the pool. "I came out here to think about that little bet of ours."

Raquel raised a brow. Her favorite form of communication.

"And then I realized..." Taylor let a smirk pull slowly and suggestively at the edge of her mouth. "What's better than getting a little wet?"

Raquel's lip twitched, her attention dropping to Taylor's hands. The ones unfastening her jeans. When Taylor pulled down her zipper, Raquel's head swiveled around to check for prying eyes.

"There's no one here," Taylor assured her.

Raquel turned her gaze to the five stories of windows overlooking the pool. "What do you call that?" She gestured toward the hotel.

"My room is right up there." She left her jeans hanging open, exposing her lower belly and hipbones. "All I can see is that awful black cover."

No part of Raquel appeared convinced.

Taylor took Raquel's towel and tossed it on the deck chair. "Are you afraid of getting in trouble, Dr. Alonso?"

The challenge produced a tiny spark in Raquel's dark eyes; the momentary flicker of flint and steel and tinder.

Yanking off her jeans, Taylor stepped out of them and threw them on top of the towel.

"Do you plan on swimming in the nude, Miss Lopez?" Raquel couldn't hide the excitement brightening her face.

Taking longer than she needed to, Taylor pulled off her T-shirt.

She hoped Raquel was eyeing her with the same hunger burning in Taylor's body.

Satisfied by the unrestrained lust on Raquel's face, Taylor tossed her T-shirt onto the growing pile. "What's a bathing suit if not underwear made from different material, right?"

Raquel smirked, forcing her gaze back to Taylor's face. "That's some very creative logic."

Stepping into Raquel's space, Taylor slid her palms over the curve of her hips, taking her time finding the hem of her coverup. At her touch, Raquel's smile disappeared.

Raquel didn't stop her from dragging up the sheer black fabric. When Taylor had taken the material up to her waist, Raquel lifted her arms so she could remove it completely.

Biting her bottom lip, Taylor drank in Raquel's body and wished there wasn't so much fabric on the strapless, navy blue, one-piece.

Pulling her close, Taylor hovered close to Raquel's mouth. She loved the heat of her body pressed against hers. Mimicking the move Raquel had pulled earlier, she leaned in to whisper against the shell of her ear.

"What do you say? Do you want to get a little wet?"

CHAPTER 12

RAQUEL WATCHED TAYLOR, her lean body exposed by her bra and microscopic underwear. She remembered when she wore things that small. Things that didn't need to be shaping or control-top or sliming. They could just be cute without pulling double duty.

Glancing back at her, Taylor grinned. She flashed a single dimple that made Raquel forget what she was worrying about, and dove headfirst into the pool. It was much more graceful than Raquel expected. Jumping off from muscular legs, Taylor cut through the surface like a scalpel.

When Taylor popped up on the far side of the pool, she slicked back her dark hair. She looked at Raquel expectantly, waiting for her to follow.

On paper, it was probably the worst idea she'd ever had, which was saying something considering she'd had a tribal tramp stamp removed. She could envision the headline. *All-girls Catholic school teacher caught in pool with half-naked student.* There wouldn't be any nuance in the clickbait. No mention of the terms *adult* or *former* or *consensual* or *clothed.*

Creeping doubt forced Raquel's attention behind her again. Looking up at the hundred rooms facing the pool, she couldn't be sure none of them had a view of the water. When she'd imagined this moment earlier, she'd forgotten about the potential for an audience.

"Are you coming?" Taylor's voice drifted over the gentle waves created by her disruption of the water, her arms moving slowly to keep her afloat.

I'm not doing anything wrong. It's not a crime to be in a pool just because it's closed. It's not trespassing if I'm a guest.

Trusting Taylor that they weren't visible from above, Raquel eased into the pleasantly cool water. As she descended the steps, Taylor swam to meet her.

"Hi," Taylor said, droplets of water hanging precariously from her long, dark eyelashes.

Raquel stopped walking when the water reached her chest. "Hi," she whispered, transfixed by the way the smudged black eyeliner made Taylor's eyes look incandescent even in the low light.

With surprising confidence, Taylor reached out and took Raquel by the waist. Like she'd been waiting to do it all day. As if she'd been unable to think about anything else, Taylor pulled her close.

"Maybe this is a good time to ask if you're still married." Taylor's lips hovered playfully over Raquel's mouth. A sea lion taunting a hungry Great White.

Allowing herself to be lifted off her feet, Raquel wrapped her legs around Taylor's hips. "Now you ask?" Throwing her arms around Taylor's neck, she kissed her as if they'd danced the dance before.

The moment she parted Taylor's lips and slid her tongue into her waiting mouth, Taylor moaned. The sound echoed and multiplied in Raquel's body, igniting her desire like a match tossed haphazardly onto a gasoline-soaked pyre.

Taylor cut through the water, spinning Raquel and pressing her back hard against the side of the pool. The rough stone ledge cut into Raquel's upper back, scraping her skin. Raquel couldn't find the will to care.

All that mattered was Taylor's mouth on hers. Taylor's hands gripping her thighs so hard she was sure there'd be ten tiny bruises from where her fingers dug into her soft flesh. Her body pushing into her, urgent and insistent.

"I haven't stopped thinking about you," Taylor whispered breathlessly before her searing hot mouth slid down Raquel's throat.

She wanted to say that she'd been thinking about her too, but Taylor's teeth dragging against her sensitive neck made it impossible to speak. All she could do was gasp when Taylor bit down and applied an excruciatingly perfect amount of pressure before letting go.

Raquel cursed. Making a fist in Taylor's hair, she pulled her head back hard.

With a groan, Taylor closed her eyes. Watching her openly enjoying her hair being pulled obliterated Raquel's resolve. Claiming her mouth again, Raquel kissed her hard and deep and undeniably.

Taylor's palms glided up her thighs and over her hips and up her chest. Through the thick material of her bathing suit, Taylor squeezed her breast.

Needing to feel the contact, Raquel slid her hand over Taylor's. Guiding her hand, she urged her to pull down one side of her strapless bathing suit. Without hesitation, Taylor clasped her hand over her breast, her touch soft and warm and debilitating.

Taylor moaned into their kiss, caressing Raquel's newly exposed skin like it deserved reverence. She raked her blunt fingernails over her hard nipple, sending a wave of aching desire pulsing between Raquel's thighs.

All of her senses focused on Taylor's touch. On the mouth sliding down her chest. On the hands yanking down her bathing suit until it was around her waist. On the teeth teasing her sensitive nipple.

Throwing her head back, Raquel bit down on her bottom lip to keep from moaning. Just because they couldn't be seen didn't mean she wanted to be heard.

Indulging in Taylor's lips and tongue and fingers all working together to drive her desire to nuclear meltdown levels, Raquel rocked her hips, wishing she could feel Taylor's bare skin against her aching core.

It had been so long since she'd been ravished. Since someone touched her like they wanted to devour her. Like she was the sexiest person they'd ever encountered. Like they couldn't get enough.

Eager to cause a meltdown of her own, Raquel tore herself away from Taylor. Sending water splashing over the ledge, she traded places with her. With a confident, sweeping move, she turned Taylor around, making her face away from her.

Following her lead, Taylor stuck her arms out of the pool, resting them on the stone, her chest pressed to the ledge. "From behind, Dr. Alonso?" she whispered over her shoulder, her voice husky, her words dripping with lust.

Pulling Taylor's long hair to one side, Raquel ran the tip of her tongue up the back of her neck. Immediately, Taylor shuddered, pushing herself backward into Raquel.

With her bare chest pressed to Taylor's mostly exposed back, Raquel let her lips graze the shell of Taylor's ear. "Is this what you were thinking about today?"

Slipping her hand into her bra, she immediately found Taylor's stiff nipple.

Taylor's reply was a breathy moan as she swung her hips backward into Raquel's pelvis with more urgency. "This is way better," she admitted before turning her head again and capturing Raquel's lips in a kiss.

"Touch me," Taylor begged, her kiss growing messy and unfocused. "Please."

Keeping one hand in her bra, Raquel slid the other down Taylor's torso. Beneath Raquel's hands, Taylor's belly tensed, anticipating her touch.

Raquel found the edge of her underwear, her fingertips gliding along Taylor's smooth skin before sliding down the wet fabric.

Arching her back, Taylor made a sound somewhere between a cry and a groan. Biting into Taylor's shoulder, Raquel slid her hand between her thighs.

At the light touch, Taylor cursed. She dropped her head to rest her forehead against the pool's edge. Raquel pressed against her, intending to tease her before pushing the fabric to one side and feeling the hard flesh slide between her fingers.

"Excuse me," a man's voice boomed and skittered over the surface of the water like moonlight.

A second before a flashlight beamed in their direction, Raquel pulled up her bathing suit. As if she'd devised the plan ahead of time, Taylor pulled herself half out of the pool and pretended to choke.

Guessing her ploy, Raquel patted her hard on the back and tried very hard not to laugh.

"Hey, there's no swimming after sundown."

Taylor continued coughing so convincingly Raquel started to doubt she was faking.

"You okay, lady?" the voice behind the blinding point of light asked.

"Fine," Taylor replied, struggling to catch her breath. "I guess I didn't wait long enough after eating."

All Raquel could see was a shiny bald head until the man mercifully pointed the flashlight at his patent leather shoes.

"Didn't you see the sign saying the pool was closed?"

"Oh, gosh, is it really?" Taylor managed to look mortified while still recovering from her near drowning charade. "I'm so sorry, sir. We would never have come in if we'd known it was closed. We're part of the reunion and just wanted a little break from all the action, you know?"

Without glasses or contacts, Raquel couldn't see anything but the man's outline. She couldn't read his expression. Despite having no idea whether Taylor was selling her story, she followed her to the pool's entrance.

"That Catholic school?" he asked, clicking the flashlight off as Taylor took the steps out of the pool first.

"That's us." Taylor flashed him her dimples. "You're not going to call the principal, are you? It's been ten years since I had detention and I'm not looking forward to scraping gum off the bottom of desks." She laughed.

Instead of ogling Taylor in what was obviously soaked underwear, the man dressed in black averted his eyes, reached for Raquel's towel, and handed it to Taylor.

"I won't have to call anyone as long as you ladies go on up to your room, alright?" He glanced at Raquel as she stepped out of the pool.

Without missing a beat, like breaking the rules was no big deal, Taylor handed Raquel her coverup once she was on dry land.

"Not a problem, sir." Taylor assured him. "We'll be right behind you. I promise."

By the time Raquel pulled on her coverup, the security guard was walking toward the gate.

Taylor slid her hand in hers. "Should we go up to your room or mine?"

The delivery was so smooth, anyone would've thought they'd already agreed.

Raquel gave her hand a squeeze before letting it go. "I think I'll say goodnight now."

Taylor wrapped the towel around her body and scooped up her clothes and shoes. "Won't you let me thank you for saving me from drowning?"

Raquel smiled and padded toward the man waiting for them at the gate.

"Breakfast tomorrow? Okay, perfect. I'll see you then."

Raquel didn't drop her smile until well after she was back in her room. Alone.

CHAPTER 13

UNSURE OF WHEN Raquel intended on having breakfast, Taylor stretched out on a couch in the lobby at seven. She had a good view of the restaurant entrance and the elevator bank from there.

Mindlessly scrolling through her phone, Taylor's thoughts were fixed on the night before. She'd been hardly able to think about anything else, and even after falling asleep, she spent all night dreaming of her.

Taylor's skin still buzzed from all the places Raquel's hands had been. Where her mouth had electrified her neck.

When she closed her eyes, she could still feel the pressure of Raquel's body pressed against her back, her bare chest soft against her. The feel of her arms, strong and sure around her, still lingered on her skin.

If she strained, Taylor could trick her memory. She could make it advance beyond what actually happened. Could feel Raquel's hand slipping underneath her underwear. Could hear Raquel gasp when she discovered just how incredibly turned on she was.

The man dressed in black appeared in her fabricated memory, disrupting it. If it hadn't been for the security guard interrupting them, Taylor was sure that Raquel would've gone up to her room.

She was sure that Raquel's desire was just as intense as her own. That she would've given in to it if she hadn't been so rattled. So stunned by the intrusion.

Wistfully, she returned to the memory of Raquel's lips on hers. On how heart-stoppingly passionate her kiss was. It didn't surprise her that beneath the still, cool surface churned something scorching and powerful and vast.

Taylor felt her before she saw her; an increasingly familiar presence moving toward her. Flicking her gaze over the edge of her phone, she smiled at the sight of Raquel.

There was no pretense in Raquel's stride. She moved straight toward Taylor as if she hadn't considered going anywhere else as soon as she saw her.

"You could have called my room," Raquel said, her voice low and gravelly, like those were the first words she'd said that day. "How long have you been waiting here?"

Taylor sat upright before getting to her feet. Even in jeans and a short-sleeve top, Raquel evoked a certain poise. With her wavy hair tossed to one side and damp from the shower, and her face free of anything but her glasses, she was even more beautiful than she'd been the night before.

"What would be the fun in that?" Taylor replied without pointing out that she didn't know what room she was in, and it would be weird to ask the front desk.

Raquel tipped her head to the side, the ghost of a smile lurking at the edges of her full lips. "What if I would've ordered room service?"

With a shrug, Taylor slid her hands into the back pocket of her shorts. "Then I guess I would've had a super boring morning," she said with an exaggerated sigh.

Raquel chuckled. "Just that easy, huh? No big deal?"

At the sound of Raquel's subdued laughter, Taylor's heart floated to the top of her chest like a wayward supermarket balloon. She would've traded music for that sound. Traded anything to hear it over and over.

"The best things in life usually are," Taylor replied, so lost in

Raquel that she was disconnected from the words coming out of her mouth.

Raquel seemed to consider her for a moment, her honey eyes searching her face. "I owe you a meal, don't I?"

With a grin, Taylor crossed her arms over her chest. "God, Raquel. You're so pushy. If you want to eat with me, just say so. No need for all this pretense. You don't have to try so hard. I'll do you the favor of a little breakfast."

Replying with a playful roll of her eyes, Raquel turned and started for the hotel's restaurant.

The restaurant was populated by a dozen other guests helping themselves to the extensive brunch buffet.

"You know you can tell a lot about a person by what they do at a buffet," Taylor said after they dropped off their things at a table along a far wall.

Raquel took a plate off the warmer and handed it back to Taylor before taking one for herself. "How so?"

"Well, if you're really high maintenance, you'll go right for the omelet station."

Raquel glanced over her shoulder at her, her face creased in confusion. "How is an omelet high maintenance?"

"Oh, come on, who needs that much customization?" Taylor took a banana nut muffin off a tower of baked goods. "Plus, you have to stand there and watch some poor person mix spinach and onions into your food. There's nothing to do but stare at them while it cooks." She shook her head. "It is the egg equivalent of an eight-shot macchiato and five pumps of four different flavors of horrific syrup poured over thirteen ice cubes and shaken by an Italian monk." She pointed at her eyes with her index and middle fingers. "But with eye contact."

Raquel skipped forward and served herself a scoop of fruit salad. She couldn't bite back her smile, no matter how hard she tried.

Powerless to stop amusing Raquel, Taylor continued. "You are probably greedy if you go for the most expensive food."

"Or getting the most bang for your buck." Raquel lingered on the word *bang* just long enough to raise Taylor's body temperature a fraction.

Taylor followed behind Raquel until they reached the waffle station. "This is how you know someone's a keeper." She dispensed a pre-measured amount of batter onto the waffle iron and closed it. "I'm willing to put in the work to get what I want." When the light on the machine turned green, she flipped it over.

"Is that so?" Raquel's eyes radiated her amusement.

Taylor propped her hand on her hip. "Mm-hmm. I'll even make you one." She took a single dimple out of its holster and aimed it with practiced skill. "I've always believed it's better to give than to receive."

Raquel moistened her lips as she leaned in, her attention dropping to Taylor's mouth. Sure that Raquel was about to kiss her as a reward for being adorable, she nearly closed her eyes.

Passing over her lips, Raquel neared her ear, her breath warm and sweet and inviting. "Make sure mine's not burned."

It wasn't until Raquel turned away, taking the haze of heat and lust with her, that Taylor detected the scent of scorched waffle.

CHAPTER 14

WHILE THEY WAITED under the covered breezeway in the school's courtyard with dozens of other alumni and faculty, Taylor hatched a plan. She decided she was not going on the scavenger hunt around Miami with the rest of the group.

"Hey, Bri. Can I borrow your car?"

"Why?" Brianna, her round cheeks pink from the afternoon heat, looked up at Taylor, her hand shielding her from the sun.

"So I can slip away with Raquel, obviously," Taylor whispered, even though she was a grown adult and she couldn't get in trouble for skipping the field trip.

"Okay, but why her car?" Alexis chimed in, dark sunglasses covering half her face. "It's a minivan with like three car seats in it." She turned her face down to Brianna. "You know you only have one kid, right?"

"They're different sizes," Brianna snapped as if that explained everything. "Danny had them all installed at the fire station before we brought DJ home from the hospital."

"Why didn't you just have them install the infant one and change it when he—"

Brianna didn't let Taylor finish posing her logical question. "Do you want to borrow it or not, fancy-ass-New-York?"

"No, she doesn't." Jessica extended her keys. "Take mine. The backseat isn't blocked."

"No offense, Jess." Alexis unzipped the waist bag secured across her chest. "Your Prius might make Mother Nature wet, but it is no pussy wagon," she added, her voice low as she leaned in to avoid being overheard.

"Oh, and I'm the vulgar one, right?" Brianna complained loudly enough to draw judgmental eyes.

Laughing, Alexis placed a huge black car key in Taylor's open palm. "I want you to succeed on your mission, okay? So much so that I'm trusting you with my baby."

"That's kind of offensive when some of us have actual children." Brianna tossed her ponytail over her shoulder.

"Hey, you can always make another baby. There's only one Heart Stopper."

Jessica chuckled. "That's an interesting choice of words for someone who works in the emergency room."

"Trust me." Alexis grinned. "She's a lady magnet. Like me." She pretended to dust off her shoulder.

"Thanks, Al." Taylor smiled. "I'll fill 'er up."

Alexis winked before her gaze drifted behind Taylor. "Go get 'em, killer."

Following Alexis' line of sight, Taylor glanced over her shoulder. With her face half-hidden behind her beige, wide-brimmed hat, Raquel was walking toward them with a group of former faculty.

"Wish me luck," Taylor said, before turning around. It had only been a few hours since they'd had breakfast together, but Taylor was already yearning to be near her again.

"Luck, bitch."

"Get in where you fit in, girl."

"Good Lord."

"Dr. Alonso!" Taylor pulled out the receipt for an iced *café con leche* she'd jammed in her back pocket. Waving it in the air, she picked up her pace.

"Miss Lopez," she replied in her sober, professional, definitely-nothing-untoward-going-on-here voice. "Good afternoon."

Flashing a smile at some of her former teachers, Taylor hoped they'd keep walking. "I have our list." She flashed the paper quickly enough to avoid anyone catching the *Pastry King* logo at the top.

"Our list?" Raquel's eyes were liquid bronze, brightening in the heat.

"They paired us together." She stuffed the paper back in her pocket. "For the scavenger hunt," she added, giving Raquel a have-you-forgotten-what-we're-here-for look.

As soon as her former colleagues were out of earshot, Raquel straightened. Her expression was severe as she leveled Taylor with her gaze. "Just the two of us?"

"Isn't it crazy that they randomly selected us to go together?" The sun tickled Taylor's back where her skin was exposed by the loose tank top.

"Despite the fact that everyone else appears to be splitting off into groups of four?"

Taylor's attention drifted to where people were pouring into the parking lot in very obvious quads and not duos. She rocked on the balls of her feet. "Yup."

"Well, then. Far be it from me to disobey the rules." Raquel started walking down the breezeway again. "We're going to have to go in your car. I left my lights on the other night and I haven't had a chance to get the battery fixed."

Taylor laughed. "Oh, no. That sounds like such a headache."

Raquel's smile in her peripheral vision warmed Taylor from the inside out. She would never have expected Mrs. Alonso to have such a playful side. Although she guessed maybe she didn't. Raquel did.

As they neared the parking lot, emptying as people raced off to cross things off their scavenger list, Taylor fished the huge key out of her shorts' pocket.

"When did you get a car?" Raquel scanned the lot.

"I've got a lot of friends." She hit the panic button on the key fob.

At the sound of an alarm blaring, their heads turned in unison toward the noise at the far end of the parking lot. Parked all by its self was an olive-green Jeep, its headlights flashing along with a massive bar of lights running above the windshield, just above the GO TOPLESS decal painted in bright orange letters.

"Who is your friend?" Judgment weighed down Raquel's words.

"Alexis Abreu."

Raquel nodded as if to say *that checks out.*

When Taylor was within ten feet of the Jeep, she realized that the tires, with their matte orange rims, were enormous. Before she worried about how she was going to catapult into the doorless, roof-less Jeep, she noticed the bright orange steps to help them up.

"This is a lot," Taylor said as she walked around the rear.

On the black material covering the spare tire mounted on the back were the words: *You didn't wake up today to be a weak ass bitch*, surrounded by an orange stethoscope.

"Charming," Raquel said in a tone Taylor couldn't decipher before adjusting her hat.

"She saves lives, you know."

Raquel tipped her head to one side and in a serious tone said, "Well then, I'm certainly glad she's not a *weak ass bitch.*"

With surprising confidence, Raquel planted her Sperry-covered foot onto the orange step, grabbed a handle on the doorframe and launched herself gracefully into the passenger seat.

Jogging up to the driver's side, Taylor tried to match Raquel's elegant entrance into the exaggeratedly tall car. As she wondered what Alexis did when it rained since her Jeep was exposed to the elements, she took the orange and green University of Miami visor cap sitting on the dashboard and slid it on before picking her hair up in a messy bun.

"Hold on to your hat," Taylor warned.

"Where are we going?" Raquel asked, posing an excellent and logical question.

Taylor bought herself some time while she strapped on her orange seatbelt. Nothing came to her in those three seconds. "I don't know. I hadn't really thought this far ahead," she admitted with a chuckle. "Where do you want to go?"

Raquel's gaze bored into her. They were a challenge and a dare and a promise that she was keeping all kinds of secrets locked away. "Surprise me."

With a grin, Taylor hit the ignition and Heart Stopper roared to life with a deafening rumble. Whitesnake's *Is This Love* blasted them with the clamor of hair metal.

Before Taylor could turn the volume down, Raquel lunged forward and turned it up. Pulling off her hat, she looked up at the sun streaming into the naked Jeep and belted out the words.

Eternally grateful that she hadn't gone for fuel efficiency, Taylor threw Heart Stopper into drive and peeled out of the parking lot.

CHAPTER 15

THE DRIVE from the mainland across the bridge straddling Biscayne Bay to connect Miami and Key Biscayne—a small barrier island between the bay and open ocean—was painfully short. Raquel would've been happy to drive all day with the wind in her hair and the sun in her face and Taylor's hand resting on her thigh. The move had surprised Raquel in the most pleasant of ways, and now she wished she could memorize the weight of it on her body.

While they drove, Raquel considered trading her sedan for a Jeep. She hadn't had time for a midlife crisis yet, and driving something slightly less ostentatious than Heart Stopper felt right.

Leaving the small town of Key Biscayne behind, they continued on the tree-lined road to the southernmost point of the island. A place Raquel hadn't visited since she was a child.

"Have you ever been here?" Taylor asked when the road through the state park ended in a long, packed parking lot.

"To *El Farito*?" She only knew the name of the beach by the Spanish term for small lighthouse.

Taylor nodded while she hunted for a spot.

"I used to come here a lot as a kid. With my parents." Her mother's raven hair shone in her memory the way it used to shine in the sun.

"My mother loved the beach. She said it was the only thing that ever felt like home."

Taylor looked at her, bright brown eyes reflecting a level of emotion she wasn't expecting. "Wow. That's beautiful."

Raquel smiled, accessing more of the memory. The warmth of her skin. The poetry and song of her mother's laughter.

"Are your parents still in Miami?" Taylor was delicate when she asked, like she sensed the particular longing in Raquel's spirit.

"My mother passed some years ago. My father lives with me in Vermont." She wasn't ready to say more than that, so she steered Taylor's sweet expression elsewhere. "What about you? Did you ever come here?"

"With my grandma once or twice," she replied mercifully fast. "My dad always bitched that parking and traffic were too much of a hassle, so we were a Matheson Hammock family. Or, as I like to call it, the sandy *charco*."

Raquel smiled. She'd only been to the fabricated beach once. It did have a certain puddle quality. She imagined Taylor running along the sandy ring separating the beach from open water, trying to get to the bay beyond the atoll.

While Taylor did another lap looking for somewhere to park the outlandish Jeep, Raquel let a question escape.

"How old are your parents?"

Taylor flashed her a glance and removed her hand from Raquel's thigh. "I don't want to tell you." She gripped the steering wheel with both hands.

"What?" Raquel chuckled at the unexpected response. "What do you mean, you don't want to tell me?"

"My parents were young when they had me, and this is the kind of thing I can imagine you getting all weird about."

Raquel put her hat back on when her scalp started tingling. "I don't get weird," she replied defiantly.

"Oh, sure." Taylor switched on the turning signal when a family started toward their parked SUV. "Like you're not going to immediately do the math in your head. I don't know how old you are, but—"

"I'll be forty-seven in January."

Taylor remained undeterred in her point, making Raquel sure that she wasn't far off from her parents' age. At least one of them. "I don't want you getting all I'm-old-enough-to-be-your-mother. You're not my mother and that's what matters. End of story."

Before an approaching car could sweep in and steal it, Taylor whipped into the parking spot. "Okay?" Taylor demanded more than she asked.

Raquel put her hands up in surrender, but didn't concede that Taylor wasn't wrong. When she was with Taylor, she didn't *feel* so much older than her, but as soon as she thought about it, it was apparent just how far apart they were in age and life experience. Nearly twenty years was a lifetime.

Taylor beamed when Raquel didn't argue. "Good." She leaned forward, capturing Raquel's lips in a kiss like it was a perfectly ordinary thing they did all the time. "Now let's go. Adventure awaits."

Raquel watched Taylor leap out of the Jeep, a smile on her tingling lips.

Adventure came in the way of Raquel sitting at a picnic table under a thatched roof pavilion while Taylor continued harassing a man named Chet. Raquel had been happy to take no for an answer when he said they were booked solid for snorkeling, jet skis, boat rides, and parasailing trips. She would've at least stopped asking when he laughed in their faces after Taylor asked if there was anything available on a Sunday afternoon. In Miami. On a cloudless summer day.

Despite not having brought any swimwear, Taylor had decided they were doing at least one thing on Endless Summer Ocean Escapades' menu. The fact that none of the events were on offer didn't seem to be an obstacle.

While Raquel watched, Taylor moved on from the guy running the little shack at the edge of the grassy beach, to a trio of men waiting by an empty stand that presumably once held the many kayaks dotting the blue water on the other side of the old lighthouse.

Raquel was too far to make out what Taylor was saying, but every so often her laugh was carried toward her on a warm, salty breeze. Less than a minute after approaching the men by the stand, they were all smiles.

Taylor was charming, that much was obvious, but it was how she wielded it like a sword that Raquel found intriguing. Another minute later, Taylor was pointing in Raquel's direction, her smile blinding.

One of the men, tall and tanned and athletic, smiled at Raquel. When he waved, she cautiously lifted her hand in a noncommittal acknowledgment.

What the hell are you doing, Taylor?

The four of them produced cell phones. A moment later, they'd all earned hugs from Taylor, who was happily jogging back toward Raquel.

Cheeks bright pink and perspiration gathering at her temples, Taylor was vibrating with excitement when she reached the pavilion. "Ready to fly?"

She eyed her suspiciously. "What did it cost you?"

"I bought their parasailing tickets."

"And?"

Taylor replied with a sheepish grin. "And I gave them my number, and the number for the hotel because I very strangely don't have yours." After a beat, she laughed. "Don't worry, I worded the deal very carefully. I didn't make any promises. If the two single ones filled in the blanks with the assumption that they were getting dates." She shrugged. "That's not my fault. They should listen more carefully."

Raquel shook her head, but she couldn't help her amusement. "Did you swindle them?"

Her eyes widened in exaggerated shock. Holding her hand to her chest, she pretended to be wounded. "Raquel, how could you think so little of me?"

Raquel slid off the picnic table and decided she liked the way her name sounded on Taylor's lips. "Did you con your way into something for us to wear?" She looked down at her suffocating jeans.

Taylor's ready smile didn't waver. "Leave it to me."

After Taylor talked Chet into a discount on merch, she convinced him to let them change in a storage shed.

Light filtered in through the wooden slats, giving the otherwise dark room littered with tools and gear an otherworldly glow. There was nowhere to seek privacy in the small space and as soon as they closed the door behind them, it became swelteringly hot.

Raquel looked at the neon orange shorts with *Endless Summer* emblazoned on the back. It clashed quite nicely with the neon yellow-green, long-sleeved fishing shirt with logos running down the arms.

"I'll turn around." Taylor spun away from her and started changing into her matching *Endless Summer* get up. "Let me know when you're done."

Raquel wasn't usually shy or body conscious, but as soon as Taylor turned away, she realized she'd been hesitating. The last time she'd been naked with someone in her twenties, she'd been in her twenties too.

Max had been her high school sweetheart before they got married. They'd discovered everything about their bodies together, and it wasn't until she was in her mid-thirties that she'd slept with anyone else.

Now, with her back to Taylor and no lust clouding her judgment, she felt more aware of herself than she ever had. Had Taylor picked up on a mild anxiety Raquel hadn't even noticed?

Suffocating heat pushed Raquel to hurry. As smoothly as possible, she peeled off the denim that had tried to fuse to her body. While she changed, Taylor didn't move, only turning around when Raquel announced that she was ready.

Leaving their clothes in the shack, since there was no secure place to store them in the Jeep, Raquel and Taylor shuffled through the hot sand toward the small boat waiting in the water.

The moment they were locked into the contraption in the boat's rear, Raquel realized it was a mistake. In a minute, they were going to be human kites, tethered to the back of a boat by ropes that could easily snap.

While Chet gave the safety rigging an alarmingly cursory glance, panic started to bubble up in Raquel's body. Taylor slid her hand into hers.

"It's going to be fun," she promised. "There's no reason to be scared. I'm sure Chet isn't going to let us die. Imagine that lawsuit."

Unamused, he didn't look up from something he was cranking on the boat's platform.

When Raquel didn't respond, Taylor gave her hand a squeeze. "If you don't want to—"

"No," she snapped, embarrassed by how high pitched and breathless she sounded. "I want to."

Taylor smiled. "It's gonna be awesome."

Chet jumped into the white, molded plastic driver's seat. "Neither of you are wearing contact lenses, are you?"

"And if we are?" Raquel raised a brow.

"Then I suggest you pop those suckers out because you're not going to like what the salt spray'll do to 'em." He glanced at Taylor. "If you'd booked ahead of time, you would've received a guide—"

"It's fine." Raquel wished her hands were a little cleaner, but she'd done worse. "They're disposable."

"I'm sorry, I didn't—"

Raquel took the first one out. "I just won't be able to read any street signs on the way back to the hotel." She removed the other one and slipped them into the little pocket square on her shirt. "Adventure, right?"

Intertwining their fingers, Raquel gripped Taylor's hand harder than necessary when Chet pulled back on the boat's throttle, sending a torrent of wind through her once nicely styled hair.

A rush of adrenaline and nerves tore through Raquel as the boat cut through the small waves and carried them out to the open ocean. It felt like a point of no return.

"Ready?" Chet called over the screaming engines and wall of wind.

No.

"Hell yeah!" Taylor offered a thumbs up with her free hand while Raquel threatened to break the bones in the one she was still clinging to.

With a little too much delight, Chet disconnected them from the boat and sent them flying backward. Raquel's eyes slammed shut to save her from the shame of freaking out.

Her stomach lurched as she bared down and tried desperately not to throw up. The feeling of being unmoored, unattached, untethered, was too foreign. Too much to assimilate.

"My God, this is incredible," Taylor gasped.

Raquel didn't want to know how high up a thousand feet were. She wanted to keep her eyes closed, hold her breath, and simply endure the ride.

Taylor leaned in. "You have to see this." Her voice was soft and warm compared to the cutting, cool wind.

The intense desire not to make a fool of herself pried Raquel's eyelids apart. On one side, there was an endless blue ocean. On the other, the most incredible view of the city she'd ever seen.

It was a vibrant painting coming to life just for them. Exhilaration washed over her, chasing away her terror. The freedom of flying was like nothing she'd ever experienced before.

Raquel eased her vice grip, but didn't let go of Taylor's hand. She marveled at the power of nature, at the visceral, unmistakable thrill of being alive.

"Incredible, right?" Taylor watched her expectantly.

Looking away from the downtown skyline, Raquel took a full, deep, cleansing breath. She met Taylor's bright brown eyes. "Breathtaking," she agreed.

CHAPTER 16

TAYLOR STUMBLED backward over a spool of cables and a pile of snorkeling stuff on the shack's dusty cement floor. Her back hit the wooden slat wall a nanosecond before Raquel's lips were on hers.

"Does this mean you liked parasailing?" Taylor joked between frenzied kisses.

Raquel's response was to take Taylor's bottom lip between her teeth and pull. Hard.

Taylor groaned, a stream of heat rushing out of the momentary pain and spreading through her body. "I'll shut up now."

Without a word, Raquel peeled off Taylor's wet shirt. Chet had dunked them in the water right before hauling them back onto the boat, even though she'd told him they didn't want to get wet. Instead of getting upset, Raquel had shrieked with excitement, then laughed. A true, born in the belly, laugh.

Now Raquel was dead serious and focused on very little other than getting Taylor's clothes off. The wet shirt landed with a slap on the floor.

Taylor responded in kind. In the same quick motion, she gripped the drenched fabric, pulled Raquel's shirt over her head and tossed it aside.

In the low, glowing light of the late afternoon sun streaming in through the gaps in the wood, Raquel was breathtaking. Like she was lit by the gods themselves.

Raquel's ample chest strained against her sexy black bra. Her soft, smooth belly trembled, giving away her breathlessness. Hips curved dangerously before easing into perfectly thick thighs. Taylor wanted to drop to her knees and pay homage to her beauty, but Raquel pulled her in again.

"We should get dry," Raquel whispered, her lips hovering over Taylor's but staying just out of reach.

"Then we're doing this all wrong." She kissed her again, parting her lips with her tongue and moaning when Raquel slipped her thigh between her legs.

Unable to help herself, Taylor started grinding against her, desperate for the release that only kept building.

Raquel smirked against her lips before grabbing Taylor's hip and pulling her hard over her thigh. A clamoring beneath them made her guess that Raquel had propped her foot up on something and bent her leg to give Taylor something sturdier to work with.

With her arms flung around Raquel's neck, Taylor leaned back and pulled Raquel flush against her gyrating body.

"I need you," Taylor begged, not ashamed to be the first to yield.

Raquel kept one hand on Taylor's side, slowing the swing of her hips, but slid the other up her abdomen and over her chest. Taylor imagined a bioluminescent show, her body lighting up everywhere Raquel's fingertips grazed.

"What do you need?" Raquel pulled down the cup of Taylor's bra, exposing her to the increasingly oppressive, stale air in the shed.

Taylor's jaw dropped open in a silent scream as Raquel slid off her lips, her mouth hot and her teeth sharp as they moved over her neck.

"Touch me," she managed in little more than a whisper.

Raquel paused, her smirk brushing over Taylor's clavicle. "I am touching you." She squeezed Taylor's breast as if to prove the point.

"Not there."

Slipping her hand out of Taylor's bra, Raquel whispered against her ear. "Tell me what you want, Miss Lopez."

The hushed demand was a destabilizing rush of lust pulling hard between Taylor's trembling thighs.

Taking Raquel's roving hand, Taylor slid it over her torso and down her inner thigh. With growing confidence, she eased Raquel's hand under the loose leg of her shorts.

Putting her out of her misery, Raquel stopped playing coy. She broke away from Taylor's grasp and found the edge of her underwear.

As soon as her fingertips brushed her throbbing, hard flesh, Taylor cursed. Tipping her hips, Taylor desperately sought more pressure, more friction, more contact.

"Raquel, please. I need to feel you inside me."

With something like a pained sigh, Raquel's mouth crashed into her lips hard. Hooking her fingers around the wet fabric of her underwear, Raquel pushed it roughly to one side.

The sound of the material ripping sent another hard pulse of painful arousal rocking Taylor's decimated body. Tossing her head back, there was nothing but Raquel's fingers discovering the overwhelming evidence of her arousal.

Raquel dropped her head, resting her forehead against Taylor's shoulder while her fingers glided along Taylor's soaked, sensitive flesh. Her quiet moan vibrated in Taylor's body, pushing her to the edge.

Maddeningly slow, Raquel moved in lazy circles before dipping the tips of her fingers into Taylor.

"You're killing me," Taylor cried, digging her blunt fingernails into Raquel's back. She needed more. More of Raquel's body. More of her touch. More of everything.

A hard bang at the door sent Raquel flying back like a ghost had yanked her.

"Ladies, you need to hurry in there. I want to go home, you know," Chet shouted through the closed door.

Dazed, Taylor watched Raquel start to change into the dry clothes she'd left folded on a stack of boxes. Her body was still humming, still ready for Raquel to slide inside of her.

"We should go," Raquel said, not looking back at her.

"And you should take those off." Taylor moved toward and put her hands on Raquel's hips before kissing the back of her neck.

Raquel stopped with her jeans in her hands and her wet shorts on the floor. She relaxed beneath Taylor's touch, allowing her to snake her arms around her waist and kiss her from behind.

"It's never a good idea to wear wet underwear," Taylor said with her lips on her shoulder.

Hooking her thumbs into the waistband, Taylor took her time pulling the fabric down an inch at a time. Raquel reached back, tangling her fingers in Taylor's damp hair.

"Ladies!" Chet banged again. "Please don't make me come in there! No one takes this long to change!"

With a sigh, Raquel wiggled out of her underwear and pulled on her jeans before Taylor could enjoy her body.

"Hurry, I don't want him to come in here," Raquel said over her shoulder as she finished dressing.

Begrudgingly, Taylor peeled off the rest of her wet clothes and went commando right along with Raquel.

Bundling her newly purchased Endless Summer merch and shoving her underwear in the middle, Taylor couldn't resist kissing Raquel again. It was like the more she did it, the more she needed it.

After apologizing to an irate Chet, they strolled through the sand and back to the parking lot. With the sun well on its way to setting, nearly all the cars were gone.

Taylor slipped her hand into Raquel's as they walked. "I can't believe we're leaving tomorrow. I feel like we just got here."

Raquel lingered at the front of the Jeep, her fingers intertwined with Taylor's as if she didn't want to let her go. Taylor stepped closer, memorizing how Raquel's sun-kissed cheeks brought out the auburn in her eyes.

"I've had a really nice time with you." Raquel's voice was soft and low and too much like goodbye.

"Hey." Taylor tucked a wayward strand of wavy brown hair behind Raquel's ear. "It's not over yet, right? There is still the reunion tonight and breakfast tomorrow." It sounded worse when Taylor said it out loud.

Raquel's weak smile was a punch to the gut. Taylor didn't want to think about what would happen when the weekend was over. It's not like Vermont was that far from the city, but if they weren't even talking about what they were doing in the present, she doubted they'd discuss the future. She didn't want to admit that Brianna was right about this being a fling, but she wasn't stupid.

"You're right," Raquel agreed abruptly. Throwing one arm around Taylor's neck, she pulled her in and kissed her deeply and openly and publicly. "It's not over yet."

The drive back to the school was much quieter than the ride to the beach. It was impossible to ignore the reality that had settled over them like a fog. Whatever they had, it was coming to an end.

CHAPTER 17

"Trust me." Brianna, dressed in a mid-length floral-print dress, snapped the curling iron in her hand.

"It's a fine line between whatever you're going for and *boucles.*" Behind Brianna, Alexis was sitting cross-legged in the hotel room's armchair by the window. She was already dressed in her Havana Nights best; a crisp, cream-colored linen suit, her undercut freshly buzzed and bun painfully tight.

Perched on the edge of her bed in nothing but a towel, Taylor was also dubious about Brianna's plan for her hair.

"What do you know, topknot?" Brianna pointed her curling iron at Alexis like a dueling pistol. "She's gonna look like the Cuban Lauren Bacall."

"Who the hell is that?" Jessica emerged from the bathroom in a short, bright yellow guayabera dress and matching flats.

Brianna rolled her eyes. "You know that Gloria Estefan *Mi Tierra* album cover? Very that."

"And how do I get this thing in my hair?" Jessica was wearing her hair natural and curly for the event, probably at Brianna's behest.

"Sit," Brianna barked at Jessica before making Taylor hold the hot curling iron. Once Jessica was seated, Brianna gathered her hair on one side and pinned the tropical yellow and orange flower in Jessica's hair.

Alexis looked at her smartwatch. "You know we're going to be late, right? Why aren't you dressed?"

Taylor smirked. "Because I was out with Raquel a lot longer than I expected."

Jessica made a swooning face. "Oh, *Raquel.*" She laughed. "I can't believe you got so lucky. You should play the lottery. Cash in while you can."

"I told you Heart Stopper was a—"

"Whatever you're going to say," Brianna warned, "don't."

Alexis scoffed. "You're so inconsistent. Did you forget about making me look at your nipples when you picked me up an hour ago?"

"That was for your medical opinion. Now, when I asked you about Danny's—"

"Okay, let's get back on track, yeah? Just do my hair however the hell you want, Bri."

Brianna smiled triumphantly and snapped her curling iron again. "So, are you two going to get married and have babies, or what?" She took a segment of Taylor's hair and wrapped it around the metal rod.

"We haven't talked about... Well, we haven't really talked about much of anything," Taylor admitted.

"Too busy getting it in," Alexis guessed with a brow wiggle.

Taylor considered it for a moment. "Yeah, I guess so. Bri is probably right. She's here for a fling and nothing else."

"Don't sound so bummed, T." Jessica put her hand on her bare shoulder. "How many people can say that they got to be with the object of their teenage affections? Even if just for a weekend. Wouldn't you have given anything for this ten years ago?"

"Yeah, bro. Enjoy it," Alexis agreed.

"Plus, wait until she sees you tonight." Brianna curled another segment of hair. "Bitch, you're going to look drop dead gorgeous."

"What are you going to wear?" Jessica crossed the hotel room to the closet by the door.

"It's hanging in the front," Taylor replied.

Pulling out her outfit, Jessica smiled. "Okay, girl. This is cute."

White, high-waisted, linen trousers were the flowing partner to a white, linen guayabera she'd had tailored into a cropped halter top. Living with an ex who worked in costume design off Broadway had some perks.

"That tan is going to pop against that white linen, and your hair and makeup is going to look banging. I'm giving you a blood red lip. Oof, sexy as hell. Alonso might just pass out, bitch. She's not going to be able to take it!"

The others echoed Brianna's encouragement until Taylor shook off the gloom that had started drifting over her. They were right. If all she had was this weekend, she wanted to enjoy every second of it.

An hour later, the trio walked into the hotel's ballroom. Decorated like Havana's Tropicana circa 1940, the bland space had been converted into a casino complete with roulette, card tables, and a silent auction.

"Why do private schools use every opportunity to raise money? Isn't all that tuition enough?" Brianna asked as they perused the silent auction table they had to pass before getting to the cash bar in the back.

"And why is it literally always pre-World War II Havana?" Alexis jotted her name down on a boat-related auction item.

"Nostalgia, man. It always works." Jessica picked up a brochure for a fancy, private gym membership.

Taylor scanned the sea of flower hairpieces and fedoras looking for Raquel. "Yeah, well, I don't think more than one percent of this room was alive in the forties, and it was certainly nobody's heyday."

"Yeah, but it's not like the nineties are ever going to have that kind of glamor." Alexis shrugged. "Who are people going to dress like? Kurt Cobain and Lenny Kravitz? It's like the twenties and the gilded age and shit like that. Some eras are just kinda sexy."

"Exactly." Brianna pointed at her husband braving the line for gambling chips dressed in a white suit and matching fedora. "Look how handsome he looks. You think you're going to get that with flannel?"

"Yeah, let's romanticize eras of legalized oppression, so hot. I'm sure we all would've fared *so* well," Jessica added.

Taylor took Jessica's side. "Jess is right. We would be in a back-room somewhere trying to cobble together a community. It's not like being out and proud would be an option for us."

Taylor wanted to continue the conversation, but she'd spotted Raquel across the room. She couldn't waste a second. Taylor gave Brianna's forearm a squeeze. "I'll catch up with you guys."

"Yeah, right," Jessica said with a laugh.

"Live the dream." Alexis patted her on the back, sending her on her way toward Raquel, who was being swarmed by a mob of Taylor's former classmates. The half of the class who hadn't participated in any of the weekend-long activities.

In a ruffled, off the shoulder maroon dress and gold hoop earrings, Raquel had slicked back her dark bob and done something with her makeup to make her tanned skin glow. Her full lips painted a glossy nude, only made her bright brown eyes more beautiful. Brianna had been wrong. It was Raquel that was serving a lethal look tonight.

Waiting on the periphery, Taylor chatted with people she hadn't seen in a decade while wave after wave of admirers crashed into Raquel. Apparently, her reputation for being tough hadn't stopped her from being everybody's favorite.

After dozens of conversations about what everyone was doing, even though no one had really lost touch thanks to social media, Taylor jumped at the chance to slip alongside her.

Without looking at Raquel, Taylor sipped her Pinot Noir and pretended to be casual. "I didn't remember you being so popular, Mrs. Alonso."

She felt Raquel's smile. It was the sun warming her skin. "And here you thought you were the only one who appreciated my history lessons." She tipped back her glass and finished what remained of her white wine.

Taylor's attention drifted to the glass' rim, envious she wasn't the one wearing Raquel's lip prints.

"Have you played any of the games?" Taylor remained in her spot next to Raquel like they were a couple of spies pretending to be strangers on a park bench, identical briefcases placed next to each other and ready for the illicit trade.

Raquel's eyes were the only things that moved as she swept over the room. "I've never been one for gambling."

"Come on, Mrs. Alonso. Doesn't it feel like the kind of night to get lucky?" Taylor grinned.

Raquel wrestled a momentary smirk into submission. "That's the thing with luck, isn't it? It's not something you can count on."

Taylor pressed her hand to her chest and mimed pulling an arrow from her heart. Pretending to recover, Taylor bounced back. "Look around you. We come from an immigrant people and accomplished all this. We make our own luck. Tonight is a sure thing."

"I didn't know you had such an entrepreneurial spirit." Raquel's lips twitched, but she managed to subdue her smile.

Taylor nodded, trying so hard not to give in to the urge to kiss Raquel right then. "There is so much you don't know about me. So many parts I'm dying to show you."

Raquel shifted her weight between her high-heel-clad feet. That one got her, Taylor realized with supreme satisfaction.

Before she could capitalize on the moment, another one of her former classmates appeared. While she bombarded Raquel with pictures of her twins, Taylor slipped away.

Rejoining her friends who'd glommed onto a larger group, Taylor couldn't stop watching Raquel. Judging by the eye contact she made every few minutes, Raquel was just as distracted. Just as focused on her. Just as starved.

Well after Raquel was honored with her teaching award, and most people were a little tipsy and spending way too much money on casino games, Taylor watched Raquel break off from a tangle of students.

Buzzing from a few glasses of wine, Taylor followed her with her gaze. When Raquel reached the ballroom's side door, the one leading to the bathrooms in the hallway, she looked back at Taylor.

She hadn't needed to search for Taylor in the crowd. With the precision of a laser-guided missile, she caught her gaze, making it clear she'd never lost sight of her either. The corner of her full, glossy lips pulled into a dangerous little smirk. One that screamed: *Come get me... I dare you.*

When she disappeared through the door, Taylor's thumping heart rallied the rest of her overheated body and propelled her across the large room.

Like a hunter tracking dangerous game, Taylor slipped through the same door, her senses on high alert. As soon as she saw the line of women waiting for the bathroom, Taylor's heart dropped.

It lifted as soon as she realized Raquel wasn't in the line.

Where the hell did you go?

Taylor's heels clicked on the white tile floor as she meandered out of the corridor and into the lobby, her anticipation growing with every step.

Away from the music and the crowd, a handful of husbands and partners had taken over couches and armchairs scattered around the front desk to chat. Raquel was not among them.

Thrilled by the unexpected cat-and-mouse game, Taylor continued her search.

At the end of a lonely hallway near the hotel's empty business center, Taylor found another bathroom. She bit the inside of her cheek to keep from grinning and pushed open the door.

Leaning over one of three sinks built into a perfectly standard vanity, Raquel was re-applying the nude gloss on her lips. Her eyes, dark and dangerous, shifted. With a nearly imperceptible hint of amusement, she watched Taylor in the mirror's reflection.

Behind her, Taylor locked the bathroom door. Bending over, Taylor quickly scanned the three stalls to make sure there were no feet visible in the gaps.

Raquel turned, leaning against the vanity as she popped her

lipstick back in her bag. She was primed to say something, but Taylor didn't give her the chance.

Unleashing the pent-up desire that had been building all night, Taylor lunged. Capturing Raquel's lips with hers, she pressed her hard against the countertop.

A moan rumbled in Raquel's chest as she threw her arms around Taylor's neck. Pulling her in hard and flush against her body, Raquel kissed her like she meant to consume her.

Aware that their privacy was limited and there was no time to waste, Taylor slid her open palms over Raquel's smooth, thick thighs. Gripping her tight, she yanked. In a fluid movement, Raquel slid back on the vanity, her legs hooked around Taylor's hips.

"You look so fucking good tonight," Taylor groaned breathlessly against Raquel's full lips. "Watching you has been driving me absolutely insane."

Raquel's lips brushed against Taylor's mouth when she smirked. It lasted a fraction of a second before she kissed her again.

Taylor tossed her head back, letting Raquel leave a trail of lightly tinted lip gloss over her throat. Sneaking a glance in the mirror, she nearly combusted at the sight of Raquel, her head bobbing just a little while she grazed Taylor's neck with her teeth.

It was too much. The desire that pounded in Taylor's body was too much to take. She couldn't keep doing this without relief.

Raquel's blunt fingernails rolled over the thin linen of Taylor's top and dug into her lower back. "Tell me," Raquel demanded. She was just as breathless. Just as desperate.

Gliding her palms up Raquel's thighs, Taylor reached around and grabbed the awe-inspiring swell of her ass. Digging her fingers into her perfect flesh, she confessed. "All I could think about was getting you alone. Waiting until no one was looking so I could slide my hands up the back of your dress."

Moving around to the front of Taylor's pants, Raquel unfastened them without fumbling with the button. Her fingers were confident and sure when they found the zipper.

At the glorious sound of the metal unzipping, Taylor's body pulsed with an aching, ardent desire.

"Don't start something you can't finish, Raquel," she warned more harshly than she intended, letting her trousers fall open and down her hips.

Undeterred, Raquel slipped her hand inside Taylor's pants. Her fingers brushed Taylor's hard flesh over the thin fabric of her underwear. The contact, light and teasing, tore through Taylor's body like the start of an avalanche.

"You really have been thinking about me," Raquel said with breathy delight.

Bracing herself against the counter, Taylor rested her weight on one palm. With her eyes closed, she was overwhelmed by the heat of Raquel's mouth on her neck, on her fingertips rolling over the wet fabric of her underwear.

"Please," Taylor whined, "let's go upstairs. I can't keep doing this. I'm going to die."

"Die?" Raquel chuckled. "That's extreme."

Taylor opened her eyes and leaned back to look at Raquel. Her kiss-swollen lips were bare and inviting. "You won't be laughing at my funeral."

Raquel responded by shoving Taylor's underwear to one side and touching her bare, soaked flesh with her elegant fingers.

The contact was too much. Taylor crumpled forward, the intense sensation rushing over her. Her eyes slammed shut, her brain unable to process any more information.

Taylor dissolved into two single points. The place where Raquel's mouth was on her neck and where her fingers were pressing against her.

A jiggling at the door ripped Taylor from her reverie. Nearly crying at the loss of Raquel's touch, she dropped her head and rested her forehead on Raquel's shoulder.

"I can't keep doing this," Taylor whispered. "I'm sick of being interrupted. I just want to be with you." She could hear herself whining, but was powerless to stop.

Raquel slid off the counter and smoothed down her dress. Giving Taylor her back, she reapplied her lip gloss.

The person at the door pulled on the handle again. It rocked loudly against the frame.

Jesus! Who the hell needs to get in here so badly?

When Raquel turned around again, Taylor had zipped up her pants. Raquel opened her clutch and handed her a room key. "Room 505." She kissed her cheek. "Give me an hour to wrap up here."

Taylor's smile bloomed from somewhere deep inside of her. The rattling door stopped her before she could say anything. "For the love..." She glared at the door and the irritating person behind it.

"Get in the stall," Taylor whispered.

"What?"

"Trust me." She smirked without spelling out that she didn't want to explain what they were doing in there with the door locked.

Looking suspect, Raquel slipped into the stall and closed the door. Collecting herself, Taylor tried to clear the lust from her body, or at least from her face.

When she opened the door, Mrs. Fraga, the Dementor, was waiting for her.

"Miss Lopez," she croaked. "What were you doing?"

Throwing away the paper towel as if she'd used it to open the door, Taylor tipped her head to the side. "What am I doing in the bathroom?" She pretended to be embarrassed by the question. "I'm using—"

"What are you doing in here with the door locked?" The old, miserable woman pointed a boney finger at her.

"Was the door locked?" Taylor skirted Fraga and slipped out of the bathroom. "How strange that the door locked behind me. I'll go tell the front desk there must be something wrong with the hardware."

Despite Fraga's suspicious scowl, Taylor smiled and disappeared.

As she bounded down the hallway, with Raquel's room key in her hand, she resisted the urge to skip and whistle and cartwheel.

CHAPTER 18

AFTER SHAVING her legs again for good measure and washing the product out of her hair, Raquel paced her hotel room. Wearing the complimentary thick terrycloth robe and nothing else, Raquel stared at her open suitcase on the luggage rack in the closet.

There wasn't a style guide for what to wear when sleeping with someone nearly twenty years younger than her. She'd Googled. Nothing. There should be some magic negligee that made her boobs sit higher and her belly flatter.

Looking through her limited clean clothing options for the third time, Raquel couldn't find anything suitable. Everything hanging in the closet was too formal and everything folded was too casual.

It was too soon to let Taylor see her in a baggy T-shirt and leggings. Raquel shook her head. This wasn't a *too soon* kinda thing. It was a one-time thing, and she wished she had something sexy to wear.

"You pack enough underwear for a month and you couldn't throw in at least one thong or something?" she grumbled at the version of herself who packed the suitcase, the one who had clearly forgotten about sex.

The last thing she wanted Taylor to see was her wearing something beige or utilitarian. Or worse, something beige *and* utilitarian.

"Nothing says I want to rip your clothes off like a skin-toned control top."

Paralyzed by indecision, Raquel had managed to accomplish nothing more than putting on a little eyeliner when the knock came at the door. Her heart rocketed into her throat like it was seeking refuge from a hungry lion.

Tossing her hair to one side, she gave herself another once-over. Robes were hot, right? Who didn't like a woman in a robe?

For the first time in a long time, Raquel was nervous. She smoothed the terrycloth and tightened the sash before shaking her head and loosening it again.

Frozen in the bathroom, she didn't know what to say. She wanted to call out a breathy, 'Come in,' but she couldn't make herself speak. She'd given herself too much time to think about this. Too much time to realize what a terrible idea it was.

A moment later, the door creaked open. Taylor, her chestnut hair falling in deep waves after having shaken out the evening's hairstyle, peeked in. "Can I come in?"

Raquel stood in the doorway to the bathroom. The sight of Taylor filled her with a sudden sense of calm. She wasn't preparing to meet a stranger. It was Taylor. They'd already shared a year's worth of laughs together.

Taylor's bright brown eyes and expectant smile chased away Raquel's fears. Destroyed her nerves and replaced them with excitement. With anticipation.

Raquel sauntered toward the door, wearing her delight in her eyes and letting it tug at the edges of her lips. Reaching for Taylor, she pulled her into the room with a decisive yank.

Freshly washed skin and delicately perfumed hair and a clean T-shirt combined to make a fragrance that was uniquely Taylor. Raquel inhaled it greedily, like her body wanted to store it and take it as a souvenir.

On her bare feet, Raquel was a little shorter than Taylor, something she realized she enjoyed as she wrapped her arms around her neck.

"I've missed you." Taylor's breath was warm against her lips, her hold on her hips tight and confident.

Without saying a word, Raquel showed her that the hour they'd spent apart had been long for her too. That she hadn't been able to think about anything but kissing her since their encounter in the bathroom. That even before then, she'd been inundated with thoughts of her. That since the first time they'd kissed, she left her lips and skin and chest vibrating.

The moment Taylor's lips touched hers, Raquel's body ignited, releasing all the energy that had been gathering, waiting to be unleashed.

Kissing Taylor as she walked backward, Raquel pulled her out of the small hall and into the bedroom.

Taylor's hands were everywhere; sliding down her back, over her ass, climbing up her sides, tangling in her hair as she deepened their kiss. It was like she couldn't get enough. Like she wanted every part of her all at once. Suddenly, what she was wearing didn't seem to matter.

As soon as Taylor hooked her finger in the knot of her robe, Raquel closed her hand over hers to stop her. "Wait," she whispered breathlessly. "Maybe we should turn off the light."

Leaning back to look at her while she was still holding Raquel's face, Taylor furrowed her brow. "Why?"

A flash of heat swarmed over Raquel's face. The light from the floor lamp in the corner was soft, nowhere near as bright as the recessed lighting in the ceiling would be, but it still felt like she was showing too much. Exposing too much.

"I'm happy to turn it off if that's what *you* want." Taylor's palms were so warm against her jaw. Her eyes were so open and bright and sincere. "But if you think I don't want to see every single reckless curve on your body, you're absolutely crazy. You're perfect, Raquel. You're incredible."

Raquel hesitated. She'd never been shy before. Never had inhibitions about being seen naked. The only thing holding her back was Taylor. If she wasn't so much younger, she wouldn't have thought twice about disrobing.

"I don't want to pressure you." Taylor dropped her hands and shifted her weight like she was going to turn off the lamp and plunge them into darkness.

Raquel caught one of her hands before she could get away. "No," she said in a soft, low voice. The sexy tone she'd been searching for when Taylor knocked on the door. "You're not pressuring me."

Taylor quirked one an eyebrow. "No? You sure?"

Raquel nodded. She was sure.

Moistening her lips, Taylor let her gaze drip slowly down Raquel's body like spilled honey. "I have been fantasizing about this for so long." She ran her fingertips along the edge of the collar. Her touch was scalding.

"Far be it from me to stand in the way of your dreams, Miss Lopez."

Both dimples cut deeply into Taylor's smooth cheeks when she grinned. "You're seriously perfect, you know?"

Raquel kissed her again, stopping whatever else Taylor was going to say.

Different from the desperate and deliciously messy kisses she'd come to expect, Taylor moved slowly. Her tongue slipped beyond her parted lips like a scalpel instead of a battering ram. It reverberated in Raquel's body, lifting her like a novel flavor, a brand-new color, a revolutionary song.

Taylor's hands found the knot in the sash again. She tugged on it just a little. Just enough to loosen. Just enough to create a plunging neckline all the way to the middle of Raquel's torso.

Kissing a line down Raquel's chin, Taylor maintained her slow, intentional pace. The pace that was building a quickly spreading heat, pulsing and pulling, between Raquel's thighs.

Tipping her head back to give Taylor more access, Raquel gasped at the sharpness of Taylor's teeth scrapping against her neck. The minor pain amplified by her increasingly sensitive skin.

Raquel tangled her fingers in Taylor's hair and pulled her closer. She wanted more. Needed more.

In response, Taylor slid her open palm down Raquel's neck and over the center of her chest. Her mouth followed a moment later. She left a long, wet line where her lips were; evidence of her slow descent.

Before Raquel could tumble into the king-sized bed with her, Taylor eased to her knees.

She looked down at the woman kneeling at her feet. "What are you doing?" Her voice was deep and covered in unmasked desire.

Taylor looked up at her, her eyes a dark storm threatening the coast, dangerous and chaotic and intent. Without responding, she tugged gently on the sash, sending the robe sliding apart.

Raquel watched Taylor's expression change to something she could only describe as awe. Like she'd been favored with a great privilege. Like she was honoring a goddess come to Earth.

Flushed with heat, Raquel didn't know what to do with a reaction like that. Not only had no one ever looked at her with such overt reverence, she was positive no one in the world had ever admired anyone the way Taylor looked at her. It was like she was a Renaissance painter studying their inspiration. Like she wanted to immortalize her in fresco or tempera or oils.

Taylor kissed her hip lightly, filling Raquel with an incredible sense of power. She slipped her hand through Taylor's silky hair and lost herself in the act of being lavished.

Closing her eyes, she focused on the warmth of Taylor's lips as she blessed nearly every inch of Raquel's thighs and torso and everywhere in between. Each kiss was a rush of electric heat racing and building and aching.

Reaching up to her chest, Taylor found her sensitive nipples with her fingers. Her light touch produced a fresh wave of mounting desire.

Raquel tightened her grip on Taylor's hair. She directed her mouth away from her upper thigh, moving her attention to where she needed it.

In response, Taylor slid her hands down Raquel's chest and over the curve of her hips before reaching back and digging her blunt nails into her soft flesh. Without warning, Taylor buried her face between

Raquel's thighs as if needing to feel her with her nose, her chin, her lips.

At the sudden contact, Raquel stumbled back before regaining her balance. Taylor was undeterred.

In a display of control, she slid one hand down the back of her thigh to hold her in place. The other, she used to spread Raquel open and drink her in.

The moment Taylor's mouth found her dripping arousal, Raquel gasped.

Taylor's moans echoed against her, obviously pleased to discover just how wet she'd made her. She slid her tongue along the length of her before capturing her aching hard point between her lips.

Wishing she had something to brace herself against, Raquel grew increasingly unsteady on her feet. She let Taylor go where ever she wanted. Let her use her fingers, her tongue, her lips, however quickly or slowly or softly or hard. Everything felt good. There was infinite pleasure in the exploration for her, and Taylor's moans vibrated against her with the increasing rumble of nearing thunder.

Reaching down with her free hand, Raquel relieved Taylor of her duty and held herself open for her. Taylor paused long enough to sigh a curse before pressing her mouth to her again, taking her in more fully.

Raquel threw her head back, gyrating her hips to grind against Taylor's skillful tongue. When her thighs started trembling and she couldn't stand being on the edge anymore, she pulled Taylor to her feet, relieving her of her supplicant pose.

This time, Raquel was the battering ram instead of the scalpel. She captured Taylor in a crushing kiss. She tasted herself on Taylor's mouth and chin and throat, drunk off the combined flavor of her and Taylor.

Moaning and desperate, Taylor pulled off Raquel's increasingly stifling robe. It slid easily off her shoulders and landed in a puddle on the floor.

Raquel tugged at the bottom of Taylor's T-shirt. Their increasingly frantic kiss paused only for the second it took Raquel to pull Taylor's shirt over her head, damp with perspiration, and flung it across the room. Clawing blindly at the clasp on Taylor's bra, she unhooked it with a practiced move; a soundless snapping gesture that unfastened the material.

Spinning Taylor around, Raquel gave her a playful little shove. With a devilish grin on her swollen lips, Taylor let herself fall back onto the mattress, the lust in her eyes thumping like a wall of speakers at a heavy metal show.

Raquel lingered at the foot of the bed and let herself be admired. She didn't admit to herself that she needed a second to recover. To regain control.

Propped up on her elbows, Taylor's gaze fell over her body. Raquel felt it everywhere it landed. Like Taylor's lips, her eyes were ravenous.

When Taylor's expression turned pained, Raquel responded with a decisively villainous laugh and rested her knee between Taylor's denim-covered legs. The contact sent a shockwave through Raquel she hadn't expected.

Confirming what she didn't think could be true, she shoved her hand between Taylor's thighs. Raquel closed her eyes to absorb the new level of desire screaming in her body. Taylor had gotten so turned on, she could feel it through her jeans.

Raquel opened her eyes in time to watch Taylor throw her head back and moan at the muffled friction caused by Raquel pressing against her through the fabric.

"Lie back." Raquel's voice was a deep, sultry growl.

Taylor obeyed, scrambling up the bed and resting her head on a stack of two pillows.

It was Raquel's turn to appreciate the beauty of Taylor's body; the definition of the lean muscles in her arms, the abstract lines tattooed on her forearm, her nicely toned abdomen and smooth skin.

Taking her small breast in her hand, she slid her mouth over her flushed throat. Immediately, Taylor moaned so close to Raquel's ear that she felt the sound inside her own body more than she heard it.

Raquel slid between Taylor's thighs more completely, pushing them apart. Using both her hands, Taylor grabbed Raquel's ass again with unshakable confidence, her blunt nails digging into her proceeded a pleasurable jolt dancing up her spine.

"Kiss me," Taylor cried, rocking her hips and grinding against Raquel like she could will her inside of her, like the thick fabric separating them didn't exist.

Raquel couldn't resist her pained pleading. She kissed her hard and deep. Beneath her, Taylor unraveled. She tightened her grip, forcing Raquel's pelvis to grind harder against her.

Tightening her core muscles, Raquel gave Taylor what she wanted, grinding rhythmically against her. Indulging her until she was afraid Taylor might come before Raquel had a chance to touch her.

Abruptly, Raquel broke their kiss and stopped grinding against her. As she moved down Taylor's chest, Taylor continued rocking her hips. Her body hadn't gotten the message that Raquel was no longer there, or maybe it had refused to believe it.

Taylor tangled her fingers in Raquel's hair. "Please," she whined.

Raquel glanced up at her as she slid the tip of her tongue down her hot belly, lapping the delightfully salty sheen of perspiration. She grinned, but didn't stop until she reached the waistband of her jeans.

Taylor watched her with half-shut eyes and her eyebrows drawn together, as if it took great effort to keep her eyes open, but she didn't want to miss a thing.

Raquel wanted to memorize her expression in that moment. To take it with her, along with her fragrance and the weight of her lips on hers.

Slowly, she made a show of unbuttoning Taylor's jeans, biting on her bottom lip when the material eased apart.

Once Taylor's jeans were hanging open, Raquel brushed her lips over the newly exposed skin well below Taylor's navel. She rewarded Taylor's breathy moans by running her tongue just beneath the waistband of her small, black underwear.

Taylor bucked her hips, urging Raquel lower. When Raquel tugged at her tight jeans, Taylor quickly lifted her butt off the bed and pushed them halfway down her thighs.

With a hard yank, Raquel slipped what remained of Taylor's

clothing off her legs and tossed them over the edge of the bed.

Leaning forward, Raquel kissed the side of Taylor's knee. Blazing a quick trail up the inside of Taylor's thigh, she stopped short of sliding her mouth over where Taylor needed her most.

Infinitely pleased with her decision to leave the room bathed in light just bright enough to see by, Raquel eyed Taylor's smooth flesh glistening with arousal. She was sure that the moment she touched Taylor with her tongue, it was going to be over. She was too close to the edge.

Testing her theory, Raquel touched Taylor. Letting her very hard, very swollen flesh slide between her fingers. Taylor shuddered, her body stiffening and her thighs trembling.

"You're not going to last two seconds like this." Raquel hadn't intended to use her professional tone, deep and measured, to sound like she was scolding her.

Taylor's hips lifted off the bed as she groaned, as if just that voice might do her in.

"What am I supposed to do with you?"

"I can control it," Taylor promised, her voice little more than a whimper.

"I think we both know that's a lie." Proving the point, Raquel teased her soaked entrance with a featherlight touch.

Taylor cursed, her body tense and rigid.

Using all the self-control she'd ever possessed, Raquel withdrew her fingers. Pretending to be dismayed instead of painfully aroused, Raquel sighed.

"I'm afraid I'm not going to be able to touch you like this," she said with exaggerated regret.

Taylor's eyes shot open, her face dressed up in unmitigated horror.

Before Taylor could ask questions, Raquel drew herself up to her knees. Instead of getting off the bed like Taylor might have feared, she turned around.

Pulling out a move she hadn't done in years, Raquel faced away from Taylor as she straddled her. Reverse cowgirl had always been her most dangerous weapon.

As soon as she was settled over Taylor's pelvis, Taylor devolved into a string of curses. Knowing her power, Raquel tossed a lazy glance over her shoulder. She didn't want to miss Taylor's expression when she started swinging her hips.

Giving her something she probably hadn't imagined in her fantasies, Raquel slipped both hands into her own hair, holding her arms above her head, and rolled her hips slowly.

Taylor didn't disappoint. With her mouth hanging open, she was obviously overwhelmed in the very best way.

Closing her eyes, Raquel's attention slid away from Taylor's face and into the sensation of grinding against her. Raquel had also let herself get way too aroused. She wouldn't last much longer than Taylor.

After a beat, Taylor gripped Raquel's hips and changed her rhythm, speeding it up. It only took a moment for Taylor to counter each swing of Raquel's hips with a thrust of her own.

Each time they collided made it harder and harder for Raquel to hold herself up on trembling thighs. Each time Raquel came up to the edge, but couldn't drop over it.

"Lean forward," Taylor demanded, her voice hot and husky.

Raquel bent over, resting her weight on the hand she splayed on the bed. The shift gave her better contact, but she doubted that had been Taylor's motive.

Losing Taylor's hands on her hips, she suddenly felt their return with a hard, possessive slap on the sides of her ass.

Surprised and aroused, Raquel cursed before dipping her chest closer to the bed, resting her weight on her elbow instead of her hand.

Alternating between gripping her hard and well-placed smacks, Taylor drove Raquel to the very limits of her arousal.

"Can you come like this?" Taylor asked, like she'd been holding back and was desperate to let herself go.

"I'm close," Raquel confessed, her words breathy and pained. "But I can't—"

Taylor snaked her hand between their bodies, giving Raquel her curved fingers to grind against. At the adequate friction, Raquel nearly cried.

Slowing her pace, she rolled her hips to make small, languid circles in Taylor's hand. Raquel crossed the barrier she'd been unable to climb before. She let the heat gather at her core, collecting like elastic energy ready to uncoil and redistribute it throughout the rest of her body.

Using the hand that wasn't trembling as it held her up, Raquel slid it underneath herself. Stretching, she found Taylor.

She'd never used the backs of her fingers like this before, but the moment the knuckle of her middle finger found Taylor, she started to curse, encouraging her to continue. Like Raquel, she was probably just relieved to have something stiff to grind against.

The sound of Taylor moaning and cursing combined with her body stiffening beneath her was enough to send her spiraling over the edge. The building energy snapped.

Raquel announced what was obvious as she bared down, her body tense as it absorbed the orgasm days in the making. Taylor was a fraction of a second behind her, shaking hard between Raquel's thighs as she cried and cursed and thrashed.

With the aftershocks still pulling at her, Raquel slid down a few inches, letting her slick, sensitive flesh slide over Taylor's.

Breathless, Taylor cursed before her breath hitched. She'd only meant to brush against her as they came down from their incredible high together, but Taylor came alive beneath her.

Sliding one leg out from beneath Raquel, Taylor repositioned herself until Raquel could feel her fully against her sensitive core.

Resting her chest against Taylor's thigh, Raquel planted both her forearms against the mattress. She loved the feeling of Taylor's hands on her hips. Of how easily she moved her around.

Overriding the fact that she was too tender to go again, Raquel kept up the quick pace Taylor needed. Even when Taylor's hands dropped off her hips and made fists in the bed.

Raquel kept up the frenzied rhythm until she felt Taylor climax hard against her. Into her.

CHAPTER 19

"SO ARE you going to tell me whether I broke a couple of the Ten Commandments?" Taylor closed the mini-fridge with her foot and carried two bottles of water across the room with her.

Raquel, her wavy bob a perfectly sexy mess, sat up in bed. She pulled the sheet up to cover her bare chest before accepting the water bottle. "What?" Her voice was even more seductive now that she was hoarse from surprisingly loud sex.

Taylor cracked open the plastic top and plopped down next to her, leaving her nudity on display. She might not have lost her voice like Raquel, but with the sun nearly up, she was wiped out. "I'm just saying." She shrugged. "I haven't gotten a direct answer from you, but I tried my best not to covet or commit adultery." She looked up at the ceiling. "Intent has to count, right?"

Resting against a tower of pillows, Raquel watched her while she sipped her water. She was taking her time drinking, that much was obvious.

"Adultery is only one down from murder." Taylor chugged half the bottle to quench her thirst. "Which, I'll admit, is surprisingly low on the list. Like is ignoring your mother's reminder to sit-up straight really worse than *killing* someone?" She put the top back on the water bottle and set it on the nightstand. "You'd think murder would at least make the top five."

Raquel didn't rush to comment, but there was something dark dancing in her eyes. She was playing with her.

"If you *are* married," Taylor continued, "then I have to say that you're remarkably good at this for a straight woman."

Raquel's throat bobbed when she chuckled. "Those are so many assumptions packed into one sentence."

Taylor smirked. She was finally going to get an answer.

"I've been divorced close to eight years now, and you're not the first woman I've taken to bed." She curved her dark brow as if waiting to see whether Taylor would be scandalized.

Taylor tried not to react, but she couldn't help being surprised. She would never have clocked Raquel.

Flipping to her side, Taylor propped her head in her hand. "Is that why you got divorced? Ladies in your bed?"

Raquel finished her water and set the bottle on her nightstand before sliding down. Adjusting her pillow, Raquel curled up on her side. Lying face to face, a few breaths away, Taylor felt closer to her than when they'd been having sex. There was a new closeness, a lack of pretenses; the pull of intimacy.

"Max and I were high school sweethearts. He went to St. Francis," she explained before Taylor asked how that was possible. St. Francis was the all-boys Jesuit school Solitude often mingled with. "He was my first kiss, my first love, my first so many things."

Taylor picked up on the wistful but sad tone that had crept into her voice.

"We loved each other in that unfettered, uncomplicated way that's only possible when you don't know heartbreak. When you're so full of youthful hubris you can't imagine anything but a charmed storybook life."

Taylor ran her fingers through Raquel's hair as she talked, indulging in how the soft tresses felt against her skin. She wished she'd known her then. She couldn't imagine Raquel ever having an awkward teenage phase like Taylor's cringeworthy obsession with *Twilight*. It took her a few years to realize her passion was less about a diehard devotion to *Team Edward*, and more about Kristen Stewart's persistent lower lip biting.

"What happened?" Taylor asked after Raquel went silent.

Raquel shrugged. "We realized we were almost forty and hadn't really experienced anything. It was like we hadn't figured out how to start living yet. I'd stayed in my same tiny circle. I didn't even leave my high school." She offered a weak smile. "We lived in the same neighborhood we'd grown up in. Max had been expected to take over his parents' import-export business, so he did. He wanted to be a carpenter, and what he *wanted* was just never a factor. We were kind of just trapped in these limited molds doing what was expected of us and never considering our own desires." She closed her eyes. "One day we just looked at each other and knew we needed to live. To really live whatever time we had left. Neither of us had ever wanted kids, so we were each other's only anchors."

"That sounds so sad." Taylor rubbed her thumb over Raquel's high cheekbone.

"It was," she agreed. "It wasn't that we were unhappy, or that we didn't love each other, we'd just never experienced anything." Raquel sighed. "Letting someone go when you don't want to is so incredibly difficult. Max was my best friend. We'd done everything as a duo. I was thirty-eight, and I'd never really been on my own. I'd never made choices based on what I wanted."

"Did he know you were attracted to women too?"

Raquel nodded. "He was always incredibly supportive and affirming."

"Where is he now?"

"He moved to the Mexican west coast and started building bamboo cabins on the beach." Genuine happiness seeped back into her eyes. "He remarried and has turned out to be an excellent stepdad."

"And your Mexican carpentry dreams are teaching in Vermont?"

"When you put it like that," Raquel chuckled, "it doesn't sound like such an adventure."

Taylor sensed Raquel pulling back. She didn't want her to feel overexposed, so she switched topics. "Have you dated a lot since? Anyone serious?"

"Some," Raquel replied, her tone rather distant and noncommittal. "I dated a woman in my doctoral program for two years." She smirked. "I was nowhere near the stepdad Max is, although he had the benefit of toddlers rather than teens."

"I bet you were a fantastic stepdad." Taylor laughed. "I would've been excited if one of my parents brought you home." She couldn't stop her lips from curling into a mischievous grin.

When Raquel laughed, she covered Taylor's hand on her cheek with hers. "Are you only interested in wildly taboo and illegal entanglements, Taylor?"

As exciting as Raquel's use of her last name was, her comfortable dropping of her first was thrilling. Combined with her easy touch, the moment was a rush of intoxicating delight.

"Be honest, you're going to miss me," Taylor said before she could stop herself.

Raquel locked her in her fractured honey gaze, the burned caramel and copper tones dancing like ancient witches in a primeval moonlit forest. "I will," she said so softly that her raspy voice was barely intelligible.

The confession was so small, so open to interpretation, so ambiguous. It had no business thundering inside Taylor with such beautiful and wonderful violence.

She wanted to mention that Vermont and the Bronx weren't so far apart. Three hundred miles was far, but not insurmountable. If she left in the morning, she could be at Raquel's place by lunch. The fact that she didn't have a car didn't matter. There were buses, trains, planes.

"We can still—"

Taylor's suggestion that they could continue seeing each other was cut off by Raquel's sudden kiss. Raquel invaded her, her lips hungry and hard as she pounced.

Consumed by her, Taylor lay back, memorizing the weight of Raquel straddling her hips. Of her chest pressed against hers. Of her mouth sliding down her body until she parted her thighs and slipped her head between them.

CHAPTER 20

GATHERED TOGETHER in the hotel lobby, Taylor found it harder than she expected to say goodbye. Since breaking up with Robbie, her circle of friends had shrunk so much. Plus, no new acquaintance could ever come close to the women she'd known since childhood.

"Bitch, you better not wait another three years before coming home." Brianna flung her arms around Taylor's neck. "We miss you, okay?"

"I miss you too, Bri." Taylor bent forward and gave her a crushing hug without mentioning that Miami hadn't been home for a long time.

"Don't squeeze me too hard, or I'll squirt milk all over your cute Guns 'n Roses T-shirt," she replied, hiding the fact that she'd gotten a little emotional.

"Jesus, Brianna, can we go ten seconds without being reminded of your lactation?" Jessica, towering over her, shoved her playfully with her hip. "We really do miss you, Tay. It was so good having you back in the *grupito*." She pulled Taylor into another embrace.

"You guys could come visit me too, you know?" she reminded, the back of her eyes tingling. In that moment, she couldn't remember why she'd ever moved away. "You can stay with me and we'll paint the town Miami pink. The city won't know what hit it."

From behind Jessica, Alexis popped out holding a large brown bag, the red *King of Pastries* logo emblazoned on the side. "I'm not doing all this mushy shit. I show you my love with fattening food, like a real Cuban."

Taylor exchanged her hug for the surprisingly heavy bag. "Thank you and give my best to Heart Stopper."

Alexis laughed, but Taylor didn't miss the mist in her eyes. "You got it."

"I love you guys!" With her backpack strapped on and the strap from her stuffed duffel bag digging into her shoulder, Taylor watched her friends leave through the hotel's sliding glass doors.

"Those are some good friends you have," Raquel said when she appeared next to her out of nowhere. "To brave Monday morning traffic to see you off."

Quickly wiping her eyes, Taylor nodded. "They're the best."

Turning her attention to Raquel, she looked down at her suitcase. "I thought you were leaving this afternoon."

They had spoken little, but when Taylor slid out of her bed a couple of hours earlier, she distinctly recalled being disappointed they weren't leaving on the same flight.

Raquel shifted her weight between her cute white canvas sneakers. In her cropped black pants and striped boat neck top, Raquel looked so composed. Taylor wished she'd packed something a little nicer than denim shorts and a cut-off, thrift store T-shirt.

"There was no fee to change it." Raquel's voice, still hoarse, was sober and unemotional. "I have a great deal of work waiting for me at home."

Taylor smirked. She'd called the airline about switching her flight to the afternoon. Not only was there a crazy change fee, she'd also have to buy a whole new ticket.

Without calling her out on her obvious lie, or asking whether work was really the impetus for the change, Taylor tipped her head to the side. "I'll see whether I can convince the shuttle driver to take you with us."

Behind her wide rimmed glasses, Raquel's brown eyes sparkled. "I was going to take a cab, but I guess if you're already going." She shrugged.

Taylor laughed, unable to keep up the farce. Raquel knew full well she'd be leaving on the shuttle. She'd told her so they could meet and say goodbye before she left.

"We better get going then." Taylor gestured toward the entrance where the shuttle was waiting.

Pretending to be indifferent, Raquel gripped the purse hanging off her shoulder and rolled her bag toward the sliding doors.

After a slow, traffic-congested drive to the airport, Taylor waited for Raquel to check her suitcase. Because she'd agreed to carry Alexis' exaggerated offering as her personal item, Taylor insisted on giving Raquel half of the *pastelitos* and other treats to take with her.

At the gate, Taylor tried and failed to persuade the agent to switch her seat next to Raquel's. There wasn't any point in flying together if they were sitting on opposite sides of the plane.

Armed with the suggestion that she could ask individual passengers if they would be willing to trade with her, Taylor boarded the flight with a plan.

Because they boarded the aircraft from the back to the front, Taylor had to wait forever for her group to be called. When she got on, she skipped her aisle right behind First Class and headed straight for the back.

Painfully close to the bathroom at the tail end, Taylor spotted the top of Raquel's head. In the aisle seat, she was looking down at her phone, something she did often.

Taylor was a row away when Raquel looked up, sensing her. Most of Raquel's face didn't change. She didn't smile. She didn't put away her phone. But her eyes. They shifted. They brightened. They gave away that she was pleased to see her.

"Your seat is at the front." Raquel had to raise her husky voice to be heard over the ambient noise.

Taylor smiled and turned her attention to the man crammed into the middle seat between Raquel and a young woman wearing huge headphones, her eyes closed and face pressed against the closed window shade.

"Excuse me, sir." When he looked up from his phone, he did not try to hide that he was annoyed at her intrusion. "Would you be interested in an aisle seat at the front?"

He narrowed his eyes like Taylor was offering him the opportunity to make six figures without leaving his couch.

Taylor pulled out her phone and showed him her ticket. "It's gonna be way better than being shoved in that seat and spending three hours next to a flying toilet."

The man looked over at Raquel and then back up at Taylor, hunting for a gimmick. "She your ma or something?"

"If I say yes, will you give up your objectively undesirable seat and stop pretending you don't want to move?"

He broke into a smirk and stood.

Visibly annoyed, Raquel moved into the aisle so the man could grab his stuff and get out.

When he was gone, Taylor slid into the middle seat and waited for Raquel to sit down again. Her energy shift hit Taylor like a bullet train.

"Did I do something wrong? If you didn't want me to sit with you—"

Raquel's posture was stiff, rigid. She kept her attention trained on the tray table folded into the seat in front of her. "You heard what he said." She didn't look at Taylor when she spoke.

It took Taylor a beat to replay the interaction. "The mom thing?" She laughed. "He was just being a dick. I bet he was angling for me to give him money. He didn't—" Taylor stopped herself. It didn't matter what she thought, or the dude's intent. It had bothered Raquel. Embarrassed her. "I'm sorry. He was rude."

Raquel looked over at her, her face expressionless. Taylor could practically feel her defenses rising like car windows being rolled up during a sudden rainstorm.

Undeterred by the chilly blast, Taylor slid her hand into Raquel's lap and clasped it over hers. She hoped Raquel understood her position. That what others thought of them could never matter.

"I only have a few hours left with you," Taylor whispered. "I don't want to waste them."

Raquel's expression eased. She shot off a message on her phone and then dropped it into the purse wedged at her side.

"You know you'd be more comfortable if you stored that in the space provided." Taylor gestured toward the space at her feet with her free hand, the other still nestled in Raquel's lap.

With the reaction Taylor was anticipating, Raquel's honey eyes widened.

"Superstitious?" Taylor exaggerated her surprise. "My grandma could be on her deathbed and she would still be making sure her purse wasn't on the floor."

"Flattering comparison to your *grandmother* aside," Raquel's words were sharp, but Taylor sensed the playful tug lurking beneath them. "She's a wise woman. I bet she hasn't lost all her money."

The immediate and sudden rush that accompanied Raquel's amusement was an all-consuming high. "And you think that would change if she placed her purse on the floor rather than a chair? Like money is literally going to drain out by osmosis and be lost forever?" She laughed. "And once the plane takes off, does it still count as the floor when we're tens of thousands of feet in the air?"

"Who are we to question generations of observational wisdom?" Raquel's smile was sly.

"So you think some poor sucker ancestor of ours brought home a bunch of shells from the beach and dropped dead?" Taylor chuckled. "The rest of the Cubans made a cause-and-effect determination, and for generations thereafter, we all had to dump our buckets of scrounged shells before stepping foot off the sand?"

Raquel's eyes were alive again, lit from within with amusement. "Let me guess, Miss Lopez, you pick pennies off the sidewalk and swim immediately after eating?"

Laughing, Taylor gave her a what-can-I-say shrug. "I live on the edge."

The light spread from Raquel's eyes, brightening her lips as they curved, lifting her face. "It's a wonder you've survived."

By the time they reached cruising altitude, Raquel had relaxed. She'd slipped her hand in Taylor's and intertwined their fingers.

Taylor glanced over at Raquel's phone sitting in her lap, her playlist open. "What the hell is a *Bananarama*?"

Raquel closed her eyes for a moment, as if appalled by the question. Fishing the case out of her purse, Raquel handed her the other headphone.

As she listened to a bunch of women lament the cruelty of summer, Taylor bobbed her head to the beat. It was catchy, she had to admit. When the next song up was an Outkast jam she'd never heard, Taylor got an idea.

"Here." She handed Raquel the headphones she pulled out of her backpack. "Let's trade."

When Raquel accepted, Taylor queued up her playlist, starting with Dua Lipa's *Love Again*.

It only took a second for Raquel to settle back into her headrest and closed her eyes. Pleased that she'd enjoyed her selection, Taylor grinned. She would've been happy to stay in that moment, listening to music, Raquel's hand in hers, for the rest of her life.

All too soon, the pilot announced their descent. Taylor's chest heaved. It was time to put their devices away. Time to say goodbye.

CHAPTER 21

FROM THE MOMENT they'd been told to put their tray tables back and shut off their electronics, a dark haze had fallen over Raquel. When she'd changed her ticket, she'd been impulsive; rash. She'd only been thinking about extending her time with Taylor, even if by a few hours.

What she hadn't considered was how much harder it would be to say goodbye. Each minute together prolonged her happiness and her dread.

Neither of them spoke when they joined the others trudging off the plane. They didn't say a word as they walked through the busy terminal and toward Raquel's connecting flight.

Goodbye loomed over them and grew heavier with every step. It had settled deep in Raquel's belly, choking her like bile.

The kind of night she'd shared with Taylor, the simple joy she'd experienced, the dizzying passion... it had been the respite she hadn't known she needed.

By the time they reached Raquel's gate, it was obvious neither knew how to say goodbye. Deciding that it was best to just get it over with, Raquel stopped at the outer edge of the rows of chairs filled with passengers waiting to go from New York to Vermont.

"There's still, like, half an hour before they board." Taylor's eyes floated over Raquel's head to the flight information above the gate. "Do you want to grab some lunch? I know a great place for terrible Cobb salad."

Taylor's dimples were on display, her brown hair parted down the middle and cascading in long waves far below her shoulders. Looking at her produced a cold, empty pain, but Raquel didn't avert her eyes when she said what she knew she must. "It's best if we say our farewells here."

Taylor's light dimmed. A rolling blackout systematically darkening a city. The darkness moved in phases, snuffing out her bright brown eyes last. "Yeah, okay." She adjusted the pack on her back, moving the duffle's strap to the other side. "So should we exchange numbers, or…" She rocked on the balls of her feet.

Raquel broke her own heart before she spoke the words aloud. "You said it yourself. I was a fantasy. Now you've fulfilled it. Let's leave it at that."

Clenching her jaw, Raquel watched Taylor crumble like a balled-up piece of notebook paper.

"That's not—" Taylor's voice cracked. "Raquel, you have to know that you're more than that." She stepped forward, taking her hand. The touch, so soft, so earnest, was an iron fist to the center of Raquel's heart. "We've had an amazing weekend. I don't want it to end like this."

Raquel drew air so deep into her lungs, she hoped it would steel her, but it made her ache instead. It was too much oxygen. It saturated and expanded and burned. "We had a wonderful few days together." She squeezed Taylor's hand, wishing her life was different. "And I won't forget them."

Taylor's eyes, beautiful and bronze and fathomless, glistened. She dropped her shoulders, accepting that this was goodbye. With a weak smile, she tugged Raquel forward.

She didn't resist, allowing herself to float into Taylor's increasingly familiar arms.

Closing her eyes as she hugged her, Raquel breathed in the shampoo of her hair, the salt of her skin. Three days. It had only been three days. How could she grow so attached in such a short time? How could leaving be so hard? It made no sense that they'd spent such little time together. It was an eternity in a blink.

Taylor tightened her hold before letting her go. "Maybe I'll run into you at JFK next time, or Newark."

The joke only added to the knot growing in Raquel's throat, but she managed a weak smile. "I should be so lucky."

Without warning, Taylor dropped her duffle bag. She lunged forward, cupping Raquel's face with both hands. She captured her in a kiss. The first one they'd ever shared that lacked the promise of more.

Raquel kissed her again and again, wishing she could store Taylor's kisses and pull them out later. To use them when she was alone. When she needed them. She covered Taylor's hands on her cheeks and held them tight. "Take good care of yourself."

Taylor held her gaze. "I'm going to miss you."

"Me too," Raquel said, her voice barely above a whisper.

While Taylor picked up her bag and heaved it over her shoulder, Raquel held her breath. She didn't let it out until Taylor turned away and she lost her in the crowd.

Numb, Raquel dropped into the nearest empty chair. Clutching her paper bag full of *pastelitos* to her chest, she tried to untangle her feelings, but all she could feel was exhaustion.

The night they'd spent not sleeping and the burden of goodbye, had shown up at the same time to collect what they were owed. It was only when she fell to a low so low it was subterranean that she realized just how high in the stratosphere she'd been.

Popping her headphones back in her ears, Raquel closed her eyes. She inhaled the sweet confections in her bag and let one of the songs she liked from Taylor's playlist fill her ears. Swiping the tip of her tongue over her bottom lip, she could still taste her.

CHAPTER 22

HOLDING her bags in her lap, Taylor swayed with the rhythm of the D-train as it carried her home. It had a lulling effect, and it matched her impossible to identify mood.

Saying goodbye to Raquel had been so strange. She'd known it was inevitable, and yet somehow parting had come as a shock. Without realizing it, she'd become addicted to her; to anticipating the thrill of seeing her next and the thrill of being unable to take her eyes off of her.

She played back their last moments together. Could Raquel really think she was just some kind of wish fulfilled? *Maybe it was about the fantasy at first,* Taylor admitted to herself. But that had dissipated so quickly.

They'd really enjoyed each other's company, hadn't they? They'd laughed together and talked about things like history and music and food and culture. It had been more than lust. More than sex.

Taylor closed her eyes hard enough to see a constellation of tiny silver spots and wished she'd never confessed her stupid crush. It had set the contours for their relationship, confined it to a fling-shaped box.

Imagining how she would have done things differently, Taylor replayed the entire weekend in her mind. She wouldn't have kissed her in the classroom. She would've taken her as far away from Our Lady of Solitude as she could. Maybe if Raquel had seen her in a different light, she would've given her a real chance.

When the subway car lurched to a stop at Fordham Station, Taylor followed a pair of kids who were obviously cutting school and exited the train.

By the time she'd jogged up the steps and onto the busy street, passed the smoke shop, beauty supply, and place for people to buy calling cards and send money to Central and South America, Taylor accepted that she was officially down in the dumps.

Even though people liked to talk a lot of shit about her neighborhood, she liked the packed together brown brick buildings crammed along the main road. She liked the chaos of a thousand businesses creating larger and larger signs to get people's attention as they walked by.

Instead of feeling invigorated, Taylor had a ship's anchor tied around her neck. Her bags were suddenly too heavy and her body too tired. The lack of sleep had finally caught up with her.

Still a few blocks from her apartment, Taylor stopped at a hole-in-the-wall pizza place. The kind of restaurant with a single chair and peeling old, brown booth in the corner no one ever sat in because everyone within a mile radius ordered delivery.

When Taylor asked the guy behind the counter in the stuffy closet of a restaurant whether she could sit, he grumbled and muttered in an Eastern European language she couldn't quite discern while moving the boxes of napkins and plastic utensils over to one side of the table.

Jamming her bags at one end of the hard, cushion-free booth, Taylor grabbed a slice of pepperoni pizza and slathered it with Parmesan cheese and red pepper flakes. She sat, popped open a can of soda, and worked on her tolerance for no air conditioning.

While she waited for her slice to cool from scalding to edible, she scrolled mindlessly through her phone. It took three seconds to stop lying to herself and search for what she really wanted.

Lucky for her, there weren't many people named Raquel Alonso in

Vermont. Navigating to the page of a quaint college that looked like it was ripped from a movie, she found her in the faculty directory.

Dr. Raquel Alonso, Professor of History, was written next to her photo, just a few down from the department chair. Taking her first deep breath since she'd walked out of the airport, Taylor pressed her fingers against the glass and zoomed in on Raquel's image.

Her hair was longer in the picture. Sleek, dark brown and straight from her side part to the tops of her shoulders. Her frameless glasses left her perfect face open and lightly obstructed.

Taylor grinned when her attention snagged on Raquel's sober expression. In her sharp black suit jacket and string of pearls, she met the camera's lens like she was putting it in its place. An effortless establishing of who was boss.

It didn't matter that Raquel's portrait was only visible from the shoulders up. Taylor could envision what hadn't made it into the frame. Her body was tight and controlled. Her legs crossed at the ankle. Her hands folded in her lap.

Closing her eyes, Taylor drifted away from the pizza shop, its air stifling and fragrant thanks to the roaring ovens. She was back in Miami. Back in the air-conditioned hotel room, pulling Raquel's hands off her lap so she could straddle her hips and throw her arms around her neck and kiss her deep and full.

Taylor's lips came alive at the memory of her kiss. Raquel's perfume filled her nose. Her ghost touch sent her skin blazing. Diving in head first into the fantasy, Taylor heard Raquel's breathy moans in her ear, watched her toss her head back as she bared down on her fingers and cursed as she unraveled so spectacularly, so singularly, for her.

A jingling bell was a polar plunge, snapping Taylor back to the present. She opened her eyes, her surroundings foreign for the briefest second.

"Ay, you high or something?" the man behind the counter stared at her while he handed a delivery driver a stack of pizza boxes. "I don't care what you do with your life, kid, but you can't be nodding off in here."

Clearing her throat, Taylor sat up and took a bite of her food. Despite the aroma of melted cheese and piled on spices, it didn't taste like much of anything; a product of her mood more than the chef's skills.

While she chewed, she opened her music streaming app and searched for Raquel's username. *TheRaq1976* was painfully easy to remember. Deciding she liked the idea of calling Raquel *Raq*, Taylor smiled to herself. It probably made the dubious man slinging pizza even more suspicious, but he wasn't wrong. She just wasn't the kind of high he meant.

"What the hell is a Lilith Fair?" she muttered before scrolling down to a playlist titled *Those days*. A little research told her most songs on the list had been released somewhere between 1994 and 1998. Some arithmetic later, Taylor guessed the list coincided with Raquel's college years.

Popping her headphones in her ears, Taylor closed her eyes again and willed her mind back to the plane ride. She could almost feel the weight of Raquel's hand, the inert power of their intertwined fingers.

Ani DiFranco sang to her about the enraging pain of unrequited love while she strode through the sticky Bronx neighborhood on her way home. Erykah Badu filled her with moving neo soul as she danced up the stairs. The Cranberries, showcasing a woman's voice that pulled at her heart like a lamenting violin, made her stop at the top of the landing, drop her bag, and press her palm to her chest.

By the time *Fast Car* hit her, all Taylor could do was drag herself over the threshold of her apartment and collapse onto her gray IKEA couch.

"Jesus, Raq. No wonder you're so intense. You're bopping to Irish protest music and the pruning of a young life before it could even start," she muttered to the high ceiling in her tiny apartment.

Grateful Robbie wasn't home, Taylor closed her eyes and let the day land on her like a cartoon anvil.

CHAPTER 23

Hazy and dim, late afternoon in Vermont lacked the blinding quality she'd already become accustomed to in Miami. Rolling her suitcase behind her, Raquel shuffled to the garage attached to the airport. Her joints were stiff and her body sluggish, like a cold was lurking, but she guessed it was something worse.

Despite her brain's best efforts to explain that her time with Taylor would be limited from the start, her body missed Taylor like it had already absorbed her; already let her in and made a place for her. One warmed by a crackling fireplace and rich wine.

When Raquel slammed the truck shut on her bags, she aimed to leave the useless longing in there with them.

The drive from the airport in Burlington to her house in Lockwood took an hour on the two-lane country highway. The small city quickly gave way to even smaller towns interspersed between long, beautiful stretches of green; hills and farms and woods and verdant open land. There was a sense of space here that she'd never experienced in Miami. A vastness.

Gripping the steering wheel of her sensible sedan, with its side impact airbags and best-in-class fuel efficiency, she wished it might morph into Alexis Abreu's Heart Stopper. Or maybe a less outlandish cousin.

With a smirk, she let her foot drop on the accelerator. She imagined driving her own Jeep. The wind whipping around her hair; the sun warming her skin thanks to the absent roof. Next to her, Taylor would belt out a song, her eyes bright, her wide smile on display. Happiness emanated from her passenger, seeping into Raquel's body like a contagion. Raquel let herself feel the joy for only a moment.

Easing off the gas, she stopped herself from indulging in the fantasy. It would not do her any good. Taylor and the Jeep were both decadent dreams, and she would only hurt herself if she let them grow.

She switched from music to an audiobook on a thriving, matriarchal village in Kenya. Started by survivors of violence, the egalitarian society banned all men not raised as children in the community.

When Raquel pulled up to her white farmhouse, its front door newly painted a dark navy blue, she almost stayed in the car to finish listening to the story. But she didn't have time for that now.

Parked next to Nadia's minivan in front of the two-car garage that doubled as a storage unit, Raquel hauled her bags up the stone walkway to the front porch crowned with flowering hanging plants and pots full of shade-loving ferns.

She'd purchased the house for next to nothing compared to Miami real estate costs. It had been properly advertised as a fixer-upper. No major structural issues, but it promised to provide years of weekend warrior projects. Projects she'd had to hire professionals to complete before her dad moved in.

Nadia opened the door while Raquel scrounged for her key hiding somewhere at the bottom of her purse.

"Look who's here, Ramon!" Nadia, her face bright and framed by her dark curls, called to Raquel's father sitting at the breakfast table in the kitchen behind her. "I told you she was coming back today," she said in Spanish.

At the sight of her dad, happily sitting in front of an empty plate after finishing his early dinner, the scent of Nadia's Dominican *mofongo* still in the air, Raquel's heart lifted.

"Thank you so much." Raquel greeted Nadia, wearing her usual colorful scrubs, with a crushing hug. Every word she knew to express appreciation fell short. Nothing captured her relief. Her bone-deep gratitude.

Hugging her in return, Nadia patted her back warmly. "He did great."

Leaving her luggage in the foyer, Raquel kicked off her shoes. The restored hardwood floors, original to the 130-year-old house, were smooth and warm beneath her feet. Despite having installed central air conditioning, her father preferred an open window and strong fan. Nadia was the same. As soon as the temperature dropped below seventy, they'd be wearing sweaters and wool socks. A product of their island blood, Nadia always joked. Despite having been born in the same corner of the world, Raquel didn't share their tolerance.

"Hi, *Papi.*" Raquel smoothed her dad's feather-soft white hair, still full and glossy, before kissing his cheek.

He looked up at her, his faded brown eyes welling with unshed tears—a signal he didn't have the words for what he was feeling. Sliding into the banquette built into the window overlooking half an acre of open field bisected by a creek, Raquel put her arm around her father.

She waited patiently while he tried to communicate, his words increasingly tangled and garbled. When it was obvious that he was stressing himself out, Raquel put her hand over his balled up fist.

"I missed you too, Papi. I promise I won't leave you again, okay?"

"Don't let him fool you." Nadia spooned ground espresso beans into the metal filter of the percolator. Despite a fully automatic machine on the clean, white marble counter, Nadia insisted that her father only liked his *cafecito* from the real *cafetera.* "He was talking about you all day." She smiled at him. "*Verdad*, Ramon?"

"And how old was I today?" Raquel ran her thumb over the back of his hand until he eased his grip.

"Judging by the trouble you were in?" Nadia put the percolator on the gas stove. "I would say ten."

Raquel chuckled. *"Que pasó,* Papi? Was I climbing that tree in the front yard again?"

When Nadia laughed, her father smiled too. *"Raquelita,* get down from there!" he shouted in Spanish, delighted at the imaginary girl causing mischief.

"I brought you something." Raquel produced the enormous paper bag she'd dragged across several states. The one Taylor had been thoughtful enough to share with her.

At the sight of the familiar bakery's logo on the bag, his eyes widened. *"Raquelita,* come! Your Mami brought you *pastelitos!"*

Raquel swallowed hard and rolled with it. She didn't pretend to be her mother, but she didn't disabuse her father of the notion either.

"These are the best, Nadia. You have to try this." Raquel motioned for her to sit with them.

Sitting around the table together, they shared one of the enormous coconut puff pastries. When the coffee was ready, Raquel jumped up and served them each a little shot glass of Cuban coffee. For her dad, she served just a splash of the high-octane drink. Just enough to wet his beak, as he sometimes joked. Too much and he would spend the night screaming in his sleep.

After they chatted for a while, Raquel insisted Nadia go home a few hours early, but she refused. She also refused to take the additional cash Raquel had picked up from the bank.

At Nadia's insistence, Raquel went upstairs to unpack and get herself ready for the night shift. Most nights, her father's medications helped him sleep, but any disruption in his routine could throw that off. They couldn't be sure Raquel's return wouldn't trigger an episode.

Upstairs, Raquel showered with scalding hot water, but she couldn't shake the chill in her body. It was like the cold had slipped directly beneath her skin. She didn't let herself think of Taylor. Not once.

Dressed in an old University of Miami T-shirt and soft pajama shorts, Raquel left her wet hair wrapped in a towel when she returned downstairs. In the laundry room right off the mud room around the side of the house, Raquel zipped open her suitcase.

As soon as she flung open the top, she closed her eyes. It was too late, though. The damage was done. The sight of fluorescent orange shorts with *Endless Summer* emblazoned on the back had been as hard to take as an uppercut to the heart.

CHAPTER 24

FINISHED with her first week back at work after the reunion, it was nearly seven when Taylor finalized the last transcript and sent it to her boss. Listening to the recorded deposition in a pharmaceutical patent case had been long and painful. Even with a spelling guide for all the scientific jargon like *kilodalton* and *copolymer*, her brain had started to liquify and run out of her ears.

She stood from the desk in her bedroom. The long table held two monitors and a laptop, but it also took up half the room. Three steps away from her orange bungee cord chair, the most colorful thing in the mostly white and neutral-toned room, Taylor dropped into her bed. A daybed was the only thing that would fit in the narrow room.

When she and Robbie found the apartment, she was thrilled to have a dedicated office. If she'd realized it would become her bedroom when they split up, Taylor would've continued hunting for something much bigger. At least it had the trusty split AC unit keeping it frosty.

As a consolation for giving up the bigger bedroom, Robbie promised to install shelves above the bed to give Taylor some storage, but the landlord had a fit before the first anchor was drilled into the drywall-covered brick.

Taylor hadn't really minded moving to the smaller space with the minuscule closet. She had a quarter of the amount of clothes and crap Robbie did. It just made sense for her to go.

Sensing her thoughts, Robbie's face lit up her cell phone. Flipping the phone over to banish the image, Taylor curled on her side and nestled against the cool, fluffy white pillow before pulling the duvet around her shoulders.

She might have drifted off to sleep if her phone hadn't dinged a few minutes later. A text message.

Reaching back blindly for her phone, Taylor unlocked the screen. Even though they lived together, she rarely saw Robbie unless they were exchanging physical custody of Phillip twice a month.

Armed with the excuse that it was less of a hassle to commute from Jersey City to any of the Midtown theaters she worked in, Robbie almost always stayed at Bellamy's place. Taylor had never seen the house Bellamy shared with three other artist friends, but she begrudgingly agreed that Phillip loved playing in the small, fenced-in yard—assuming the photos were to be believed.

Robbie: *I've let you think about it all day! Come onnnnnn*

Taylor: *Thanks for the invite, but I think I'm going to pass.*

Just so she didn't seem like the disgruntled ex-girlfriend, Taylor added several festive, birthday-related emojis. For good measure, she threw in a GIF of a dancing panda too.

Robbie: *Oh, come on. You've been cooped up all week. I KNOW you have. Fraya, Bryce and Liam are coming! You haven't seen them in forever.*

The friends she hadn't seen in months were schlepping across the city into New Jersey on a Friday night. How thoughtful.

Robbie: *And everyone is staying over. You don't have to worry about getting back to the city. It's going to be so much fun!*

Yes, as fun as hanging out with an ex and her current flame and your former friends can be.

A moment later, Robbie texted her a picture of Bellamy's backyard. The fenced in square was crowned with overlapping strings of lights. In one corner, a bar had been fashioned out of wooden crates. In another, a small inflatable pool was filled up and sitting in front of perfectly mismatched lawn chairs. Hanging at the center of a small white tent was the reason Taylor wouldn't consider attending. An enormous papier-mâché lion.

Taylor: *She knows she's not a Leo, right?*

Robbie: *Don't start. It's just a birthday party, and she made that out of reclaimed materials.*

Taylor: *I'm just saying being on the cusp of something is not the same as being IN it.*

Robbie: *WHO CARES?!*

Taylor: *I mean, if you don't care that you're with a fraud, ROBERTA.*

When Robbie didn't immediately respond, shame tugged at Taylor's usually shame-free Aquarian heart. She didn't really care about Bellamy, but the few times she met her, she'd mentioned being a Leo so many times that it forced Taylor to correct her. The justification that followed was an obviously weak, and practiced, attempt to support what she wanted to be true.

Robbie: *Tay, I don't want you being all isolated. So many people are coming. A lot of really cool girls.*

Sighing, Taylor flipped onto her back. There was the real motivation behind the invitation. Pity. Robbie had no reason to feel it, or the guilt that was obviously crushing her. She hadn't done anything wrong by moving on and being happy, and she wasn't responsible for Taylor.

Taylor: *Thanks for the invite. Honestly. I really appreciate your thinking of me. I was just being a little shit. Tell Bellamy I wish her a very happy thirtieth birthday, and that I would love to travel to another state to celebrate her being a Cancer-Leo cusp, but I have a date.*

Robbie: *Shut up! Do you really?!?! You didn't tell me! With who?*

If it hadn't been for Robbie's exaggerated excitement, Taylor would've let the lie stand.

Taylor: *Perhaps that was overstated. What I meant to say is I'm reactivating my dating profile.*

Over the course of nine months, she'd deleted and re-installed the app on her phone about a dozen times. There had been good dates and bad, but no one who threatened to shift her foundation.

Robbie: *Okay, well that's exciting! If you make a connection, you should bring her!*

Taylor: *Well, that would be the queerest first date LOL bringing a person I just met to my ex-girlfriend/roommate's girlfriend's birthday hang.*

Robbie: *ORRR you could just come here... Bellamy invited the welder from the studio next to hers and they are JUST your type.*

Taylor chuckled. Unless the welder was a forty-six-year-old college history professor, she doubted that very much.

After promising Robbie she would think about coming to the party, which she dutifully did before discounting the possibility, Taylor re-installed her dating app.

She swiped left repeatedly while waiting for her perfectly spicy order of Xi'an Biang Biang noodles to be ready to pick up from the restaurant downstairs. It wasn't that there was anything wrong with any of the smiling faces on the app, it was that none of them were *her*.

With a belly full of Michelin-star-worthy noodles, Taylor expanded her dating radius three hundred miles. When the results were overwhelming, she narrowed it to forty-six-year-old females identifying women with no children.

Bummed she couldn't find Raquel on any social media platform, dating site, or image search, she returned to Lockwood College's directory.

None of Raquel's scholarly articles were freely available, so she was left with looking at her faculty photo. Staring longingly at the bespectacled woman she couldn't get off her mind, Taylor couldn't stop herself from reaching out.

To: Raquel Alonso
From: Taylor Lopez
Date: Friday, July 23, 2022 09:14:33PM EST
Subject: Public Access to Scholarly Materials

Good Evening, Dr. Alonso,

My name is Taylor Lopez. I was a student of yours about a decade ago when you taught at Our Lady of Solitude High School. I'm sure you won't remember me, and I hate to bother you, but I came across a publication of yours in a journal. It's titled: *Making Space: The Valiant First Women of the Intelligence Community.*

I was wondering if you could send me a copy? The topic looks absolutely fascinating. I'll leave my phone number at the bottom of this email in case you need to reach me. I'm more than happy to facilitate this academic exchange.

Very Best,

Taylor.

SHE HIT SEND BEFORE she could stop herself. Sprawled out on her couch, she chewed the inside of her lip and waited for a response. While she waited, she texted the STATE CHAMPS '12 to see what Brianna, Jessica and Alexis were doing.

Nearly an hour later, her phone dinged. The chime of a text from an unknown number.

CHAPTER 25

EYES tired from sitting in front of a computer screen for a solid fifteen hours, Raquel finished grading the last assignment of the summer term. Being done didn't mean that she didn't have another long day ahead of her on Saturday. Whoever said professors had summers and weekends off had no clue how long it took to plan courses and perform near constant research and writing.

Before she closed the laptop she was using while sitting in her kitchen's breakfast nook, the familiar pop of an email was followed by a notification on the corner of her computer screen. She might have let it wait until the following morning if she hadn't noticed the sender's name.

A smile tugged at the corner of her lips, but Raquel didn't rush to open the message. Instead, she picked up her stemmed wine glass and sipped the rich merlot.

Excitement thumped through her veins like techno music delivering high energy beats and filling her with unrelenting delight. Part of her was surprised Taylor was reaching out. The other part of her was shocked it had taken her a full week.

Two hasty sips was all she managed before she nearly broke the glass by slamming it down against the wooden table. Opening the message sent to her Lockwood College account, Raquel's skin tingled from the top of her scalp to the bottom of her bare feet. Her entire body wanted to connect to Taylor again, and her brain was powerless to stop it.

Without giving her rational mind a chance to talk down her eager heart, Raquel plugged Taylor's number into her phone and shot off a text.

Raquel: *Miss Lopez, I am sure the college library can provide you with a copy of my research. I will forward the contact information.*

The response came so quickly, Raquel didn't have a chance to reach for her wine.

Taylor: *I was hoping to get it directly from the source, Dr. Alonso. Perhaps you would even indulge me in a private discussion about your bibliography.*

Grinning, Raquel surged with the familiar thrill of amusement. She clutched her phone with both hands, her thumbs flying over the screen as she texted like a revved-up teenager.

Raquel: *That's how you want to play this, Taylor? You want to make your way into my... bibliography?*

Taylor: *Well, when you say it like that, I sound like a weirdo.*

Taylor: *I bet you've been so bored without me, sitting in your ivory tower all alone.*

Raquel chuckled, her heart leaping into her throat. There was no denying she'd missed the brightness Taylor exuded. The blinding essence that vibrated through the phone and filled Raquel with the otherworldly flash of a comet burning up in the atmosphere.

Raquel: *Is that how you see me? Aloof and secluded, perched far above the real world?*

Conversation bubbles appeared and disappeared. Needing to discharge the energy building in her body, Raquel padded around the large kitchen island and down the short hall to her father's room. It had been a den and formal living room before she had it converted to a large bedroom with a private and completely wheelchair accessible bathroom should that need ever arrive.

Pushing the door open to peek into the room instead of going upstairs to retrieve the baby monitor in her room, Raquel made sure her father was asleep.

She checked the front and side doors to make sure they were locked and that she hadn't left the key nearby. It had been a long time since her father tried to leave while in a bout of confusion, but she didn't take any chances. She couldn't be sure the sensor in his bed wouldn't malfunction and fail to alert her that he'd gotten up.

By the time she served herself a second glass of wine and nestled into the white, slip-covered sofa in front of the stone fireplace flanked by built-in bookshelves, Taylor had finally responded.

Taylor: *Fiiiiiine. I just wanted to know whether you were by yourself on a Friday night, okay? Make a Federal case out of it already.*

Biting down on her bottom lip, Raquel decided not to torment her. Maybe it was the wine, or the long week, but she was happy to know Taylor was angling to find out whether she had company.

Raquel: *I had dinner with a very handsome older man earlier this evening, but I'm by myself now.*

Taylor: *Older man? Is it serious?*

Raquel: *Oh, very. We live together.*

Taylor: *WHAT? Pretty sure you failed to mention this before.*

Raquel: *We've been together for such a long time. It'll be 47 years in January. Haven't lived together all that time though.*

Taylor: *Damn it, Raquel! I thought you were serious!*

Chuckling, Raquel reached for the wine she'd set on the coffee table. As she sipped it, she felt drunker than she had in years. She couldn't blame the wine. It had taken hours to finish the first glass while she worked.

Raquel: *I am serious. I had dinner with my father. He lives with me. He's handsome. Is it my fault that you made assumptions?*

Taylor: *You should have been a lawyer instead of a history professor with the way you like to play with the exactness of words. You almost gave me a heart attack.*

Whether Taylor was being playful or not, Raquel had to admit she liked the idea of her being a little jealous.

Raquel: *A heart attack? Over dinner? That's a touch extreme, isn't it?*

Taylor: *I guess you wouldn't care if I had dinner with a handsome older companion then.*

Folding her leg beneath herself, Raquel shifted around. She wasn't thrilled at the notion of Taylor going out with someone.

Raquel: *Is that what you did this evening?*

A moment later, a photo popped up on Raquel's screen. A simple black coffee table with no decorative rug covering the parquet wood floor was littered with two open Chinese food containers and a torn paper bag, a smattering of condiment packets forming an orange, yellow, and black river at the center.

Taylor: *Dinner and probably breakfast tomorrow. Not even a dog to share it with. Not that he's a fan of spicy food.*

Raquel: *Where is Phillip the Papillon?*

Taylor responded with a photo of a backyard set up for a party; a rather stylized paper lion on display.

Taylor: *My ex-girlfriend's girlfriend is having a birthday party. I was invited, but decided eating takeout and re-organizing my spice rack was more appealing. Phillip is probably wearing a suit to the festivities.*

Raquel: *I don't know what I find more surprising, that you have a spice rack or that you and your ex-girlfriend are so evolved.*

Taylor: *Ha!*

Taylor: *Your turn. Let's see what you're doing.*

Hesitating, Raquel looked around her living room. Her glass of wine looked so sad. Should she move over her hardcover copy of *The Architecture of Trees*? Maybe add a candle and a bowl of decorative wicker balls? Was that trying too hard?

Before she could overthink it, Raquel snapped a picture of the wine glass and sent it.

Taylor: *Are you under the influence right now, Dr. Alonso?*

With a grin, Raquel almost admitted that any intoxication had nothing to do with the wine. She held herself back.

Raquel: *It would explain my terrible lapse in judgment.*

Taylor: *Oh, come on. You've missed me. Admit it.*

Hovering her thumbs over the keyboard, Raquel couldn't bring herself to admit that it was true. That she did miss her. That she hadn't let herself realize just how much. That she'd busied herself not to notice.

Taylor: *Do you want to FaceTime or is that too weird?*

Taylor: *I'd really like to see you.*

Unsure how to respond, Raquel looked down at herself. In shorts and a black cotton camisole, she wasn't exactly camera ready. As if reading her mind, Taylor texted again.

Taylor: *It's not a big deal. I'm already in my PJs.*

A photo followed a moment later. Taylor was smiling wide, her dimples cutting deep swaths in her smooth, makeup-free cheeks. Her long brown hair was piled on top of her head in a very messy bun. Wearing the kind of baggy T-shirt with a bank logo Raquel was sure was only given away and never purchased, Taylor was sitting on a couch in front of a plain white wall.

Taylor had no right to send a ripple of warmth skittering over her skin with just a picture. No right to make her chest tighten and her stomach flutter with anticipation.

It was a bad idea. What was the point of talking? They were just going to waste each other's time entertaining something impossible.

Raquel grabbed her glass and stood. Neither of them was doing anything else tonight, so no time was wasted there. What was the harm? Video chatting one night didn't have to become a whole thing.

Raquel: *Give me a minute.*

She jogged upstairs, wine and phone in hand. There was no way she could talk downstairs without waking her dad.

Hurrying into her bedroom at the top of the stairs, Raquel darted for the bathroom. It was too late to put in contacts, so she traded her boring frameless glasses for her wide rimmed green ones. She'd already washed her face free of makeup, but she threw on a little eyeliner and *zhuzhed* up her hair by tossing her wavy bob to one side.

"Alright, not bad," she said to her reflection as she pushed up her boobs. She almost considered putting something on that didn't show so much cleavage, but she remembered how much Taylor liked to see it.

Back in her bedroom, Raquel only had two options: sit in the tufted armchair by the window she'd bought to read books in, but ended up as a repository for her clothes, or get in bed.

Pretending not to know what message calling from the bed would send, Raquel piled all the pillows on her king-sized bed on one side. It gave her something to lean against other than the black iron frame.

She slid under the white cotton quilt and pulled it over her lap as she adjusted the pillows behind her. On a tray table she only used for decorative purposes—to give her bedroom that romantic, magazine-quality, farmhouse feel—she propped up her phone using a few books from the ever-growing TBR pile on her nightstand.

Taking a deep breath to still her nerves, Raquel fluffed her hair one last time and opened her phone.

Raquel: *Ready.*

CHAPTER 26

TAYLOR DIDN'T EXPECT Robbie to come home unannounced, especially not tonight, but not wanting to take any chances, she cleaned up the food on the coffee table and dashed to her room.

As if Raquel might notice, she brushed her teeth before jumping into bed. She considered talking to her from her desk, where she had a much better set-up for video calling, but it felt too sterile, like she was on a work call or job interview.

With her back against the low frame of her daybed, she crossed her legs under her and put a pillow in her lap to rest her elbows while she held up her phone.

With the exhilaration of diving off an Acapulco cliff and barreling headfirst into blue waves crashing against the rocky coast, Taylor called Raquel.

In the moments it took for Raquel to answer her call, Taylor pulled her hair tie out and tossed the wavy mess to one side. What she wouldn't give for Brianna to live nearby so she could work her beauty school magic.

Raquel appeared on her screen. The sight of her was a church bell being hit with a sledgehammer, the reverberations echoing in Taylor's body. Reclined against her headboard and tower of pillows, she looked like she had on the night they spent together—regal and poised and perfect.

"Hi," Taylor said, her voice just above an awe-struck whisper.

Raquel's full lips eased into the kind of smile that ignited her entire face, but she pulled it back before it singed her hair. "Hi."

It took a few minutes for the awkwardness of the video call to melt away, for Taylor to give up her tense position and lay on her side with her head propped in her hand.

"So, why don't you have a date tonight? Do people not go out on Friday nights in Vermont?"

Raquel raised a dark brow. "I could ask you the same thing."

"You could," she agreed with a tip of her head, "but I asked you first and there are rules about these things."

She loved making Raquel laugh, especially when it was accompanied by a little eye roll.

"I'm sure there are all kinds of people out tonight."

"Are you sure you didn't go to law school? You always answer the limited call of the question."

Raquel smirked. "Didn't I teach you to think critically, Miss Lopez?"

"Man, you'd make an impressive witness and frustrate the hell out of whoever was doing the cross-examination."

Tipping her head to the side, Raquel appeared to receive the compliment in the spirit it was given. "Your turn."

"Why aren't I out at a bar or something?"

Raquel nodded.

"Well, despite what you might have seen this last weekend, I'm not a big drinker. And…" She debated telling the whole truth. "I rejoined a dating app for about thirty minutes before deciding I rather be alone than without you. No one is going to measure up anyway, so let's save ourselves the disappointment and unnecessary shaving of legs."

Raquel's laugh was a rumble in her throat. "Razors are very expensive these days. How very thoughtful of you."

When she didn't shoot her down for abandoning her attempts to date in favor of being with her, Taylor's heart soared.

"Has it been a long time? Since you've been out with someone?" Raquel's tone sounded like she'd chosen the words carefully.

"Since Robbie and I broke up last year, I've been on dates. A bunch of them, actually."

"And not a one person was to your liking?"

Taylor shook her head. "It's not that. They were all nice, well, except the one who asked for a mold of my feet on our third date. She may have been trying to eat my soul."

"What?" Raquel asked with a chuckle, her honey eyes glistening. "You're kidding."

"I wish I was! After dinner, we went back to her place. When she asked me to take my shoes off at the door, I didn't think anything of it. The moment I sat on her couch, she asked if she could look at my feet and it only got worse from there."

"So… no fourth date?"

Taylor laughed. "Stepped all over any hopes of that."

Raquel gave her a little groan, but couldn't drop the smile on her lips.

"But the truth is, it wasn't going anywhere. Even without the foot mold. I think you know with someone pretty quickly whether there's a spark there. It might not be enough to sustain a relationship and you might find out you're not compatible, but without that little some-thing"—she rubbed her fingers together—"there's no chance. I'm not going to settle for less than that spark."

Raquel tucked her fist under her chin as if engaged in a philosoph-ical debate. "You don't think you can build something enduring based on something other than attraction? That spark is usually lust, isn't it? Look at how much more successful arranged marriages are, and they're based on objective compatibility rather than lust and emotions. Two people can come to love each other."

"I adamantly disagree, Dr. Alonso. At least for me. I need that undefinable something special. That chemical reaction. That pull. That feeling like you've arm wrestled a bear or climbed a burning skyscraper. Like you'd do absolutely anything for that person. Trade anything for their happiness."

Putting aside her academic exercise, Raquel's eyes widened. "That's what you think love should feel like?"

Taylor nodded.

"Is that how you felt with your Robbie?"

The question caught Taylor off guard. Buying a moment to think about it, she rearranged herself on the bed, tucking a pillow between her knees as she got more comfortable on her side.

"I *wanted* to feel that way," she admitted.

"But?"

"But I didn't, no. I think that's why it's not all that hard to keep living together. Even though I had to request that she not have sex here while I'm in the apartment. Thin walls and I don't know that I want to hear anyone making those sounds."

Raquel agreed with a nod.

"We were what we both needed at the time we met. We'd both moved here from somewhere else around the same time, and were kind of safe harbors while we figured this place out. Then, we just held on a little too long. Morphed into friends and then roommates before we broke up."

"It's hard to let go of things that are comfortable."

"Did it take you a long time to date after the divorce?"

Raquel took a deep breath and Taylor tried not to notice the mouthwatering swell of her full breasts.

"It was a tough adjustment. Everyone felt so alien. Max and I never had to tell each other anything. We'd had front row seats for all the major events in each other's lives. I knew every scar on his body, probably better than he did. The prospect of getting to know a complete stranger was daunting. And then the physical intimacy was a major change. It took a while to stop feeling like I was cheating on him."

"All those years together, didn't you ever wonder what it would be like to be with someone else?"

"Not really. Not until I knew it was over. It was a long time before I understood the difference between being desperately in love and loving someone because they'd become part of you." Raquel shook her head. "It's hard to explain."

"If you guys hadn't felt trapped for other reasons, do you think you would've stayed together?"

Raquel took a deep, cleansing breath. "Maybe. I don't know. We both valued stability so much, we traded that mad, passionate, bear-wrestling love for it."

Taylor considered Raquel's words for a moment. "So you were playing a little devil's advocate earlier," she said. "You wouldn't make a logical, dispassionate choice. You're looking for that spark too."

Replying with a coy little smirk, Raquel shrugged. "I mean, I've already had one. It's probably about time I had the other."

A Roman candle detonated in Taylor's being, emitting a fountain of colorful sparks. The brightness cleared away any doubt that Raquel felt the same way she did. That there was something more than lust and fantasy between them.

"Would you get married again?"

"Yeah, I think so." Raquel slid down her pillow tower and got more comfortable. "If it was the right person. I don't want to get divorced again. What about you?"

Taylor winced. "Should I play it cool or admit something embarrassing?"

Chuckling, Raquel turned on her side like they were face-to-face in bed. "Now you have to admit it."

Taylor covered her face before peeking between her fingers. "Alright, so I've kind of been planning my wedding since I was twelve."

"A romantic? Seriously?"

"Okay, okay. You didn't have to shriek with giddy surprise, Raquel."

"Women my age do not shriek, Taylor." She tried to sound serious, but there was too much amusement playing on her wine-stained lips. "Now tell me about this wedding of yours."

"So you can make fun of me? No way."

"I promise I won't."

"Lies!"

Raquel laughed. "I swear."

"What do I get if you break your vow?"

Raquel moistened her lips. "Why are you always trying to get something?"

Taylor let her gaze fall very obviously over Raquel's mouth and neck and chest. "Because there are a lot of things I want."

Biting back a grin, Raquel's teeth lingered over her bottom lip. The bottom lip Taylor wanted very much to taste again.

"Well, I'm not going to break my promise, so out with it."

Making a show of giving in, Taylor let out an exaggerated sigh. "Fine. If you really want to know so bad. I've always envisioned a little mountainside chapel. White, of course. Covered in just enough snow to be magical. A small gathering of family and friends. No more than ten tops. Then my new wife and I steal ourselves away to a cabin further up the mountain where there is nothing to do but build fires of all kinds." She shook the faraway, dreamy tone out of her voice. "Okay, you can laugh now."

"I'm not laughing," Raquel said softly, her dark eyes wide and dewy. "That sounds absolutely gorgeous."

Flushed with heat, Taylor winced again. "You're just saying that."

Raquel shook her head. "You've dreamed up something beautiful. What made you come up with it?"

"My dad absolutely loved traveling, especially going north in the winter. My wanderlust was definitely inherited." She grinned. "One year, he decided we were going to spend Christmas and the New Year in a cabin in Tennessee. When we were driving through Gatlinburg, we stopped at this little white chapel tucked into the snow-covered pines. I was maybe ten and completely enchanted by the woman traipsing through the snow in her wedding dress, her new husband's black tux littered with snow flakes and their loved ones circled around them as they exited the church. It was this like slow motion moment in my mind. It really looked like magic. And then I imagined myself looking at a partner, how that guy looked at his bride. Like she was this otherworldly impossible-to-comprehend goddess who'd blessed him with her presence."

"God, Taylor. You're going to make me cry."

She laughed. "Are you a closet softie?"

"Absolutely not." Raquel cleared her throat, but she couldn't erase the mist in her eyes.

"I think about those people sometimes and wonder if he still looks at her like that."

Raquel's face softened again. "I hope so."

"Yeah. Me too. I guess since then I've always waited for the person who's going to look back at me like that. Everything that falls short of that feels like settling."

Raquel's expression turned sympathetic. "Real life might have a hard time living up to pre-teen expectations."

"I know," Taylor agreed with a sigh. "And yet I can't seem to stop looking for her." She smiled, saying more with her eyes than her mouth. "My goddess dressed in white."

Raquel held her gaze for a long beat. "Not a lot of us left who can wear virginal white in a church without bursting into flames."

At the image of Raquel in a wedding dress, Taylor's heart launched into her mouth and beat as hard as dragon wings. "Come on, Raquel. Don't tell me you believe in the misogynistic, patriarchal construct of virginity."

Her laugh was husky and brimming with mischief. "Certainly not after I didn't leave an inch of your body untouched."

Heat pulsed and pounded through Taylor's body like it had been waiting for any excuse to be set free. Unable to recover from the unexpected comment, she bit her bottom lip and let the pain of desire wash over her instead.

CHAPTER 27

SUNLIGHT, weak and hazy, broke through Raquel's uncovered window and pestered her like a younger sibling. She was going to turn away from it and eke out a few more hours of sleep when she realized that she'd fallen asleep at all.

The last thing she remembered was talking to Taylor. They'd realized how late it was; nearly five in the morning. Hours had evaporated without their notice as they talked about a hundred different things.

They'd started to say goodbye, but had somehow been pulled into another conversation. Raquel couldn't remember what about. At some point, she must have fallen asleep.

Opening her eyes, she reached for the phone that had fallen back on the pillow she'd been using to prop it up. Expecting a dark screen, it surprised her to find Taylor.

Asleep, Taylor's hair was wild and covering part of her face. Raquel reached out to push it out of her eyes before she curled her fingers into a soft fist.

She wanted more than anything in that moment to touch her. To wake her with featherlight kisses placed down the column of her neck. To slide down her body and part her thighs and drink her in until Taylor woke up mid-moan and reached down to tangle her fingers in Raquel's hair. To pull her closer so she could go deeper and harder, tasting her so completely that she couldn't breathe. She wouldn't stop until her name was on Taylor's lips and intertwined with her pleas for mercy.

Regret was a sour, cold pang in Raquel's stomach. They could've slept together last weekend. She could *know* what Taylor's body felt like asleep in her arms rather than guessing. Know how heavy her breaths were when she slept. But it had taken her way too long to realize that she wanted to know those things. That she wanted to actually sleep with her and not just have sex with her.

Raquel let herself watch Taylor for a little while. Let herself long for her until the baby monitor on her nightstand crackled to life and reminded her that she had more to do than stare at a sleeping Taylor. Her father would be up soon.

With a heaviness in her chest she didn't expect, Raquel pressed the red button and ended the call. Nine hours and twenty minutes they'd spent on the phone and it had barely felt like any time at all.

Rolling out of bed, Raquel plugged her nearly dead phone into the charger and dragged herself into the shower.

Thoughts of Taylor swirled in her mind like nothing else in the world existed. She recalled the passion on her face when she talked about her dream wedding.

Raquel hadn't been expecting that. She didn't think people even cared about getting married anymore.

Her own wedding had been a forgone conclusion—a ceremony at the Catholic Church she and Max's family attended since they had immigrated from Cuba. A reception followed where they hadn't gotten to pick the guests or the music or the food.

Washing the conditioner out of her hair, she imagined herself in Taylor's fantasy. It was crazy to envision herself as the woman in white traipsing through the snow, but she did it anyway. As long as it didn't leave the confines of her mind, it wasn't hurting anybody. It would only be a dream.

What would Taylor wear? She could easily see her in a white dress herself, or in a sharp tux, or anything in between. Taylor had that sort of energy. Like she didn't need to abide by femme or butch rules. If Raquel envied anything, it was the younger generation flouting the need for boxes to fit into. They could just be whatever suited them, and it didn't have to be some permanent declaration. It could be fluid or fixed, and no one seemed to care.

Out of the shower, Raquel threw on a pair of jeans and a loose pink button-down with the sleeves folded up to her elbows; the kind of outfit she could never wear in Miami without sweating, but was perfect for the mild Vermont summer.

Once in her father's room, she woke him gently and helped him into the bathroom. Mornings were always her favorite. He was always at his clearest then and most likely to recognize her.

Every now and again he would be so close to completely lucid, and while she loved those moments with him, she hated the realizations it brought with it. The memory of her mother's passing would always re-emerge and break his heart all over again. If the cruel disease of dementia could be thanked for anything, it was the gift of forgetting all the bad along with the good.

Most mornings, her father merely expected his lovely wife to be home later, after her shift at the factory. He wasn't alarmed at her absence, merely trapped in the excited expectation of his soulmate about to walk through the door. His was definitely a love capable of arm-wrestling bears, and probably man-eating gators and lions too.

Once Raquel had helped her dad shower, shave, and comb his hair, she ushered him to the banquette in the breakfast nook. Despite having a rather large house, it seemed like they spent all their time in the kitchen. It had been that way when she was a child too.

As she cooked him over-easy eggs and toast the way her mother made, they chatted happily about nothing at all. She was halfway into her extra strong *café con leche* when her dad decided it was time to sit by the window.

While he dozed looking over the front garden, Raquel sat at her kitchen table and tried to work. Her brain was filled with pop rocks; she couldn't form a complete thought.

Raquel: *I hope you're getting plenty of rest since I have to work with sleep deprivation.*

Conversation bubbles appeared after a beat. Instead of a text, Taylor sent a photo of herself. Sitting at a desk, she was holding a coffee mug in one hand and her chin in the other. Her eyes were half-closed as if she was barely awake.

Taylor: *Feel like trash.*

Taylor: *Can't wait to do it again tonight.*

Laughing at the unexpected response, Raquel picked up her phone and leaned against the banquette's cushion, her laptop and research forgotten.

Raquel: *Haven't you learned to stop being presumptuous yet?*

Taylor: *I'm a slow learner. Teach me again.*

With a smirk, Raquel shook her head.

Raquel: *I don't have time for games, Taylor. I'm working.*

Taylor: *On a Saturday?? NOOOO*

Taylor: *What are you working on?*

Raquel: *Research.*

Taylor: *Stop talking my ear off already.*

She chuckled.

Taylor: *So I'll see you again tonight? Dinner?*

Raquel: *And how do you suppose we'll do that?*

Taylor: *Tell me what kind of food you're having and I'll have the same. Just like if we were in person. DUH. What time? 8?*

Raquel: *I don't believe I ever said yes.*

Taylor: *But you know you waaaaant to.*

Taylor: *I'm in the mood for Italian.*

Taylor: *I make a mean vegan baked ziti. I'll make it for you one day.*

Exhilarated at the prospect of spending another night with Taylor, Raquel grinned. The promise of seeing her again was a bigger jolt than the Cuban espresso in her mug.

Taylor: *Unless you have another dinner date with your man tonight. In that case, I'll be happy to be dessert.*

Taylor: *What do you say?*

She should have said no. Should have said that she intended to get a full night's sleep because she felt like she'd been hit by a truck, but she wasn't a talented liar. The best she could do was play it cool.

Raquel: *Maybe.*

Taylor: *I can't wait.*

Smiling despite herself, Raquel put her phone down and tried so very hard to think about history, but all she could see was the future.

CHAPTER 28

AFTER A LATE AFTERNOON nap and a quick jog along the Bronx River, Taylor ran errands while crossing her check-in call with her parents off her to-do list. By the time she ran up the stairs to her apartment and got in the shower, she was ready for her date with Raquel.

Raquel hadn't called it a date. She'd never exactly confirmed she was going to show up either, but when Taylor texted her around six with a picture of her dinner ingredients, Raquel responded with a photo of a pint of *Halo Top* pistachio ice cream.

Taylor couldn't stop smiling while she blow-dried her hair and listened to Raquel's playlist. As much as Raquel liked to be precise with language, she rarely answered any of her questions directly. Taylor had to interpret the dessert for a deeper meaning.

In a cropped T-shirt and high-waisted leggings, Taylor was feeling pretty cute. She'd taken the hint and eaten dinner before slipping into bed and waiting for Raquel's call.

The day's exhaustion fled her body the second her phone lit up. When she answered it, Raquel appeared on her screen.

The sight of her sent Taylor's heart hopscotching into her throat. She wanted to be so smooth, so chill, but she couldn't stop the grin that bloomed on her face.

Dressed in a pink button-down and wearing her hair straight so it ended in a severe line below her chin, Raquel was not sitting in bed this time.

"Where are you?"

Raquel's eyebrow twitched. "My bedroom."

"Let me see."

As if the request really put her out, Raquel moved the phone around the room to give it a quick scan. She was sitting on a fancy armchair in the corner, next to a round side table and picture window. The huge room had an enormous wrought iron bed and a couple of dressers that looked like treasures discovered at an estate sale. It was exactly the kind of orderly and tastefully decorated space she imagined Martha Stewart would co-sign.

"Nice," Taylor said. "You showed me yours, so I guess it's only fair I show you mine. Please don't be blown away. I'm more than just my square footage."

Raquel smirked. "I'll do my best."

Taylor got out of bed to give Raquel the grand tour. It took less than a minute to show her the entire apartment.

"Do you ever feel cooped up?" Raquel asked, instead of teasing her about it. "Working all day in the same room where you sleep? There appears to be space in the living room. Can't you set up your work station there?"

Settling back down into her bed, Taylor shrugged. "I like the privacy. Plus, when Robbie and Bellamy are here, I rather be able to get stuff done without distraction. Where's the ice cream?"

Raquel tucked her hair behind her ear, making Taylor jealous of the fingertips trailing along her neck.

"I decided I didn't need the extra calories."

Taylor shook her head. She didn't understand why Raquel monitored her food, but she didn't think it was her place to comment.

After a few minutes of catching up, which consisted mostly of Raquel yelling at her for keeping her up all night, and Taylor reminding her she was equally responsible, they moved on to other topics.

"If you could go anywhere in the world, and money was no object, where would you go?" Taylor stacked her pillows before resting her upper back on them.

Following her lead, Raquel moved from the chair to stretch out on her bed. Taylor wondered, but didn't ask, if she'd sat in the chair to make some kind of point. Or maybe she was afraid she'd fall asleep again.

"I've never given it much thought," Raquel said, her dark hair splayed on her white pillowcase after she laid down.

"Gun to your head, you have to pick somewhere."

"What kind of crazed madman needs to know the answer to this question so badly he'd hold me at gunpoint?"

Taylor laughed at her faux offense. "Come on, Raquel. Be a good sport. You've really never thought about where you want to travel?"

Something unreadable flashed in her face, making Taylor feel like she was stepping perilously close to a landmine, but she couldn't see the harm in her question.

Glancing up at the ceiling, Raquel shrugged. "I guess I've always wanted to see Greece."

"Why do you say it like that? Like traveling is a sad thing?"

Raquel's hesitation made her stomach clench like a steel door slamming closed. There was obviously something Raquel wasn't saying.

"You don't want to hear that whole thing. Let's talk about something else. How was your dinner?"

"I'm not trying to be nosey, but if there is anything you want to talk about, I want to hear it," Taylor said, asserting herself more than she intended. "There is nothing you can't tell me."

Raquel sighed. "It's been a long time since I've thought about traveling or seriously dating or much of anything other than work or..." She took a long deep breath, as if bracing herself for impact. "Or anything other than my dad."

Taylor waited patiently for her to explain, wishing she was sitting in bed next to her so she could take her hand. The subject was an obviously sad and difficult one.

"He's been unwell for a number of years. He had a stroke, probably from the stress of losing my mother very suddenly. In turn, that brought on dementia." She paused as if to gather strength. "He requires someone to be with him around the clock. Thankfully, I have help while I'm at work, but in the evenings and on weekends it's me. Not that I'm complaining," she added hastily. "I'm happy that he's home with me. That I can care for him."

"God, Raquel. I'm so sorry." Taken aback by the revelation, Taylor struggled to process the enormity of Raquel's news. "That must be so incredibly hard on you," she said softly, her chest aching for Raquel, imagining the crushing weight of her burden. Of her sorrow.

Blinking fast as if to keep any emotion from forming, Raquel swallowed hard. "It's not about me."

"Yes, it is. At least in part. You're his caregiver. That's huge. Day in and day out, I bet you're on high alert all the time. Worry always sitting in the back of your mind."

Raquel shook her head, but Taylor knew she was right. "How can you know that?"

"My grandma took care of my grandpa after he had a stroke. She refused to leave his side for a second." A knot formed in Taylor's throat, followed by the overwhelming desire to puke. "She had a heart attack within a year and then I'm pretty sure my gramps died of a broken heart a few months later." She caught a tear before it could land on her cheek. "My mom couldn't take the guilt that she didn't do more, so she let my dad convince her to move to Portugal and travel around Europe instead of dealing with any of it."

Raquel furrowed her brow. "I'm so sorry, Taylor. That must have been such a hard time for your family." She took another deep breath, as if it might cleanse her of the sadness marring her face. "Grief can warp and break so many precious things. Sometimes the only thing we can think of doing is running away from it; hiding from it. Sitting still forces you to process whether you're ready to do it or not."

The simple truth hit Taylor hard. "It was the final fracturing point in a lot of ways. We all kind of drifted off to do our own thing." She shook her head. "I regret it, you know? I could've come back from the city and I didn't. Sometimes I wonder what would've happened if I'd lent my grandma a hand. If someone stepped in and helped her shoulder the load. We're not meant to take these things on alone. You burn out. You break."

It was Raquel's turn to try to hide her emotion, but her eyes were glistening and her dark eyeliner had smudged.

"So… is that why you have cameras in your house?" Taylor recalled Raquel checking her phone all the time. Checking what appeared to be live streams.

She sniffled. "It's not that I don't trust his nurses—they are phenomenal people—but I drove away the first aides I had by calling them constantly. With the cameras, I can just pop in and see what he's doing without overburdening them with requests for updates."

"Do what makes sense to you," Taylor said with conviction. "You can't feel bad about that."

"I didn't expect you to respond this way," Raquel confessed, as if truly shocked. "This is not something most people understand."

"I just wish I could be there right now. I'd give you the best hug."

Raquel wiped her tears and sniffled before letting out a little chuckle. "I can't say I wouldn't accept it."

Taylor's chest heaved. Her skin tingled. Her body was primed to run all the way to Vermont, just to hold her. She would do anything to take care of her, to protect her.

"I'm sorry you lost your mom." Taylor dropped her voice and held her phone closer to her face as she turned to lie on her side. "Can I ask what she was like?"

Lit from within, Raquel broke into a fragile smile; a hairline crack in her marble expression. "She was wonderful. Generous. Kind. Funny as hell."

The sound of her soft chuckle lifted Taylor like a magnet drawing up her chest bone.

"You know how they say a person is likely to give you the shirt off their back?" Raquel's eyes were bright again, gleaming with pride instead of glistening with tears. "She literally did that once. A woman who worked with her at the factory came in totally drenched after waiting for the bus during a torrential rainstorm. Their supervisor wouldn't allow this poor woman to wear one of a thousand garments in the place. Not even one from the rejected pile that would either be recycled or thrown away. She'd rather this woman remain in dripping, soaked clothes." Raquel's lip curved with second-hand mischief. "So my mother took off her smock and her shirt and her pants, and gave them to her to wear. She stayed on the factory floor like that until the supervisor caved."

When Raquel laughed at the memory, Taylor did too. She imagined an older version of Raquel staging a protest in her bra and undies.

"What a revolutionary! Come through, Cuban Norma Rae! I see you!"

Raquel wiped tears away again, but these were from a full-body laughter. "My mom loved telling that story."

"I bet! Did anything happen to her? Did she get in trouble?"

Raquel shook her head, her lips still curved in a devilish grin. "My mother was twice as fast as the next best seamstress. They wouldn't hurt their bottom line like that and everyone knew it."

"She sounds like a real badass."

Raquel chuckled, her dark eyes distant, like she was looking into the past. "My dad always used to say ballerinas had no right to be so elegant and so cutthroat."

"That must be where you get your poise. You always walk like you're gliding."

"You should've seen my mother," she said wryly. "I stomp around like Big Foot in snow boots compared to her. Everything she did had such a perfect rhythm; an invisible flow."

Deciding she was falling very stupidly in love, Taylor asked more questions. She couldn't absorb enough of Raquel's childhood, of the people who made and shaped her.

A jealous spike shot through her like lemon curdling milk. Max never had to be told these stories. He'd probably been around long enough to get them from the source. To meet the badass ballerina herself and just be there while she talked.

Taylor wished for the first time that they weren't a generation apart. That she'd been the high school sweetheart. She would never have squandered a second with her. Never let her feel less than the passionate excitement of a life fully lived.

CHAPTER 29

With fewer than two weeks before the start of the fall semester, Raquel was sitting in her office, her webcam off, waiting for the faculty meeting to begin over Zoom.

The meeting just before the fall semester was always the most chaotic, and by far the longest. The reading of the spring meeting's minutes alone would take forever.

Twice Raquel had suggested sending the minutes, along with the agenda, talking points, critiques, and new course proposals to attendees ahead of time so they could have a substantive discussion rather than wasting time reading together, but each time she was shut down.

Now, doodling in the corner of her monthly planner, Raquel was preparing to lose precious time, listening to people talk in circles. When the meeting was underway, she turned on her camera, said hello, and turned it off again. Her work done. She'd read the minutes later and pull out what she needed. It's not like anyone was going to listen to her ideas.

A familiar ding catapulted her out of her annoyance. She'd assigned Taylor a ringtone and now she associated the little pop with a thrilling rush of heat prickling underneath her skin.

Taylor: *Can you believe it's been a month since we last saw each other?*

Raquel's grin spread like an uncontrolled wildfire. She double checked her camera was off before she picked up her phone.

Leaning back in her worn brown leather office chair, surrounded by walls of books shelved floor to ceiling, Raquel didn't even pretend she would not respond.

Raquel: *Really? Because I'm almost sure I've seen you every day. I saw you last night. And the night before that. And the night before that. And... well, you get the point.*

Taylor: *Don't play coy. You know what I mean. It's been a month since I saw you in person. Since I... touched you.*

Raquel shifted in her seat. The small fan on her desk was no longer capable of keeping her cool as her body reacted to the memory of Taylor's fingers.

Raquel: *Aren't you busy transcribing that eternal medical malpractice trial? How do you have time to think about the last time you were at an airport?*

Taylor: *It's not being inside the airport I'm thinking about, babe.*

The winking face emoji Taylor tacked on to the end of the text made Raquel chuckle.

Raquel: *Was it being inside a three-star hotel then?*

Taylor: *You're getting warmer.*

Raquel: *I'm working, Taylor. I don't have time to play games with you.*

Taylor: *Oh, come on. Are you engaged in the faculty meeting? You said you were going to spend two hours playing tic-tac-toe against yourself.*

Biting the inside of her lip, she was glad Taylor couldn't see her face. She wouldn't be able to hide her amusement.

Raquel: *And what is it you're doing? Since you've obviously abandoned your scribe duties.*

Taylor: *Do you really want to know, Dr. Alonso?*

Heart thumping in her neck, Raquel's body reacted the way it did every time Taylor called her *Dr. Alonso*. She did it every time she flirted like this. Every time she wanted to play.

Moistening her lips, Raquel wanted more than anything to know what Taylor was doing. What made her think about the last time they'd touched?

Raquel: *Tell me.*

Taylor: *What is it they say about pictures? They speak a thousand NSFW words? Are you very alone in your office, Dr. Alonso?*

Her gaze cut to the locked office door. The one with a note taped to it alerting everyone that she was in a faculty meeting and was not to be interrupted for any reason.

Raquel: *Completely and utterly.*

When the image appeared on her phone, Raquel's body pulsed with heat in response. Forget the fan, she was going to need a turbine to stay cool.

Sitting in her office chair, Taylor was in a dark blue plaid short-sleeved shirt and tiny, soft-looking cream-colored shorts. Visible only from her dimpled smirk down, she'd unbuttoned her shirt to the middle of her flat belly. Without a bra, the modest swell of her cleavage was visible. If Raquel strained, she could almost see the shadow of her dark pink nipple. Sitting with one long, smooth leg propped on her desk and the other on the floor, her pose was inviting Raquel to slither between her parted thighs.

Taylor: *I've been thinking about you all day.*

Raquel closed her eyes for a moment. She imagined Taylor's voice, breathy and hot, whispering the confession against the shell of her ear. It stirred the familiar ache between her thighs, awakened the longing that never seemed sated.

Taylor: *I keep having this fantasy that you'll show up at my door.*

Raquel: *To help you transcribe? I'm afraid I can't type nearly as fast as you.*

Taylor: *That's not what I need your fingers for...*

Another photo appeared. Taylor's pose was the same, but she'd slipped her hand beneath the flannel shirt. With her head tossed back, Taylor exposed her long, elegant throat. She didn't need to see beneath the fabric to know that Taylor's fingers were working to stiffen the peak shielded from view.

Cursing under her breath, Raquel wished it was her hand on Taylor's firm flesh. Her mouth on her neck.

Taylor: *Let me see you.*

She looked at the door again. Raquel wanted to give in to the swirl of lust, but the risk was too great. It was too wrong.

Raquel: *This is all you're getting.*

Unbuttoning the top two buttons on her silky, pastel pink blouse and shrugging on the black blazer hanging on the back of her chair, Raquel angled her phone above her. Making sure not to capture her face, or any part of her office, she snapped a picture of her cleavage and sent it.

Taylor: *The blazer, Raquel? Are you trying to kill me?! You know that's one of my top three fantasies. You in a blazer... maybe nothing else... I can't decide.*

With a satisfied smirk, Raquel buttoned up her shirt again. She'd guessed Taylor might like that.

Raquel: *I thought your thing was pencil skirts.*

Taylor: *Fuck. That too.*

Taylor: *Tell me one of your fantasies.*

Raquel: *I don't know that I really have one.*

Taylor: *Everyone has a fantasy. That little kink that you just can't shake.*

Biting the inside of her cheek, Raquel didn't want to divulge the silly little musing. It would probably make her look old and out of touch.

Taylor: *I promise there's almost nothing in the world you can say that I'll find strange. Trust me. I read a metric ton of erotica.*

Sitting up to rest her elbows on the desk, Raquel tried to clear her shyness.

Raquel: *It's not exactly a fantasy, but growing up in the 80s, I was led to believe that garter belts were going to be more of a thing. I was very disappointed to never see a pair in person.*

Taylor: *So, like black stockings and the whole thing? Very Gal Gadot in* Keeping Up with the Joneses?

Raquel: *I didn't see that.*

Taylor: *Oh, the movie was terrible, but Google the scene of her and Isla Fisher in the dressing room. You'll thank me.*

Taylor: *Back to this garter belt thing. I need more details. Do you want me to wear it for you? Or do you want me to worship your sexy ass in it?*

Biting down on her bottom lip, Raquel was inundated by images of Taylor in lingerie. Of her walking toward her slowly and dripping in lusty possibility.

Raquel: *I would like to admire you in it.*

Taylor: *I wish I was waiting in your bed right now. A low-cut black bra I'm spilling out of... a little black thong... lacy garter belt... black thigh-highs. After spending all day thinking about you, I'd be so wet and ready.*

Sighing a curse, Raquel let the image curl around her. Let it hypnotize her. Let it raise the heat inside of her like Taylor's body was splayed in front of her.

Taylor: *I miss you so fucking bad.*

Raquel: *Show me.*

Taylor: *What do you want me to show you, baby?*

The term, used seriously for the first time instead of as a joke, sent an aching pull surging between Raquel's thighs. She squeezed them together, trying to smother it. There was no use.

Raquel: *Show me how much you miss me.*

A moment later, an image appeared. Taylor's semi-unbuttoned shirt was askew, revealing one firm breast. If that wasn't enough to drive Raquel insane, Taylor had slipped her hand in her shorts. Raquel could feel her on her fingertips like it was her inside the fabric.

Taylor: *I need you, Raquel. Please.*

Raquel: *I bet you feel so good.*

Taylor: *Fuck, I'm so wet. I wish you were here to feel it. To slide your fingers inside of me.*

There was nothing Raquel wanted more than to be with her. To kiss her. To touch her. To lose herself in her.

She was going to tell her so before the history department chair's voice traveled through the speakers and echoed in her office. It landed like an ice bath in her sauna. She was going to have to pay attention now. Her chair might call on her.

Raquel: *Shit. Taylor, I'm so sorry. I'm going to have to get back to the meeting.*

Taylor: *You're going to leave me like this??*

Raquel: *At least you're home and can do something about it. I have to sit here for an hour at least.*

Taylor: *Do something about it all alone? That doesn't seem fair.*

Raquel: *Unfortunately, I can't teleport into your bed, Miss Lopez.*

Taylor: *No... but maybe I can wait for you? After you get home. Unwind. Meet me in bed? We can pick up where we left off?*

Raquel: *What exactly are you proposing?*

Taylor: *Video is a little better than sexting. You know... a next best thing?*

Raquel: *Maybe.*

Taylor: *I'll be waiting.*

CHAPTER 30

THE MOMENT TAYLOR submitted her completed transcript for her supervisor's review, she bolted out of her room and into the shared bathroom, a little larger than a postage stamp.

After a month of talking to Raquel every night, they'd developed a rhythm. With Raquel's fall semester about to start, she'd been spending long days on campus, but she always had dinner with her father at six. Those rituals were important to her. Cooking breakfast and dinner for him obviously brought her an immense comfort. Taylor guessed her father loved it too, even if he might not be able to convey his feelings through words.

Unless Raquel had to work late, they'd usually be on the phone by eight and talk until their eyes were heavy and drooping with sleep. On the nights Raquel had to continue working after dinner, they still talked before bed—even if only for a little while.

Good morning texts, mid-morning check-ins, lunchtime chats, and little messages shot off throughout the day. They were almost always talking; keeping their connection alive and thriving.

A few times, Taylor had suggested seeing each other in person. She was happy to make the trip to Lockwood.

Looking at her reflection in the bathroom mirror, still framed with steam from her hot shower, Taylor shook her head. "You've got it bad, Lopez," she said to herself while channeling Alexis.

At that moment, she ached for her friends. What would they say if they were crowded in her dead, silent apartment? She could imagine Briana fussing about something. See Jessica in the kitchen making sure they had something to eat apart from the seven-layer dip Alexis scrounged up from somewhere.

She'd never felt alone since moving to New York, but after returning from Miami, it had suddenly stopped feeling like home. She felt like a visitor in her own apartment. She felt... lonely.

Shaking off the heavy, gray feeling, Taylor padded across the tiny hall and back to her bedroom.

Even when she had the entire apartment to herself, as she did most days, she still spent most of her time in the tiny room that was starting to feel a little like a jail cell.

Maybe Raquel was right, she should move her desk to the living room. There was a larger window in there, and even though it faced the brick exterior of the building next door, there was a little more natural light than in her cave.

Propping one foot up at a time on her office chair, Taylor slathered her freshly shaved legs in moisturizer. Unsure how far Raquel was interested in going tonight, she'd shaved as meticulously as when expecting company.

Staring down at her open underwear drawer, Taylor decided on a pair of black low rise boy shorts and a muscle tee she'd cut out of a black vintage Batman t-shirt, its yellow insignia all but faded. Without a bra on and with all her wavy hair tossed to one side, she knew she looked sexy as hell.

When her phone rang, it displayed a picture of Raquel. Taylor had asked her to send it on one of the many mornings they woke up together. Raquel's head was on her pillow, her hair perfectly messy, her face still soft from sleep, and her eyes gently looking into the camera. It made Taylor feel like they were lying in bed together. Like Raquel was offering an expression reserved solely for her.

"Hi," Taylor said when she slid the phone open, her grin giving away her excitement. It had been hours since she'd seen her that morning. She'd missed her face. Her voice.

"Hi," Raquel replied softly. Her voice was a husky pulse that rippled through Taylor's body.

"You're in bed without me."

Raquel's bedroom was lit low. Taylor guessed all she had on was the bathroom light, which offered just enough of a glow to see her.

Raquel's full lips, even sexier when they were nude and unpainted, curved into a smirk that Taylor was dying to kiss. "You were supposed to be here waiting for me, dressed in something rather special."

Taylor moistened her lips and tried to remember what Raquel tasted like. "What are you wearing?"

"Just like that? No, how was your day? No, what did you have for dinner?"

"I know how your day was because we texted during the whole thing, and I know what you had for dinner because I was on the phone with you when you stopped at the supermarket. And I know the *carne con papa* was delicious because even in the picture you sent me, it looked bangin'."

Laughing, Raquel's throat bobbed in the way that made Taylor ache to bite the sensitive skin.

"What are *you* wearing?" Raquel asked instead of answering Taylor's question.

Sitting on the edge of her bed, Taylor shook her head. "You really refuse to learn the rules, don't you?" She sighed before muttering, "Capricorns."

"I don't know what you're talking about. I follow my rules just fine."

"You're terrible," Taylor said before giving in. Leaning back on the hand splayed out behind her, she stretched out the arm holding the phone and let Raquel get a look at her. As if it was in on her plan, the shirt, and its wide-cut sleeves, slid to one side to expose grade-A side-boob.

Raquel wasn't smirking anymore. Her eyes darkened as they slid over Taylor's body. Even from hundreds of miles away, she felt the weight of her gaze.

Taylor tore the lens away from her body and held the phone to her face as she dropped into bed. "Your turn. Let me see."

Tipping her head to one side, Raquel obliged. She lifted the fluffy white duvet covering her body to reveal a silky, white pajama top, and the very edge of frilly navy-blue underwear.

All Taylor could do was imagine what unbuttoning that top would be like. How she'd kiss every newly exposed inch of skin as she worked her way down.

"God, you look so good," Taylor said. "Open one of those buttons for me."

Raquel's response was a throaty chuckle, but her fingers moved to the button at the top of her chest. As she toyed with it, Raquel watched Taylor. "I don't recall you being quite this assertive before."

With a flick, Raquel parted one button and then another, exposing the lacy fabric of a navy-blue bra.

"Keep going," Taylor whispered.

Instead of replying with a quip or something smart-assy, Raquel moistened her lips and slid her fingers over her bare skin before finding the next button below her sternum.

"You don't know how badly I wish I was there with you right now."

"Then why don't you tell me?" Raquel let the fabric of her top slip to one side.

Taylor's attention fixed on the lacy fabric stretched over Raquel's full breast. Understanding exactly what she wanted, Raquel ran her fingertips under the material, finding her nipple beneath the lace.

"You feel so good," Taylor said slowly, infusing each syllable with breathy desire.

Raquel's approval was a tiny rattle in her throat.

"Let me put your fingers in my mouth and wet them for you. It would feel so much better." Taylor's body hummed with lust, building and pushing and throbbing.

In response, Raquel made a show of running the tips of her middle and index finger across her bottom lip before her tongue inched out and swirled around them.

Taylor cursed and shifted in her bed, pushing away the covers as she squirmed.

When her fingers returned to her nipple, Raquel let out a little moan. Unable to resist, Taylor's hand drifted down her abdomen and over her underwear.

"Let me see," she begged, desperate to pull down Raquel's bra herself.

"You first." Raquel's words were already husky and dripping with need.

Happy to give her whatever she wanted in return, Taylor rose off the bed just enough to pull up her shirt. As slowly as she could manage, which was nowhere near Raquel's distressingly glacial speed, she lifted her T-shirt just enough to expose one breast. Rolling her fingers lightly across her chest, she revealed the other.

Raquel cursed and then bit her bottom lip when Taylor teased her nipple for her viewing pleasure.

"I miss your mouth on me," Taylor moaned before squeezing her breast and wishing it were Raquel touching her. "I want to feel you all over my body." She dropped her hand, letting it glide over her belly and down her thighs.

"I think about you all the time," Raquel confessed. "I dream about you. I can still taste you. Smell you. Feel you on my skin."

It was Taylor's turn to curse. "I want you so bad it hurts, Raquel."

At the sound of her name, Raquel moaned. "Then let's see if we can do something about easing your pain."

Sure that things were about to escalate very quickly, Taylor pulled off her shirt. "Take that off," she barked in a tone more demanding than she intended.

Without hesitation, Raquel unbuttoned the last button of her pajama top. Taylor ached to feel her soft, tanned skin. To run her tongue over her clavicle and between her breasts and down to her navel.

"I want to see more of you," Taylor pleaded.

Fixing her in her gaze, Raquel fiddled with the strap on her bra. Her dark eyes glinted with mischief as she let her attention float over Taylor's exposed chest.

"I suppose it's only fair," she said before setting her phone face down on the bed. When she picked the phone up again, she had the covers back over her chest.

"Oh, come on!" Taylor whined. "Two can play that game, you know." She reached for her blanket, ready to pull it over herself.

"Patience," Raquel urged, her lips full and painfully kissable. "I promise I'll give you everything you want."

Taylor's core throbbed again, hard and sudden. She'd been turned on all day and being pushed to the edge like this was going to kill her.

"Everything?" Taylor echoed, possibility thrumming through her veins and collecting between her thighs.

Raquel licked her lips so slowly that Taylor was sure she would pass out before she spoke again. "Anything."

Relaxing into her pillow, Taylor tried to wait, but she'd been waiting all day. There was only so much she could bear.

"Do you know what I keep thinking about?" She paused, her gaze lingering on Taylor's body. "Do you remember that first night we were together?" Raquel's voice was a sultry drug, taking over Taylor's mind and sending her backward in time.

"It was a long night." Taylor smirked. "We did a lot of things."

Raquel's lip twitched. "We did," she agreed, her fingers grazing her neck before disappearing beneath the duvet. "But we only did this once." The covers slid down enough for Taylor to see her cleavage.

Taylor tried to focus, but all she could see was Raquel's skin. All she could think about was seeing more of it.

"I'm surprised you forgot. I thought you were going to leave bruises all over my ass."

A memory of Raquel riding her reverse cowgirl sprang into Taylor's mind and sent a jolt of heat to her core. Tilting her phone down, she let Raquel watch her push her hand into her underwear.

"I remember," Taylor breathed, her fingers slipping over her hard, sensitive flesh. "God, how am I so wet already?" She closed her eyes for a moment as she remembered the sensation of Raquel grinding on her. What she wouldn't give to feel her slick, wet heat against hers.

When she opened her eyes, she noticed a distinct flush spreading over Raquel's neck, spilling over her now fully exposed chest.

As Taylor watched, Raquel rolled her stiff nipple between her fingers. When her hand disappeared beneath the duvet covering her lower body, Taylor nearly cried.

Forcing herself to show restraint, Taylor moved her fingers in slow circles. Her discipline was tested as soon as Raquel furrowed her brow and her full lips parted. Taylor had to stop touching herself or risk losing control.

"Are you wet for me?" Taylor asked, barely above a whisper.

Raquel nodded, her expression pained.

Taylor wished she was wedged between her thighs, watching. "Let me see, please."

With half-lidded eyes, Raquel looked at her for a beat before her roving hand reappeared.

Even over the phone, Taylor could see it was glistening with the evidence of her desire.

"Tell me how good you taste," Taylor begged.

Raquel's grin was danger and sin and sex manifested. She ran her fingers over her bottom lip before dipping them oh so erotically into her mouth.

"I taste so fucking good," she whispered slowly, like the revelation wrecked her too.

The combination of words was too much. It sent Taylor's head spinning. Her body pulsed with a yearning so desperate it claimed every inch of her.

"Raquel, please." Taylor didn't know what she was asking for, but she needed to release the energy building inside of her or she was going to die. She was sure of it. Death by desire deprivation. It had to be a thing, or maybe no one had ever been tortured to these lethal levels.

"Do you remember what you did that night?" Raquel's voice was a low rumble rolling over Taylor's body, electrifying her with a thousand lightning strikes.

Taylor shook her head as she moved her fingers so lightly she was practically hovering. Even that felt like too much, like she was a second away from an unstoppable orgasm.

"When you came the second time," Raquel explained, her hand moving beneath her duvet.

Taylor recalled the scissoring position she'd never tried before but worked like absolute magic. Watching Raquel's ass bouncing while she was grinding hard against her core was the hottest thing she'd ever seen in her life.

Overwhelmed by the memory and watching Raquel touch herself, Taylor could barely breathe. It was sensory overload.

"Do you even realize what you did?" Raquel let the covers fall away completely, revealing her nude body and gently moving hand.

"Fuck," Taylor cried.

"Stop," Raquel demanded, breaking the start of Taylor's spiral. "Wait for me."

Taylor made a fist to keep from getting ahead of herself. She was already hot, her body covered with a sheen of sweat despite the AC blasting. She was so close she was almost too far gone.

Raquel didn't stop her own slow ministrations.

"I wish those were my lips around you," Taylor groaned, her attention fixed on Raquel's hand. "Can I see you?"

Raquel hesitated.

"You said I could have anything," she reminded her. "Everything."

The chaos returned to Raquel's gleaming brown eyes. "Just for a second."

A second of watching Raquel's elegant, manicured hands, of watching her fingers sliding over her soaked flesh was all Taylor needed. Even without touching herself, she felt pushed to the brink.

"Raquel, please." Taylor pulled the sheets at her side, crumpling them into her fist as she dug her hips into the mattress. "I need to—"

"Not until I'm close," she moaned in a way that made Taylor feel confident she wouldn't have to wait much longer. "You never answered my question."

The color spread over Raquel's stiffening body and her breathing grew heavier. She looked unbelievable as she writhed.

"What question?" Taylor tried to find her voice, to return the moisture to her mouth, but it was useless.

"What you did."

"I don't remember." Taylor bit the inside of her cheek, her core pounding hard and aching for relief.

"I haven't stopped thinking about it," Raquel said, her words clipped and her hand moving more quickly; more erratically. "I've been fantasizing about you doing it again."

"Tell me. I'll do anything you want," Taylor swore the vow with every fiber of her being.

"You came inside of me."

Raquel's words were nearly lost to her moan as her back arched off the bed, but Taylor heard them, absorbed them into her body, let them wash over her and flow into her.

Taylor's body vibrated, and she nearly dropped the phone. While she'd thought about that moment a million times, she hadn't thought about it that way.

"That's so hot, Raquel. Jesus. I can't wait to do that again. I wish I was inside of you right now."

"Call me *baby*," she moaned before her eyes slammed shut.

"Fuck, baby. Yes, come for me. Come all over me." Lust nearly robbed Taylor of her voice, as it claimed her completely. "You feel so fucking good."

"I'm close," she cried.

The moment Taylor touched herself, she started to unravel. She tried to keep her eyes open to watch Raquel, but she dropped her phone on her pillow. The sound of Raquel panting and moaning was so intense, she couldn't stop the string of orgasms that claimed her while she listened to Raquel curse and moan her name.

When she picked the phone back up, Raquel was still recovering.

"That was intense," Taylor said, unabashedly breathless.

Raquel nodded, obviously unable to speak.

"I miss you," Taylor confessed without the qualifications of flirtation or lust. "I wish I was lying next to you right now."

Running her fingers over her scalp, Raquel pushed back her hair and rolled onto her side. "I miss you too," she admitted softly, her sleepy eyes fixed on Taylor's.

Imitating her move, Taylor turned on her side. With all of her emotions heightened, she felt a swell of sadness start in her chest and push at the back of her eyes.

"This kind of made me realize how badly I want to see you again." Taylor couldn't stop confessing her feelings. "I should be there. Holding you. Kissing you."

"We'll figure something out," Raquel said in a way that made Taylor realize she didn't want to have the conversation now. "Sleep with me tonight?"

The request lifted Taylor's spirits. She propped her phone up on the pillow the way she did when she got tired of holding it during their marathon conversations. "Anything for you, *baby*."

Raquel glared at her use of the term of endearment, but her lips twitched in amusement. "That's exclusively for sex. And if you tell anyone—"

Chuckling, she stopped teasing her. When Raquel reached for her covers, so did Taylor.

They looked at each other for a while, neither talking with their lips but divulging too many truths with their eyes. As soon as Raquel fell asleep, Taylor dove in after her.

CHAPTER 31

As Taylor jogged along one of the many curves of the Bronx River, she reveled in the cool Friday afternoon. With September just a few days away, summer's tail was mild and absolutely perfect.

The wooden footpath straddling the banks where birds foraged on the slick stones creaked beneath her feet as she ran by an old man and a very excited toddler in a ladybug raincoat.

She barely felt the ground beneath her feet as she followed the path to the botanical garden. Even at the end of August, with half the flowers in the sprawling rose garden withering or gone, it was still beautiful.

Pulling the phone out of the side pocket in her leggings, Taylor wished Raquel was strolling the circular paths with her instead of at a working lunch meeting with her department. As much as she loved talking to her all day, she was starting to hate being without her. Video calls were a shitty substitute for the real thing.

Taylor was not really an *alone* kind of person. She wasn't the sort to always need to be in a relationship, but she'd always had a strong group of friends. Even the ones she'd made in New York had come quickly, but now that they'd obviously chosen Robbie, she felt adrift.

Deciding she was going to join a pottery class or book club and make new friends, Taylor started her walk back to her apartment. She only had fifteen minutes left of her lunch break, so she used it to check-in on her parents.

She was a block away from her place and finished with her call when her headphones read Raquel's message to her.

Raquel: *Those rose garden pictures are gorgeous. I got roped into another meeting. Won't be able to talk until tonight.*

She pulled out her phone and let the sass claim her fingers as she texted back.

Taylor: *Tonight? Are you asking me on a date?*

Conversation bubbles appeared and disappeared. Raquel could be so unnecessarily weird about things. She should have known that classifying the time they spent together as *dating* would make her spin out.

Raquel: *I didn't know you were interested in putting a label on things. We're having a good time. Why don't we keep it at that? I don't want to spoil anything.*

Taylor: *Oh, please. If what we've been doing for six weeks isn't dating, then I don't know what is.*

Smirking, Taylor leaned against the door to her building. The one Mrs. Lassiter from 2C had covered in fall decorations like she did every year.

Taylor: *Or maybe I should put it like this: how would you feel if I was having a GOOD TIME with someone else?*

Raquel: *Don't be rude.*

Laughing, Taylor punched the code into the door and let herself in. As she jogged up several flights of stairs, she waited for Raquel to say something more.

Her phone rang in her headphone while she was still climbing. Before she answered it, she pulled off her shirt so Raquel could see her all sweaty in just a sports bra and leggings.

"Hi, Raquel." Taylor smirked. "I thought you had a meeting."

Raquel, standing in her office, scanned Taylor's body with open approval. "I do. I only have a few minutes." She adjusted her own white earbud.

"Why the urgent call, then?" She walked the rest of the way up to her landing.

Raquel tucked her straight hair behind her ear. In her glasses and jacket, she was in full professor mode, and it was incredibly hard not to drool over her.

"Well, Miss Lopez, you might be comfortable defining our relationship over a random text, but I'm not."

Slipping her key into the door, Taylor chuckled. "Oh, is that what I was doing? Haphazardly throwing things out there over text?"

Raquel lifted an eyebrow over the rim of her black glasses; the big square ones Taylor loved.

Once inside the apartment, she found Phillip curled up on the couch exactly where she'd left him. He lifted his head when she walked in and plopped down next to him.

Making Raquel wait just a minute, she scratched behind his black ears. "Hi, buddy."

"Is he okay?" Raquel asked, looking at the Papillon with concern.

Taylor sighed. "He's been getting like this after a few days of being with me. Bellamy's roommate adopted a Collie mix and I think they're in love. I guess a couple of days is all he can handle without him."

Raquel frowned. "That's terribly sad."

"I know, right?" Taylor petted him as he slowly rolled onto his back. "This morning I had to bribe him with chicken so he'd eat his food. I think he's thoroughly miserable."

The sound of the front door opening unexpectedly caused both Philip and Taylor to look toward it.

"Oh, shit," Robbie said when she appeared in the doorway, prompting Phillip to leap to his feet and yap excitedly. "I'm sorry, Tay. You scared me."

"By sitting on my own couch?" She chuckled and tried not to feel hurt at the dog's obvious preference.

Robbie tucked a strand of blonde hair behind her ear. "No." She smiled nervously. "You're just usually in your office at this time. I didn't mean to interrupt." She looked at the phone in Taylor's hand, but didn't comment on the woman on her screen.

"It's your apartment too," Taylor reminded her while setting her phone down face-up on the couch next to her. She didn't add the '*not that you're ever here.*'

Robbie scooped up Phillip to kiss his head before setting him down on the couch. "I'm just off this week, so I wanted to grab some stuff. I'll be gone in a minute."

The entire time Robbie was milling around the apartment, Phillip was jumping at her feet and barking. When she walked toward the door with a bag slung over her shoulder, Phillip looked like he was trying to jump inside of it.

"It's okay, Rob." Taylor picked up the dog and gave him kisses while he licked her nose. "Take him with you."

"It's not my week," Robbie said, looking properly horrified at their dog's reaction.

Holding him to her chest, it broke her heart to admit the truth. To accept it. "I know, but he's been miserable cooped up here and I want him to be happy."

"You know it's not me, right?" Robbie's blue eyes were huge and apologetic. "It's the yard and Moses. He spends all day out there playing with him."

Taylor smiled and gave her dog another little squeeze. "I know. He left his heart in Jersey City." She sighed. "I know what it's like to want to be somewhere else, buddy. Go get your man," she whispered to him.

Robbie replied with a little chuckle before letting Phillip wiggle into her tote bag. When he was settled and snug, Robbie leaned forward and kissed Taylor's cheek. "You're a very excellent dog mom."

"Thanks," Taylor said, closing the door behind her.

When she returned to the phone, she expected Raquel to be gone, but she was sitting at her desk instead.

"Sorry. I know you have to go. I didn't mean to take so long."

Raquel's rich honey eyes were filled with something unidentifiable. "I still have a minute and the meeting is just down the hall," she said softly. "That was rather kind of you. To put the dog's needs before your own."

Lifted from being on the very verge of crying, Taylor managed a smile. "I know. Your girlfriend is just the sweetest, isn't she?"

Without missing a beat, Raquel smiled. "Yes. She is."

Taylor had been half joking, expecting to fluster Raquel or get a reaction at the *GF* label. Instead of shocking Raquel, she was the one who was sideswiped in the very best way.

"Alonso, are you messing with me?" Taylor couldn't handle her own wildly vacillating emotions. "Because if you're kidding, that's really messed—"

"Why would I play like that?" Raquel was grinning, straight, white teeth on display. "Did I misunderstand your earlier texts? Weren't you angling for clarification on where we stood? Well, I don't want you texting anyone else good morning, or sending them sexy pictures, or telling them when you've had a bad dream, or coordinating the exact right moment to hit play so you can watch a movie together. I don't want to spend time with anyone but you. So, here we are."

Taylor was levitating somewhere a foot above her body. In her mind they weren't seeing other people, if only because they spent all their time on the phone, but hearing Raquel say all those things out loud was a flood of endorphins and adrenaline and the only thing that could make it better would be throwing her arms around Raquel's neck and kissing her.

"So, this being girlfriends thing..." Taylor smiled hard at the sound of the word on her lips.

"Yes?"

"Does it mean I can call you baby when you're not in the throes of passion?"

Raquel chuckled before pretending to straighten her beige blazer. "Maybe."

CHAPTER 32

HIGH ON THE GIRLFRIEND DECLARATION, Taylor spent two days debating whether she should surprise Raquel in Vermont. It seemed insane that she was only a train ride away, but they hadn't made concrete plans to see each other in the month and a half since they'd been talking.

Deciding they hadn't been together long enough for her to be sure Raquel would consider her showing up on her doorstep a pleasant surprise, she broached the subject with her instead.

On weekend nights, she couldn't expect Raquel to stay up after ten. She didn't talk about it much, no matter how many times Taylor tried, but taking care of her father day and night on Saturdays and Sundays after a long work week was obviously exhausting. The one time Taylor brought up wishing she could help, Raquel stiff-armed her like an old-timey football player and changed the subject.

They'd just finished watching an episode of a mediocre mystery series when Raquel stretched out in bed and rubbed her neck.

"Does your neck hurt?" Taylor adjusted the pillows behind her as she sat up, her arm on her knee as she held up her phone.

"Just a little stiff. I must have slept on it wrong."

Taylor jumped at the chance to bring up the subject of visiting. "I would love to come rub that for you, you know?" She flashed a dimple to show she was flirting.

Raquel chuckled. "That would be amazing."

"I mean it, Raq. I could come see you. If you want that." She held the phone closer to her face, wanting Raquel to see the truth in her eyes. "I really miss you."

Raquel's tired eyes flickered like a neon light trying, and failing, to sputter to life. "I miss you too, Taylor. I swear I do."

Taylor sighed. "But?"

After a moment's hesitation, Raquel gave her a sad, weak little smile. "But nothing. Let's make a plan. A vacation. You're so good at planning those, right? How about you pick anywhere within a two-hour flight from the Burlington airport?"

The clouds that had been forming over Taylor parted, leaving blue skies and a blazing sun. Taylor's excitement was an unrestrained rocket shooting off the ground without warning. She hadn't realized how badly she'd needed this until now. To take a trip *and* see Raquel? It was too good to be true.

It took a three-second Google search to come up with an option. "Do you have a passport? Apparently, Montreal is a short drive from you."

"That sounds wonderful." Raquel smiled. "I can plan after the holidays. Maybe we can celebrate our birthdays together during the winter break."

The holidays? Birthdays? That meant next year. January at the earliest, when they were barely in September.

"Oh," was all Taylor could manage in reply.

"I really do miss you." Raquel's face dimmed. "You can't possibly imagine how much I'd love to see you." She hesitated, debating something. With a heavy sigh, she continued. "I just can't leave my dad again so soon. It's too much to put on Nadia and the only back-up nurse he likes is on maternity leave."

"Is that it?" Taylor bounced back from her low mood. "Well, that's not a big deal! I can just come there. We don't need a whole vacation. I can come for the weekend. No need to change his schedule at all."

"That's very sweet of you to offer. I can't tell you how much that means to me, but you know how the weekends are. From the moment he wakes until he goes to bed, he has all my time spoken for," she said with open regret. "I know this is a lot to deal with, and I know it's not fair. This is why I haven't dated—"

"Stop that. I know full well you guys come as a package deal, and I don't have a problem with that at all. You're such a loving and dedicated daughter. You're teaching four classes this semester. Working sixty hours a week to juggle it all, but you bend over backwards to take care of him and call it a privilege. You're incredible." Love pushed at the contours of Taylor's chest, but she stopped short of confessing it. "Do you think I care you can't travel? That's the easiest thing to overcome."

Raquel shook her head. She didn't like being complimented like this, Taylor knew, but she needed her to hear it. Needed her to understand that Taylor would extend her all the grace and patience in the world.

"You're so young, Taylor." Raquel sighed again. "You should be doing more than waiting for me. I'm being selfish. I'm keeping you from living the absolute best time of your life."

"Oh, no." Taylor shot up, her back straight. "You listen to me, Raquel. You're not going to do this. I choose what I do with my life, okay? I choose you. Every day. Every time. So don't get all noble and try to slip away from me because you think you're holding me back. And I'm not that young," she added with a grin. "Twenty-seven is almost forty, remember? We're essentially the same age."

Raquel's shoulders relaxed as she shook her head and smirked. "I'm still not convinced that math is right, babe."

Taylor beamed. "Trust me, okay. I'm a whole ass adult. I understand my choices, and that's not changing."

Relenting, Raquel tipped her head in agreement.

"Okay." Taylor was undeterred. A solution felt so possible. "So if staying over is too much for the first visit, why don't I get an Airbnb in town? One of those cute farmhouses in Lockwood has to have a guest house they rent out or something, right? I'll stay nearby and you can sneak me into your room when your dad goes to bed." She wiggled her eyebrows. "It'll be just like now, except in person. And when you're ready, we'll take another step. I just want to see you. Even if it's for a minute."

Raquel's eyes were liquid bronze while she gazed at her for a beat before speaking again. "Nearby, huh? And what do you plan to do with yourself all day? You realize Lockwood is nothing like Miami or the city."

Hope filled Taylor to bursting. Raquel wasn't shutting her down. "I know your postcard-perfect town of 8,000 people isn't the city, Raq." She rolled her eyes. "But there are, like, a million places to go hiking. Don't you worry about me. I'm very good at entertaining myself."

With a chuckle, Raquel's essence brightened. "Okay, if you're sure—"

"More than sure."

"Give me a couple of weeks to get into a rhythm with the new semester. I'm teaching two freshman classes this fall and the start is always a bit of chaos."

"Yeah? For real?"

Raquel laughed. "For real."

Taylor dropped back onto her bed, her skin tingling from the inside out. "You know what I'm going to do as soon as we say goodnight?"

Raquel waited for her response.

"I'm going on the *Savage X Fenty* website and buying everything I need to make your fantasies come true." Taylor grinned. "Unless you want to pick what I wear?"

Moistening her lips, Raquel shifted lower on the bed. "Oh, I think I much prefer to be surprised," she said in the low, slow tone she used for their more intimate conversations.

"Other than the very particular outfit, is there anything else you want me to bring?"

Raquel pretended to consider the question, but Taylor knew in her gut Raquel had something in mind already. "You look really good in those gray sweat pants you were jogging in this morning." Raquel dragged her teeth over her bottom lip. "It would be fun to balance all that feminine energy with something else."

"Something else?" Taylor had a good guess what she meant, but she waited for Raquel to say it.

"Something you can wear with those sweatpants and one of your ripped up muscle tees."

Taylor grinned, unable to help herself. "Mrs. Alonso, do you want me to strap it on?"

She raised an eyebrow. "Do you object?"

"Fuck no." Taylor laughed. "But this is an important purchase. I need to know size, color, style." She pulled up her favorite queer-owned sex shop and sent her the link.

Raquel's eyes widened as she scrolled through the site. "Who knew there were so many options?"

Taylor laughed, experiencing her delighted surprise by proxy.

"I don't even know what half of this is."

"Have you never used toys before?" Taylor asked without judgment.

"Max bought me a magic wand once," Raquel admitted with a chuckle. "That was pretty good."

"Oh, baby. There is a whole world out there waiting for you."

"Apparently," Raquel muttered before squinting her eyes. "What the hell is an air suction toy?"

"It's amazing is what it is."

After some scrolling and googling, Raquel navigated to the strap-on page.

"I already have a harness," Taylor explained before Raquel got overwhelmed with those options. "You just have to pick which dildo you like."

"Couldn't they have picked a better name for that? It sounds so clunky and un-sexy."

Taylor chuckled. "What do you want to call it?"

"I'll give it some thought," she said. "How are there over a hundred of them?"

"Spoiled for choice." She chuckled. "Do you want the texture to be realistic or smooth?"

"What do you want?"

"They each have some pros. I think smooth feels better, but if you want to role play a little... realistic could be fun."

Raquel's eyes ignited at the possibilities. "Both then."

"Am I creating a monster here?"

After selecting two silicone toys, a sleek, deep sea blue number and a modestly sized, but very realistic dildo that matched Taylor's tanned skin tone, they settled back into bed. She'd gotten Raquel the air suction vibrator as a surprise, intending to leave it behind when she left Vermont.

"Well, this is certainly not what I planned to do today," Taylor joked, still buzzing with the excitement of the package arriving in five business days.

Raquel's face was still dressed up in mischief. "What do you intend to do with your new friends?"

When Raquel's arm slid underneath her sheets, Taylor bit her bottom lip. "Well... we have to start by getting it a little wet, don't we? Maybe you can get on your knees and help me with that."

Raquel's eyes slid closed when she gasped. The sound traveled over Taylor and slid between her bare thighs before it curled into her.

"Keep talking," Raquel whispered.

Taylor eagerly obeyed.

CHAPTER 33

LOCKWOOD COLLEGE during the first week of the fall semester was not unlike a kicked over ant pile. Of the three thousand enrolled undergrads, only twenty percent of them were freshman, and yet they seemed to be everywhere; wide-eyed and learning their way through the rural campus with its old, far-flung buildings.

Considered one of the *baby ivies,* compared to its prestigious New England neighbors, the college established in 1801 was everything Raquel dreamed of when she imagined being a professor. Tucked between a pair of creeks, the sprawling campus with its rolling hills and strategically placed maple and birch trees was an absolute explosion of color in the spring and fall.

With the cool September morning breeze on her cheeks, Raquel strode from the small faculty parking lot to the building where her office was and where the upper-level history classes were taught.

L. J. C. Daniels Hall—a grand, white and gray stone structure as tough and venerable as the woman it was named after—was Raquel's absolute favorite building. Every year she told all her freshman classes about the suffragette who worked hard for all women to have the right to vote and was repeatedly jailed for her pursuits.

Raquel couldn't wait to show it all to Taylor. As she walked, she imagined pointing out every bit of history and then heading to her favorite place in town: a turn-of-the-century tea house restored to its original state in an old barn at the edge of Main Street. Owned by women and catering only to them, the tea house had been a hotbed for cultivating social change at a time where so much seemed impossible.

Two women, unmarried *best friends*, who had remained devoted to each other until their deaths, had started the tea house. She had no proof, of course, but Raquel imagined them as a romantic pair, finding a way to live together on their own terms. Imagined them decorating the barn with colonial furniture, colorful hand-hooked rugs, beautiful wooden furniture and pewter light fixtures. Taylor was going to love it, she was sure. Maybe she'd even have a guess which one of the original tea house proprietors was in charge of dispatching with the spiders.

She'd climbed two flights of stairs and was striding down the hallway toward her office when she bumped into one of her colleagues. A sweet man with an uncanny resemblance to Richard Dreyfuss who loved round glasses and sweater vests.

"Raquel, good to see you."

"Edward." She reached out and squeezed his hand warmly. "How was your summer research trip?"

He held his hand to his chest as if recalling a great love affair before recounting his deep dive into the Battle of Glorieta Pass during the American Civil War. "It's called the *Gettysburg of the West*, you know," he said with a blinding smile.

"Did Paul stay in New Mexico with you all summer?"

"Oh, yes. He was not nearly as riveted as me, but he had a good time exploring while I was buried in the annals of history. The quality of the preserved letters would absolutely amaze you. Some real gems."

His enthusiasm was contagious. As Raquel listened, she remembered the excitement of her own field trips. It had been a while since she'd been able to go on site anywhere. If so many research libraries didn't have electronic catalogs, she couldn't continue her work at all. She was grateful for that, but nothing beat the thrill of seeing things for herself; to walk in the steps of the people she studied. Even if the landscape changed, as it almost always had, there was something about occupying the space her subject once had. Of knowing that person had existed in that very spot, even if it was now a *Starbucks*.

When Raquel's phone buzzed in her hand, she put up a finger instead of stepping away. Edward was one of the few who knew her situation at home. "One sec. Don't go anywhere, Edward. I want to hear more about your trip. It's my father's aide."

She picked up the call.

"Nadia, what's up? Everything okay?"

"Ramon is okay," she replied immediately, probably to calm her, but her voice was so weak it shot Raquel's heart into her throat. "I was feeling a little funny this morning, but I thought it would pass. Now I think it might be a stomach virus or food poisoning." Her words echoed in the bathroom before she collected herself. "Raquel, I'm so sorry to call you like this. I know how busy you are, but I can't—"

"Please don't apologize." Raquel looked away from Edward and toward the carpeted floor. "You need to take care of yourself. Do you want me to come pick you up? Take you to the hospital?"

"No, no. My husband is coming with one of his apprentices to get me and take the car. I already called the agency, but a replacement is not immediately available. They're calling all the back-ups, though. I know it's not—"

"Don't worry, Nadia. I'll be right there," she promised before hanging up.

"What's wrong?" Edward's soft face was creased with worry, sending his snowy mustache into a frown.

"The aide is sick. I need to go home and stay with my dad until the agency can send someone else." Stress sharpened her consonants and sent a surge of blood pumping in her ears.

"What do you have today?" He clasped his hand over her shoulder.

"*Europe in the Twentieth Century* this morning and a seminar this afternoon," she explained, her mind going in a hundred directions.

"Send me your lecture notes." He patted her. "I can cover for you. Go home and take care of your dad."

"I can't ask—"

"Hey, you're not asking me, okay? I'm offering. You were an angel when Paul was sick. Let me help." He smiled. "What else are you teaching this semester?"

"The other two are online classes. I can handle those."

"Perfect then. Now go. Don't keep the aide waiting."

Pulling him into a hug, she breathed in his light cologne. "Thank you, Edward. You don't know how much this means to me."

He patted her back. "Oh, I absolutely do, and I'm more than happy to do it."

During her short drive home, Raquel spoke to the HHA staffing agency. Apart from the aide on maternity leave, they'd staffed the other Spanish-speaking alternate in a permanent position. They were reaching out to other agencies to find emergency coverage, but there was no chance someone would arrive before she had to teach her classes.

Thanking them for her efforts, Raquel gripped her steering wheel and prayed for a miracle. Maybe her dad would suddenly remember the English he'd forgotten after forty years of speaking it, then at least she could widen her pool of possibilities.

Pushing her panic aside, Raquel refused to be overwhelmed. One fire at a time. She couldn't think about this afternoon, or tomorrow, or next week. She still had to get through right now.

CHAPTER 34

THIRTY-FOUR HOURS without Nadia and they were falling apart. Raquel was on her hands and knees collecting pills and tablets scattered beneath the kitchen table; the vitamins and medications her father was supposed to take with dinner, but had hurled across the room instead.

Their second weekday together had started out like an ordinary day. They began with the same easy, familiar rhythm they had on the weekends.

It would have stayed that way if she hadn't gotten a call from Edward. If she hadn't stayed on the phone with him a minute too long. If she hadn't been a moment too slow behind her dad shuffling into the bathroom, she would have unfastened the belt he insisted on wearing before it was too late.

But she hadn't gotten his fly open, and he'd had an accident for the first time in a long time. Apart from drastic changes in routine, events that affected his dignity were always the most destabilizing.

There was no coming back from the small miscalculation. Her father, a man who'd never raised his voice at her in his life, who'd never uttered a bad word no matter how upset he was, snapped. He'd launched the most vicious and vile string of curses at her while threatening her that his wife would be home soon and she'd be sorry then.

She'd waited until he was sitting in his armchair by the front window to sob as quietly as possible into a towel she pulled out of the hall closet. He wouldn't understand why she was upset, and it would only scare and confuse him. Her father wasn't saying those things, it was the disease.

It took a long time to calm him, and even longer for Raquel to coax him into the shower. He'd seemed to settle after they took a walk along the creek behind the house and up to the pond where ducks were always hanging around. He'd even laughed and held her hand while they walked back, but the house seemed to remind him that something was wrong.

Combative and angry, he'd refused dinner, but agreed to drink a nutritional shake she used in emergencies. It would have been enough to give him his medications if he hadn't thrown them and accused her of poisoning him.

After a break, she'd returned to his room with his three crucial medications and deployed her nuclear option. She told him that his wife had called and asked that he take them. He'd been suspicious, but after some questions to make sure they were talking about the same woman, he agreed to take the pills. The vitamins and supplements would have to wait for a better day.

Deceiving her vulnerable father while invoking her dead mother's name had been the absolute last thing she could take. In her head, she knew it was necessary, but in her heart, she felt like a manipulative monster.

Tired and frayed, Raquel dragged herself upstairs and clicked on the monitor to hear her dad snoring and muttering in his sleep. He had to be depleted. On days like that, she wished she could take his place. Wished he didn't have to feel angry or disoriented or afraid.

With nothing but fumes left in her tank, she dragged herself into the shower and all but laid down on the tile floor. If she'd had the energy to wait, she would've filled the hammered copper clawfoot tub, her most prized possession, and sunk in it.

Needing something comforting, Raquel pulled on the neon orange shorts with *Endless Summer* emblazoned on the back. The same logos were running down the arms of the long-sleeved yellow-green shirt.

Dropping into bed, Raquel ran her palms over the material of the shirt. Like she was rubbing a magical lamp and hoping for someone to grant her a wish, she tried to take herself back there. Parasailing with Taylor, the unmatched feeling of flying so far above it all, what she wouldn't give for another afternoon like that. What she wouldn't give to feel a little less overwhelmed and alone.

After catching up on a shocking number of emails, she sent Nadia a message to see how she was feeling. When she didn't get a response, she wished she'd gotten her husband's number to make sure she was okay.

She opened her text chat with Taylor, who'd spent all day talking to herself.

Raquel: *I'm so sorry I've been MIA today. The first week of classes hasn't gone as expected.*

Taylor: *Oh no! What's wrong?*

Rolling onto her stomach, Raquel tucked a pillow under her chin to hold herself up. She debated telling Taylor what was going on, but she didn't know where to begin. What would she think of her if she knew days like this were possible? They weren't common, but they happened. Taylor wouldn't choose this. Who would? It was more than she could confront right then.

Raquel: *Just had a lot of stuff to juggle. How was your day? Did you make it to the book club?*

Taylor: *Yeah, it was cool. Except I didn't realize it was a reading and knitting book club, so a nice Cottagecore lesbian lent me some of her stuff and showed me how to make a slipknot and cast-on, so now I'm the proud owner of one very long piece of knotted up yarn.*

Raquel: *I don't even know where to start with my questions.*

Taylor: *I sent you a play-by-play...*

Raquel: *I'm so sorry, honey. It was a really wild day.*

Taylor: *I promise I'm not usually this person, but you went super quiet all day. And you've never done that. Did I do something? Are you mad at me?*

Guilt seized Raquel's chest and crushed her weary heart. She didn't want Taylor to feel ignored.

Raquel: *I can promise you're the absolute best part of my day. This semester just hasn't started off the way I planned. Things will be back to normal soon.*

Taylor: *Is there some way I can help? I'm pretty good at researching stuff. Can I help you organize? Take over any admin?*

A comforting warmth spread across her chest and eased the tingling behind her eyes. Taylor's kindness and generosity were probably Raquel's favorite things about her. She gave of herself so easily, so enthusiastically.

Raquel: *Just the fact that you're offering is more than enough. I think all I need right now is to get to bed. I'm wiped out.*

Taylor: *Then sleep it is. Sweet dreams, babe. I'll be thinking about you.*

A photo popped up after the text. Taylor was splayed out on her bed, her lips puckered up in a kiss. Next to her was the accurately described creation from her knitting book club.

The sight of her was a soothing balm. Raquel zoomed in on her face. On her frozen kiss. And wished more than anything that she could feel it.

After fluffing up her damp hair a little, Raquel sent her a similar image in return.

Taylor: *You're in the parasailing clothes!!*

Laughing, Raquel shot off the kind of response Taylor would normally give her.

Raquel: *DUH!! I miss you OKAY. I just want to feel close to you OKAY!?!*

Taylor: *You mock me, sir. ALSO, I do NOT use caps that often.*

Lifted more than she imagined possible, she allowed herself to experience bone-deep gratitude. She didn't know if she believed in fate anymore, but Taylor sure felt like she'd been put in her path when she needed her most. When she could fully appreciate her.

Taylor: *Goodnight. I hope you have incredibly restful sleep and have the best day tomorrow.*

Closing her eyes, Raquel let peace slip into her heart and relax her clenched muscles. Setting her intentions, she willed the next day to be better.

CHAPTER 35

MIRACLES FELT real at the start of Raquel's third Nadia-free day. The agency had sent a lovely woman that morning, and even though she didn't speak Spanish, her father not only understood her, but seemed to really like her.

By lunch, Raquel had started to hope that some of the English he'd spoken for forty years was coming back to him. Or at the very least, he'd been able to access enough of it. At midday, Raquel had taken a step back and let the aide take over serving his meal.

It had gone so well, Raquel had retreated to the living room to respond to emails. While he napped in his chair by the window, the aide had taken it upon herself to change his bedding. The day had been utterly peaceful.

She'd started to consider the possibility of getting back to campus the next day when Nadia finally returned her text.

Nadia: *Oh, Raquel. How is Ramon? Who is with him?*

Raquel: *He's fine! How are you feeling? Do you know what's wrong? I've been so worried about you.*

Nadia: *I'm fine. But I'm in the hospital.*

Raquel: *What? What's wrong?*

Nadia: *It wasn't food poisoning or a stomach flu. It was appendicitis, if you can believe it. They were able to remove it this morning before it burst.*

Raquel: *Oh my gosh! Nadia! I'm so sorry. Are you in a lot of pain?*

Nadia: *It's not so bad, but unfortunately it's going to be at least a week or so before they will clear me to go back to work, but that's the best-case scenario. I already called the agency. I convinced them to let me take a trainee with me when I go so I don't have to do any lifting or bending.*

Raquel: *Don't worry about us, Nadia. We're okay. You focus on getting better, okay? I'll check on you again tomorrow. Let people take care of you for a change.*

Nadia: *How much did my husband pay you to say that?*

Raquel: *It's time to take your own advice. Put the oxygen mask on yourself first.*

From the hallway, Raquel heard a sudden commotion. She whirled around on the couch to look at her dad, but he wasn't in the chair. Throwing her phone down, she leaped to her feet and raced across the living room and into the hall leading to her father's bedroom.

"*Papi!*"

"*Ladrona!*" he shouted, accusing the aide on the other side of his bed of being a thief.

"Sir! Calm down!" the aide shouted. "I don't understand what you're saying!"

Getting in between them, Raquel tried to deescalate by getting the aide to stop screaming first.

"He's confused. He thinks you're stealing—"

"I've never stolen anything in my life!"

"I'm not accusing you. I'm just saying he's confused—"

"*No me vas a robar!*"

"*Papi*, it's okay. She's not taking anything, okay? She's here to help. There's no reason to be upset," Raquel spoke as softly and slowly as she could.

As soon as Raquel took her father's hands in hers and got him to look into her eyes, he dropped his shoulders.

"You're okay, *Papi*. I'm here with you and everyone here only wants to take good care of you."

His wild eyes darted between her and the aide standing in the corner, a pillow in front of her as if needing to use it as a shield.

"Come on. Why don't we go see the ducks? That'll be nice, right?"

Three lifetimes later, he nodded. The sudden release of tension left her light-headed and queasy.

"Good. Okay, let's all go for a walk. It's a lovely afternoon, right? The sun is shining and everything is right in the world."

Looping her arm in her father's, she led him out of the room and hoped the aide would follow.

"Why don't you grab your jacket, *Papi*? There's a little chill in the air." She pointed to the lone brown jacket hanging on the coatrack by the door.

When he started for it, she turned to the aide behind her. "Listen, I'm really sorry about that. He never—"

"It's not my job to be accused of crimes."

"Of course not—"

"And when he says—"

"He doesn't understand the accusation he's making. Not exactly. It's hard for him to put together what he's seeing—"

"I could get fired for that, you know? Lose my job. Not to mention how shitty it feels to be screamed at like that."

Raquel took a step back, needing a moment to gather her scattered thoughts. "You know that he has dementia, right? I'm not going to report anything to the agency. I have no reason to believe you were doing anything other than changing the bedding."

She was a train barreling in one direction, regardless of what Raquel said. "I don't know why Nadia puts up with this. Managing this…" She pointed at him in a way that made Raquel want to slap her hand down, but she kept her hands still at her sides. "That's far outside our job description. We're only supposed to help with his hygiene, feed him, light housework. Not manage a combative, grown man."

Raquel forced herself to remain calm despite her racing heart and churning stomach. "Today was an anomaly. He's very sensitive to change, but as soon as he gets to know you—"

"They don't pay me enough for this. If Nadia wants to deal with this, that's fine. I'm not going to tell the agency about it. I'll just say it didn't work out—"

Anger was a thumping beat on her temple and dripping pain into her left eye. She couldn't keep her mouth shut for another second. "He's not a *this*. Not an *it*. He's a person. His name is Ramon, by the way. I'm not sure you've said his name once."

"I'm sorry, lady. Good luck," she said before pushing past her and disappearing out the front door.

Stunned, Raquel stood in the hallway, trying to process the suddenness of the shift in her day. The sight of her dad standing by his chair, holding his jacket, split her down the middle. He had no idea what was wrong, no idea why a woman stormed right by him and slammed the door.

"Let me just grab the food for the ducks, okay?"

She didn't make it two steps into the living room before her phone dinged; the sound of a voicemail. She played the message while she rushed to grab the tin of corn she kept in the kitchen.

The sound of her department chair's voice made her headache morph into a migraine.

Raquel, listen. I need you to call me back. I understand that you've arraigned for Edward to teach some of your classes. You know I don't mind looking the other way from time to time, but one of the deans has somehow found out. I'm going to need you to call me Raquel. If you can't resume teaching, we're going to have to discuss a formal leave of absence, but we need to talk, okay? Call me.

Numb except for the pain raging in her head, Raquel refused to give in to the overwhelming urge to cry.

"*Vamos, Papi.*" She tucked the tin under her arm. "*Los paticos* await."

He smiled and held out his arm for her to take.

CHAPTER 36

ANXIETY HAD CONGEALED at the top of Taylor's stomach. Its green, mucus-like fingers hooked into her chest formed an ever-present heaviness she couldn't shake. It had been nearly a week since Raquel said more than a few words to her and they hadn't video chatted once.

Without being able to see her, at least over video, she couldn't gage what was going on. But it left her with the unshakable conclusion that something was very wrong.

She told herself it couldn't be about her, and yet she was sure that Raquel was slipping away from her. The more space she tried to give her, the more she took. It was feeding the nauseating worry that a break-up was imminent.

Running through their conversations again and again in her mind, she tried to identify when things had changed. After the start of the semester, but that couldn't be it. Not entirely anyway.

Had she felt pressured about Taylor wanting to come visit? It was possible, even though Raquel had seemed excited about it. Was their age difference bothering her again? She hadn't commented on it in a while, but maybe something triggered her fears?

When Taylor was sure that she'd pushed too far too fast, she recalled Raquel had been the one to define their relationship. If

Raquel wasn't ready for the *girlfriend* label, she could have let the subject go untouched.

Deciding she needed to know, Taylor texted Raquel and asked for an after-dinner video call. To her surprise, Raquel told her she could talk at lunch.

Needing to work the excess energy out of her body, she clocked out of work early and went on a run. The mid-morning day was hazy and ominous, like a storm was brewing somewhere and might engulf the sky at any moment. It felt less like the arrival of autumn and more like the death of summer.

After her shower, she threw on a sweatshirt and leggings and prepared herself for the worst. Maybe Raquel wanted to get dumping her over with instead of dragging it out until after dinner.

Sitting at the edge of her bed when Raquel called, Taylor couldn't help smiling when she appeared on her phone screen. It was a physiological response to seeing her face, as automatic as breathing.

"Hi."

Raquel, dressed in a cable sweater and sitting in her living room instead of her office, looked like she hadn't slept in a week. "Hi." She smiled back, but it didn't reach her unusually puffy eyes.

Taylor's entire body clenched. "What the heck is going on?"

Raquel started to say *nothing*, but Taylor rejected it immediately.

"Raquel," Taylor snapped. "Don't say *nothing* when it's very clearly something." Worry coated her words and made them sharp and hostile. "Tell me what's happening." She gulped for air. "Please."

With her eyes closed, Raquel pulled off her glasses. She pinched the bridge of her nose and remained motionless for so long, Taylor started to wonder if the call had frozen. Desperate to push, Taylor chewed the inside of her cheek and waited for Raquel to be ready to speak.

"It's my dad." When she opened her eyes, they were glistening with unshed tears. Without the glasses, Taylor could see how irritated her eyes were, how swollen. "I mean, it's not *him*. He's fine. We actually had a pretty good day today, but um, the agency hasn't been able to send any more replacements."

"Replacements?" Taylor shook her head, unable to follow Raquel's words. It was like she'd tuned in halfway through the movie. "I don't understand. Where's Nadia?"

After a deep breath, Raquel explained. She told her about Nadia's appendicitis and her surgery and the home health aides that had not worked out. She told her about the call from her boss and the very clear directive that she had to return tomorrow or be forced to take a formal, and unpaid, leave of absence, which she couldn't really afford to do. But she couldn't leave her father alone either, so she was trapped in an impossible position. A shit rock and a turd hard-place.

"Why didn't you tell me this was happening?" Taylor yearned to reach into the phone and hold her. "I'm so sorry you've been dealing with this all by yourself."

Holding her head in her hands, Raquel shrugged. "I don't know." The words were nearly nonexistent wisps that didn't sound like they were in response to Taylor's question.

"Well, I'm glad you did, because I'm coming."

Raquel's head sprang up. "What? No, Taylor. You can't do that."

"Of course I can." She furrowed her brow. "There's gotta be a train leaving today."

"Honey, thank you so much, but—"

Taylor was already on her feet and pulling her duffle bag out from under her bed. "You're drowning, Raquel. I'm not being sweet or whatever. I'm being a normal person throwing you a life vest. You can go back to work tomorrow if I stay with your dad."

"Taylor, I don't think you understand—"

"You just told me. You can't not get a paycheck, and there's nothing I can do about that, but I can do something about hanging out with your father." She set her phone on the desk, opened her underwear drawer and blindly tossed in two handfuls. "Maybe I should bring the suitcase too," she muttered to herself before going into Robbie's room and borrowing her huge check-in sized rolling bag.

When she returned, Raquel was still trying to talk her out of what she'd already gouged in stone. "Taking care of my dad isn't just like hanging out with him. He doesn't need help with everything, but he needs help with certain things." Raquel looked away and then back at Taylor. "He needs help in the bathroom," she whispered.

Keeping her voice low too, in case he was listening, Taylor picked up the phone and held it close to her face. "I've seen a penis before, Raquel. I have no problem helping him with whatever he needs."

"He might vehemently resist your attempts. He might get mad or cranky or confused."

"So I'll try different approaches until he doesn't resist me." Taylor smiled softly. "Listen, parents literally love me. I speak Spanish. I practically never lose my temper or patience." She flexed her meager, but not nonexistent, biceps. "I'm strong. My back and knees are good." She winked. "As I'm sure you recall."

A microscopic smile pulled at Raquel's lips. "This is serious."

"I know." She dropped into her office chair. "I know it is, and I'm only joking to put you at ease because you're absolutely breaking my heart right now. Please let me help."

"This isn't what you signed up for."

Taylor tilted her head as if it would change the picture. "*Mrs. Alonso* may have been a crush or a fantasy, but you're not. Raquel, I don't want to just be your girlfriend for the fun parts. That's not real life. I want to be there for you. Please. Let me."

Raquel closed her eyes for a long time again, as if she was wrestling some great inner demons. "What about your job?"

Smiling, Taylor shot up and started packing again, her phone resting against her desk lamp so she could continue talking to Raquel while she shoved almost everything she owned in the duffle and then started filling up the suitcase.

"You mean the job I can do remotely from literally anywhere as long as I have internet?"

Raquel replied with a playful eye roll.

"I have some leave saved up so I can use that today and tomorrow. Then, if Nadia isn't back next week, which doesn't sound like she will be, I can work from your place. It's not like I have a lot going on here, Raq. Not even Phillip needs me, and I'm trash at knitting."

"It's not that I don't want to accept, Taylor." Raquel sighed. "But caring for my dad can be hard, and I don't think you realize—"

"That might be true. And maybe we realize I can't do it. I'm not going to let your dad have incompetent care. I'll be the first to say if I can't give him what he needs or if I'm upsetting him. And I'm sure you'll be watching on the cameras, but please just let me try. What do you have to lose?"

"I could lose you," she replied softly.

Taylor gave her a wide smile and flashed both dimples. "Not a chance." She waited for Raquel to return the gesture. When she did, she jumped on her computer to send an email to her boss. "Can you start looking at the trains? Is there something leaving tonight?"

"Not until tomorrow at midday," Raquel said after a beat. "Not even to Burlington."

Taylor started packing her laptop into her backpack. "How about Greyhound?"

"A bus?" Raquel's tone was far too shocked and horrified.

Taylor rolled her eyes. "Yes, *a bus*. I rather not pay an arm and a leg to rent a car, but I will if I have no other choice."

"Either way there's no way I'm letting you pay for this, but maybe renting a car would be safer."

Taylor chuckled. "Babe, your snob is showing. I've taken significantly sketchier modes of transportation. Is there a bus or not?"

A minute later, Raquel begrudgingly reported her findings. "There's one leaving from the New York Port Authority at four this afternoon, but you would have to transfer in Albany, and there are all these stops. You wouldn't get here until after midnight."

Taylor tossed in the packages that had just arrived in the mail and zipped up the suitcase. "Perfect. Then I'll be there in the morning when you have to go to work. Is the bus station in Lockwood? I can take an Uber—"

"The stop is near the college, but don't be ridiculous. If you insist on taking a bus, I'm picking you up."

Taylor smiled. "Then I'll see you soon."

CHAPTER 37

SHAKING HER LEG, Taylor was perched on the edge of her seat, ready to sprint off the bus when it arrived in Lockwood. A light drizzle had started as soon as they entered Vermont. Every time the bus doors opened at its annoyingly regular stops, a blast of cold, wet air slapped Taylor in the face. A small price to pay to sit close to the front and far from the bathroom.

Dressed in a hoodie and joggers, she regretted not having worn something warmer. At one in the morning, the temperature outside had dropped into the forties and Taylor could only get the chill out of her hands by sitting on them. As soon as she'd finished ordering a bunch of things for next-day delivery to Raquel's house, she'd gone back to warming her hands.

Staring out the front of the bus, her heart lifted when she saw the green road sign. *Lockwood Town Line.*

Taylor pulled her phone out of her hoodie's front pocket and texted Raquel like she'd asked her to when she saw the marker. Despite Taylor's insistence that she could reserve a ride-share to be sure she'd be picked up and dropped off at her house, Raquel had enlisted her neighbor, a retired school principal, to sit in her living room while she was gone.

What little Taylor could see of Lockwood in the dark was perfectly picturesque. Rolling hills and leaves changing on trees and a college campus that looked like it was right out of some cozy, watercolor dream. It was easy to see what had drawn Raquel to the quintessential New England town. It had a built-in romance and nostalgia, even for Taylor.

"This is you," the bus driver said when they pulled up along a brick church with a real-life white steeple.

Pulling on the backpack and duffle she'd stored in the overhead compartment, Taylor gave the half-empty bus a last look before following the driver outside.

Rain fell like tiny, frozen needle pricks on them while the driver opened the compartment under the bus where her suitcase was stored. Taylor rubbed her hands together and blew on them to warm them up while she waited.

"You sure you got someone picking you up?" The driver slung her bag onto the sidewalk, her breath visible in the cold air.

Taylor scanned the shockingly quiet Main Street. Unlike the city, there wasn't a single car or person walking around the center of town.

While Taylor was pulling out the cash she'd gotten at a truck stop ATM, a pair of headlights turned a corner and shone on them. She rolled up the cash and offered it to the driver with her thanks for the bag. "Yup," she said with full confidence, despite only being able to see the lights and windshield wipers. "I'm good."

With her hood up over her head, Taylor rolled her bag and jogged toward the sedan pulling up behind the bus. When the driver's door opened and illuminated the cabin, it sent a rush of excitement coursing through Taylor's body.

Raquel, wearing a buttoned-up navy peacoat and leather gloves, was jumping out of the car and jogging toward her, her breath plumes of white smoke as she hurried.

As soon as they saw each other, Raquel smiled a broad, conquering smile. She smiled with her eyes, with her teeth, with her lips. She was light and warmth. She was a long, deep, lung-burning breath after seven weeks of shallow pants. She was a song and art and laughter and Taylor felt her in every single nerve ending, every fiber, every cell of her body.

"Hi," Raquel managed just before Taylor threw her arms around her neck and inhaled her.

"Hi," Taylor sighed more than she said.

She'd expected to feel so many things when she saw Raquel again. She'd expected joy, excitement, lust. She hadn't expected muscle-melting relief.

Raquel's embrace was tight and sure as she hugged her hard. In that moment, Taylor realized they were clinging to each other more than they were greeting. Two desperate souls finding each other in the freezing rain with the fumes of a bus exhaust swirling around them. The picture of love, even if they hadn't spoken it aloud yet. In your face, Jane Austen.

"Come on, let's get you warmed up," Raquel said before taking her suitcase and rolling it toward her car.

Inside the toasty sedan, Taylor slid into the heated seat, warming her behind.

"Oh, this is nice." She laughed loudly and nervously as she balled up her cold hands.

Before Raquel started driving, she pulled off her gloves. "Here. Your hands look like they're freezing.

Taylor had considered declining, but her knuckles were starting to hurt. "Thanks," she said and pulled them on. Looking down at her hands in the leather gloves, she flexed her fingers. "Fancy."

With a grin still painted on her face, Raquel pulled onto the empty street.

Raquel drove through the town center in under two minutes and started down a country road so dark it was like they'd been dropped in the middle of nowhere.

"I can't believe you're here," Raquel said, slipping her warm hand into Taylor's lap.

"Me neither," she admitted, intertwining their fingers. "But I'm really glad I am. Thank you for letting me come."

Raquel shot her a glance. Her eyes were still glistening, but her vibe was significantly less distraught than it had been that afternoon.

"I can't imagine being this far from my neighbors." Taylor peered out the windshield, catching the houses illuminated by the headlights or the ones with their porch lights still on. "It's like a mile from one to the next."

"There are quite a few acres between us," she agreed, running her thumb slowly and rhythmically over Taylor's gloved hand.

A few minutes later, they were going up a winding road and pulling into Raquel's driveway, where a four-wheeler ATV was parked in front of a closed garage door.

"Your elderly neighbor drives that?"

Raquel chuckled. "She's rather spry for eighty."

"At least it stopped raining, but it's so cold."

"She's originally from Alaska. She's unfazed until we drop into single digits."

After getting her stuff in the gloriously warm house and thanking the woman who took off through the grass and downhill instead of driving on the road, Raquel checked in on her still sleeping father.

When she came back, she offered Taylor a tour.

Hardwood floors and a super clean farmhouse design touched every single inch of Raquel's impeccably neat house. Taylor could only imagine what a place that size, and with that much land, would cost in Miami.

Raquel took her backpack and duffle while Taylor heaved her suitcase and carried it as quietly as she could upstairs. After leaving her stuff at the top of the steps, Raquel showed her a bathroom and a room with a treadmill and stationary bike.

"I have a spare bedroom." Raquel opened the door to a nicely decorated room. "The sheets are fresh and you would have exclusive use of the hall bathroom."

Taylor didn't have time to hide her disappointment. "Oh, um. Okay."

Raquel searched her face as if trying to figure out what went wrong. "I didn't want to presume... I want you to feel comfortable."

Hooking her finger into the empty loop of Raquel's jeans, Taylor tugged her close. "If you're comfortable with it, I'd much prefer to stay with you."

"I suppose that can be arranged," she replied, obviously trying and failing not to grin.

Before they turned back down the hall, Taylor pointed to the only door Raquel hadn't opened. "What's in there?"

"Nothing. Just an attic." Raquel turned the glass knob and opened the door.

"Is it spooky?" Taylor asked with a wiggle in her brow.

"Aren't all attics?"

"I guess I'm about to find out."

Taylor flipped on the light by the door, revealing a spiral staircase. At the top of the landing was a space nearly as big as the entire second floor. Apart from some boxes stacked in the corner, there was nothing but hardwood floors, a huge window overlooking what Taylor guessed was the backyard and shiplap over the walls and pitched ceiling.

"This is like a-whole-nother house up here." Taylor walked down the center of the room where the pitch in the roof was at its highest point. If she moved off to the sides, she'd have to bow her head or risk smacking it on the beams.

"Yeah, if you don't mind crouching," Raquel joked from where she stood on the top step.

"Seriously, Raq. This is three times the size of my whole apartment. You should convert it into a bedroom or an office or something. It's so much wasted space."

"I've never used a home office," she replied with a shrug. "They end up just being a waste of furniture because I sit at the kitchen table or on the couch."

Taylor imagined the view during the day. She knew there was a creek behind the house. What kind of Norman Rockwell landscape would be out there? Scattered pines and gently sloping knolls covered in snow during the winter. The babbling, rocky stream cutting through the lush greenery in summer. She would happily spend eight hours a day transcribing up here.

"I have an air mattress somewhere, if you want to sleep here."

"Very funny."

Raquel smirked and disappeared down the staircase like a gopher dipping back into her hidey-hole. With a grin, Taylor followed.

"Last but not least." Raquel pointed toward the open door.

"It looks a lot bigger in person," Taylor said when she stepped into the room she'd seen on so many of their video chats. "Do you mind if I take a super quick shower? I know it's late—"

"This is your house." Raquel cupped her cheek, her touch rippling over her skin and sinking into her bones. "Do whatever you like."

Taylor covered her hand with hers, a sudden and keen desperation to brush her teeth rolling through her. "Thanks."

"Can I put your things away while you're in there?" Raquel gestured toward the bags piled in an ugly heap by the door. The mismatched colors looked obscene in the soothing, gray and white room.

"You don't have to worry about that. I can do it when I get out."

"I don't mind. You've already had such a long night. I want you to be comfortable," she repeated.

"Okay, then. I'll be right out." She rushed into the spa-like bathroom, complete with a real-life copper clawfoot tub and glass encased shower, and ripped off her clothes like they were burning her skin.

CHAPTER 38

AFTER BRINGING Taylor a fresh towel and leaving it folded on the usually unused side of the double sinks in the bathroom, Raquel found Taylor's toiletry bag and left it on the vanity.

She'd resisted the urge to look at her while she was in the shower. The steam covered most of the glass, but she could've seen her outline if she tried. She didn't, despite Taylor's invitation to join her.

Instead, she rolled Taylor's suitcase to the mostly empty dresser facing the bed and unzipped it. As much as she wanted to touch Taylor, to kiss her, to drown in her, she wanted her to feel at home; wanted her to find her things without scavenging for them in a bag.

As soon as she opened the suitcase, Raquel laughed. She should've known what to expect. She'd watched Taylor throwing clothes in it like a deranged otter collecting all her sea urchins. And yet, that her clothes looked like something exploded was still a surprise.

While she worked, folding some things and putting them in the drawer, and separating others to hang in the walk-in closet, Raquel was overwhelmed by the shockingly pleasant ache in her chest. She liked the feeling of putting Taylor's things away; of making space for her.

She was nearly finished when she picked up the brown box and mailing bag that had been stuffed into the suitcase. She didn't mean to snoop when she put them back in the suitcase along with Taylor's now empty backpack and duffle. Her plan had been to deposit them in the bag and roll it all into the closet to get it out of the way.

Noticing the return addresses on the unopened packages had been an accident, but one Raquel hadn't minded making. With all the chaos of the last week, she'd forgotten about Taylor's purchases. Forgotten how eager Taylor had been to find Raquel's fantasies and fill them.

Her attention flickered to the gray sweatpants she'd folded neatly in her antique chest of drawers. With a smirk, she imagined the *gal pals* in the tea house and wondered what they'd think of their future sisters in arms. Did they have sexy outfits they wore for each other?

The sound of the shower turning off prompted Raquel to change into her nightgown. She hadn't wanted to overdo it, though she had a revealing and silky slip she was very sure Taylor would like. She pulled on a soft shirt that looked like an oversized men's dress shirt and went to brush her teeth in the guest bathroom.

When she returned to the room, Taylor was coming out of the bathroom in tiny shorts and a loose T-shirt, her long, brown hair thrown into a messy bun on top of her head. Taylor strode toward her like they did this every day, like she fit there so perfectly. It made little sense that she hadn't always been there.

"Hi." Taylor wrapped her arms around Raquel's neck, her skin still hot from the shower eased over hers like it meant to melt her. "Now I can greet you like I wanted to."

Her lips, soft and minty and desperately missed, pressed against Raquel's starved mouth.

Gripping Taylor's waist, Raquel pulled her in close, but even being flush against her wasn't close enough.

"God, I missed you." Taylor sighed against her lips before kissing her again. Harder this time, like she couldn't get close enough either.

Raquel turned off the lights before walking backward toward the bed. She moved without breaking their kiss. She needed to show Taylor how much she'd missed her too.

Raquel spun her around to ease her onto the bed before straddling Taylor's hips as she climbed on top of her.

Immediately, Taylor's warm palms were gliding up Raquel's smooth thighs. Gripping her hard while she moaned into their kiss. She loved how much Raquel loved her body. How she touched her like she needed her.

Taylor's hands up her back sent a charge roaring down her spine and pulsing between her thighs. Grinding against her, Raquel lost control. She slid her mouth down her neck, unsure of whether she was biting or kissing.

The more Taylor moaned and rocked her hips against her, the more Raquel needed. She pushed up her shirt, yearning to feel her skin.

Cursing, Taylor's back arched off the bed when Raquel ran the tip of her tongue over her hard nipple before taking it into her mouth. The sounds she'd been hearing on the phone were a thousand times better in person; sounded better when she was the one causing them.

Using her knee, Raquel parted Taylor's legs and slipped between them. She was halfway down Taylor's torso when she felt the hand on her shoulder.

"If we start, I'm afraid we're not going to stop," Taylor said breathlessly and with a little groan, as if the angel on her shoulder had just won a high stakes game of rock-paper-scissor over a now sobbing Devil.

Raquel dropped her head, resting her forehead on Taylor's pelvis. She didn't want to admit that Taylor was right; didn't want to think about tomorrow or work or anything other than existing in that moment.

With a whine unbecoming a grown woman, Raquel tore herself away and climbed up the bed to lie at Taylor's side.

"Trust me." Taylor shifted her shorts before reaching for the duvet to cover them both. "This hurts me a lot more than it hurts you."

Despite the desire pounding hard in her body, Raquel snuggled into Taylor's side, her head on her shoulder and her hand resting on her flat belly. "Don't be so sure."

"Oh, I'm sure."

In a quick and unexpected move, Taylor took hold of Raquel's hand. With her fingers pressed over the top of Raquel's, she slid into her underwear and pressed the tip of Raquel's middle finger inside herself.

Raquel closed her eyes to keep from crying at the sound of Taylor's tiny gasp, at the discovery of how wet she'd made her, of the sensation of her tightening around her.

Taylor moaned before abruptly snatching Raquel's hand away and slipping it back under her shirt and onto her chest. Raquel imagined the trail she'd left along her belly and how much she'd like to run her tongue along it.

"Well, that's going to make sleeping tonight *much* easier. Thank you, Taylor." She didn't care that her sarcasm made her sound petulant.

Taylor chuckled. "Why should I suffer alone?"

Ignoring the arousal coating the tips of her fingers tested every ounce of Raquel's determination and self-control. It was hard to care about responsibilities when confronted with such alluring temptation.

As the thumping fog of lust faded, Raquel relaxed into Taylor's tight embrace. She couldn't have imagined how full Taylor being in her bed would make her feel; how annoyingly complete.

"I can't believe you're here," Raquel confessed into the dark room.

"I think you said that already," Taylor replied in the faraway, soft tone she usually had just before she drifted off to sleep.

"It bears repeating."

Without loosening her grip around her, Taylor's breaths came more slowly and deeply. Raquel listened to the gentle rhythm like it was a soothing ocean tide until sleep crept up on her too.

CHAPTER 39

SOMEWHERE BEHIND TAYLOR'S slumbering body, a monitor crackled to life. The foreign sound woke Taylor out of a sleep so deep she was disoriented when she blinked awake.

Raquel's bed. Raquel's room. Raquel's arms slung around her waist. The comfort of being the little spoon was a lullaby, coaxing Taylor back to a dream. When the sound came again, it was a high-pitched beeping.

"Sorry." Raquel kissed the back of her ear before rolling abruptly out of bed. "He's up early. I have to beat him to the bathroom."

Before Taylor's eyes and brain could work together to process her surroundings, Raquel was out the door. A second later, she heard her voice over the monitor.

Taylor rolled onto Raquel's side of the bed to pick up the monitor. The sound was so low, Taylor had barely noticed it before.

Holding the device to her ear, she heard Raquel speaking sweetly to her father in Spanish. She closed her eyes and tried really hard to keep her head and her heels in the right location.

After brushing her teeth and throwing on a pair of jeans and a sweater, Taylor debated whether she should wear shoes in Raquel's house. She decided *yes* and slipped into a pair of canvas sneakers.

While she trotted down the stairs, she pulled her hair into a pony-tail. In the early morning light, Raquel's house looked even nicer than it had the night before. There was such a well-ordered coziness; a feeling of home.

From the stairs, she crossed into a large, formal living room. It was the heart of the house, connecting to the hall to Raquel's father's room, the garage door, the stairs, the foyer, the kitchen, and the dining room too pretty to use.

Taylor imagined sitting in front of the fireplace on cold nights, plucking something from the floor-to-ceiling bookshelves on either side of the fire, and snuggling under a blanket together. The pinnacle of sapphic domesticity.

Unsure of what to do with herself, Taylor sat on the couch and waited for Raquel to come out of her father's room. She tried not to feel nervous about meeting Raquel's dad, but she wanted very much for him to like her; wanted this to go well.

While she waited, Taylor considered ways she might make herself useful. Coffee? Plant watering? Gutter clearing?

Would Raquel think that was thoughtful? Or would she think it was weird she was traipsing around her house?

"*Papi*, I have someone I want you to meet," Raquel said in Spanish from the hallway.

Taylor stood and clasped her hands together before putting them in her pockets. Then she shook them out and held them down at her sides. Were hands always so weird and in the way?

Wearing a short robe, Raquel emerged from the hall with a tall, handsome, well-dressed and well-cologned man on her arm. As soon as he made eye contact with Taylor, he smiled.

"*Papi*." She gestured toward Taylor. "This is Taylor—"

"*Como*? Tay?" He struggled to pronounce her name as he shuffled closer.

"You can call me Paloma. It's my middle name," she explained in Spanish as she extended a hand toward the man.

"Paloma, *que linda*." He reached out to give her a hug.

"Dove," Raquel translated her middle name with noticeable amusement, "this is my father, Ramon."

He embraced her like he'd known Taylor her entire life. Taylor closed her eyes and accepted the warm gesture. When she stepped back, Raquel looked like she'd been holding her breath.

"How about some breakfast?" Raquel smoothed her robe unnecessarily. She was nervous too.

"My Luz is a wonderful cook." He looked at Taylor with open adoration.

Confused, Taylor's attention darted to Raquel.

"Luz is his sister," Raquel mouthed silently when they started for the kitchen.

She nodded. If it made Ramon happy to think Taylor was his sister, she wasn't going to lie, but she wasn't going to correct him, either. Assuming another identity was a small price to pay if it made him feel safer around her.

"What's for breakfast?" Taylor asked after Ramon took a seat at the table with the L-shaped banquette built into the window overlooking the enormous backyard. The kind that was apparently too big to fence in.

"We usually start with *un cafecito*." She pulled out an old-school percolator. "And today, what do we think? A little oatmeal and fruit?"

Ramon shook his head and asked for an omelet.

"An omelet?" Taylor smiled. "A high maintenance man."

"What do you want in it, *Papi*? Ham and cheese?"

He nodded.

Taylor put her hand over Raquel's before she twisted the percolator open to fill the base with water. "Why don't you go upstairs and get ready? See how we get on here?"

Raquel furrowed her brow.

"What's better than trial by fire? I'm amazing under pressure." Taylor tried to sound encouraging. "You'll still be here if I need you, and we might as well know now whether this is going to work out or not."

"Do you even know how to use a *cafetera*?"

Taylor smirked before snatching the metal thing out of Raquel's hands. "Duh. What kind of self-respecting Cuban doesn't? My grandma made me learn. You know, because as a *señorita*, I had to be ready to provide my husband with coffee every morning, and when company dropped by, of course," she added with a laugh. "I'm sure it's like riding a bike."

She chuckled. "My aunt taught me for very similar reasons."

"Luz?" Taylor opened the espresso canister.

Raquel shook her head. "My mother's sister. Amelia."

"Where is she now?" Taylor's amusement dimmed. "Do your aunts ever visit?"

Raquel's response was something of a quick wince.

Taylor wondered how many people drifted away after her mother died. After her father started to need help. She moved off the topic. "Alright. I have stuff to do and you're in my way," she joked to ease them out of the tension.

Raquel tipped her head to the side in surrender. "Okay." She cupped Taylor's cheek before turning away from her. Kissing her father on the top of his head, Raquel squeezed his shoulder. "I'll be right upstairs, okay?"

"Luz, don't make her an omelet. You know my ballerina is always on a diet. I tell her all the time she is perfect the way she is, but she doesn't listen to me. Maybe you should tell her."

"Oh, I agree, Ramon. She's absolutely perfect the way she is. She couldn't be more beautiful." Taylor dropped her gaze over the reckless curves hiding under Raquel's robe before giving her a wink.

Raquel chuckled. "And apparently I'm my mother this morning. It might just be a good day." She flashed Taylor a broad smile. "Call me if you need me, my darling sister-in-law."

As soon as Raquel was gone, Taylor forced herself to shake off her anxiety. Ramon was just a person. Nothing to be nervous about.

Taylor scooped espresso grounds into the little cup she dropped into the base. "Do you like music?"

"Oh, yes."

She smiled and put the percolator on the edge of a front burner on the gas stove. On her phone, she pulled up a *Cuban Classics* playlist.

A high energy salsa song by the Afro-Cuban queen of salsa, Celia Cruz, painted the white room with trumpets and conga drums.

"Eh! *Azucar!*" Ramon clapped and mimed dancing with a partner from his seat.

Taylor swung her hips around the kitchen as she cracked eggs into a bowl and started on three omelets.

By the time Raquel returned dressed in a very serious charcoal pantsuit, her dark bob straight and sleek, Taylor and Ramon were singing *Guantanamera* at full volume.

"Well, this is either going well or I'm going to need someone to supervise the both of you."

Taylor laughed before pouring her a shot of espresso. She read the relief in her eyes and wasn't buying her Raquel-tone for a moment.

"Sit, sit." Ramon gestured to the food Taylor had just served. "It's going to get cold."

Raquel couldn't stop the smile tugging at her lips as she held Taylor in her gaze while accepting the small ceramic cup.

High on the indescribable feeling vibrating in her chest, Taylor grinned. "I told you." She sighed as if it were a burden. "Parents love me."

Raquel's gaze lingered on hers, and her lips parted like she wanted to say something; confess something.

Taylor's heart parkoured up her sternum and into her throat. She stepped closer, breathing in Raquel's perfume as she waited for her to say what her eyes were already telegraphing; what Taylor was thinking too.

"You weren't lying," Raquel said after a long beat, but Taylor doubted she'd been thinking about her effect on parents.

After breakfast, Raquel ran Taylor through her father's routine and mealtimes and medications. There really wasn't very much to it.

They were sitting at the kitchen table and Ramon was looking out the front window, but Raquel still leaned in close to speak. "I already gave him his bath this morning," she whispered before shooting a

220 | DESTINATION YOU

glance over at her father to make sure her dad wasn't looking their way. "And if you need—"

"Babe." Taylor put her hand over Raquel's. "You've gone over this stuff like ten times. I promise I understand what I'm supposed to do. I can't imagine how scary this is for you, but I honestly think we're going to be fine, and if we're not, then I'll call you. I promise."

Raquel looked like she wanted to relax, but was physically incapable. "Until he gets in a groove again, I'm worried the smallest thing will set him off. Everything is all well and good until it's not, you know?"

Taylor rubbed Raquel's hand. "I know, and I know you're worried about the worst-case scenario, especially after the week you've both had. I'm not going to let anything happen to him." She smiled. "And come on, no one can get mad at the dimps." She pointed to her dimples. "Can you yell at these?"

With a sigh, Raquel shook her head, but she smiled too. "If you're really sure." The worry was painted on her face, along with her mascara. "I don't teach until eleven, but—"

"I'm sure you have stuff to sort out after being out all week. Go." She squeezed her hand. "We'll be fine."

"My last class ends at four. I'll be home immediately after, okay? I negotiated to do my office hours virtually until Nadia is back, and I have a three-hour gap between classes today, so if you need me, I can come pop back over."

Taylor shook her head. She'd never seen Raquel nervous before. "You need to focus on your job. Let's leave you running back and forth as a last resort, okay?"

"You promise you'll tell me if you're feeling overwhelmed or freaked out or in over your head or anything?"

Taylor cupped Raquel's cheek and looked at her unblinkingly. "I swear."

Raquel took a long, deep breath. "Okay."

CHAPTER 40

THE FIRST THING Raquel did when she arrived on campus was find Edward and thank him for being a hero. He'd apologized unnecessarily for not being able to cover for her longer. After much persuading, and a little begging, he agreed to let her take him and Paul to their favorite steakhouse an hour away as a token of her appreciation.

"I'm so glad the agency finally sent someone who worked out," he said from his place behind his huge wooden desk.

Raquel shifted in her chair across from him. "Not from the agency."

"Oh?" He quirked a white brow.

"It's..." She shifted in her seat. "A friend. From New York. Well, not *from* New York—" Raquel abruptly snapped her jaw shut to stop rambling.

The damage was done. Edward turned his head to the side like a dog listening to a wonderfully new melody.

"A friend. From New York. But not from New York," he repeated slowly, exaggerating his confusion. "What kind of friend? The handsome kind?"

"Oh, don't play dumb, Edward. It doesn't suit you." She chuckled before gesturing toward the many degrees mounted in heavy, ornate frames.

Edward's cheeks brightened. "Tell me about him."

"She is lovely," Raquel replied, unsure of how much to divulge. She didn't want to be embarrassed by their age difference; didn't want to feel so self-conscious about their previous teacher-student relationship.

"She?" He uncrossed his legs and leaned forward. "I didn't know you were interested in the fairer sex." He wasn't scandalized as much as he was openly delighted.

Raquel gave him a wry smile. She found no reason to mention her pansexuality, and she didn't talk about her dating life unless it was serious.

"Tell me about her."

She hesitated.

"What is it?"

"I'm afraid you'll judge me."

"Judge you?" Edward chuckled. "Good heavens, why?"

Raquel forced herself to come out with it. To get a preview of the commentary, the judgement, the scandal, she'd have to deal with.

"She is my former student." When Edward didn't react, she added, "From when I taught at a Catholic high school in Miami."

His fluffy white eyebrows sprang up his forehead like sheep bouncing into the sky. "That was quite some time ago, wasn't it?"

Raquel nodded.

"And were you involved when she was your student?"

"Absolutely not, Edward. How could you—"

"Then Raquel, my dear." He smiled. "Who the hell cares?"

"She's much younger than I am," she pointed out, as if he'd missed that part.

He waved that away. "Does she make you happy?"

"Yes," she replied without hesitation.

He smiled.

"But happiness isn't everything," she felt compelled to point out. "I'm nearly twenty years older than she is." She made herself a little queasy with the fact. "Can you imagine the looks we'll get? The things people will say?"

"Oh, let them talk. What a tiny life we'd live if we fashioned ourselves to the comforts of others. Life is so exceedingly short, Raquel. We're here one moment and gone the next." He snapped his fingers. "And in this briefest of histories, what is the point of anything if we aren't living?"

"She makes me more than happy," Raquel confessed, stopping short of the complete truth. "You should see her with my father. I mean, just the fact that she insisted on coming here to help. Of putting her life on hold to show up for me…"

Edward's expression bloomed. "It sounds like you have something very special. Guard it fiercely."

Raquel's chest tingled. This wasn't the reaction she was expecting.

"We'll talk more when I get everything under control." She smiled. "I promise."

"I'll hold you to it."

Fifteen minutes with Edward had been the longest Raquel had gone without checking the cameras in her house. While she walked to the larger building housing the auditorium-sized lecture halls where she taught freshman classes, she flipped the collar of her coat over her neck and gave in to the urge to peek in on Taylor and her dad.

"What the heck is that?" Raquel zoomed in on the doorbell camera.

On her front step, there was a tower of packages. At least three.

Taylor, having deposited her father in his chair, took a few steps to the front door and retrieved the boxes. Unable to resist, Raquel opened the microphone to listen in.

"Alright, Ramon. I've got some options," Taylor said in Spanish as she tore open packages. "Dominos?" She pulled out an aluminum box that rattled when she put it on the floor next to her. "I got a puzzle, and I've got some art stuff." She pulled out a stack of coloring books and colored pencils.

Raquel held her breath while her father evaluated his options. Despite zooming in all the way, she couldn't make out his expression.

If he felt like Taylor was treating him like a child, he might react badly.

Taylor's pep was not hampered. "Oh, and I got something else." She opened the largest box. "*Pastelitos* from Pastry King. All I have to do is pop them in the oven. What are you in the mood for? Plain guava, guava and cheese, or coconut?"

When he didn't respond, Raquel stopped walking. Taylor had given him too many choices. Too many new things to process. Raquel's heart hammered so hard against her chest it was making it hard to breathe the cold, mid-morning air. She turned around, intending to run back to her office to get her car keys, but then her father finally spoke.

"All of them," he said with abject delight.

Relief flooded Raquel's overworked nervous system, weakening her legs.

"One of each it is," Taylor said conspiratorially. "I'll put the rest of them in the freezer for when Raquel gets home."

"Oh, yes." He stood and followed Taylor to the kitchen. "*Raquelita* loves those. She will be so excited when she comes home from school."

"I bet she is going to be so surprised."

Raquel switched the view from the living room to the kitchen to continue watching them. Taylor was right. She had such an easy calm way about her, she couldn't imagine her stressing him out. She also talked to him like a person, not like she was talking to a baby, or worse, behaving like he was a piece of furniture. Talking around him like he wasn't even there.

Slipping her phone back in her coat pocket, Raquel couldn't help but grin while she walked. A few months ago, she could never have guessed that she'd not only have had an intimate relationship with a former student, but that the woman would be in her home, taking care of her father, and stealing her heart right from under her nose.

As she neared the lecture hall, Raquel tried to get her teaching face on. In all her decades of experience, she had never struggled so hard to focus.

If she were being judged based on the hour and fifteen-minute class, she wouldn't have been honored with any awards. Still, a dozen students remained after the lecture to talk to her. It was another hour before she broke free and returned to her office.

At her desk, she caught up on everything she'd missed. Taylor, understanding her anxiety, had documented their day. They'd abandoned the puzzle almost immediately when Taylor realized it was more frustrating than fun.

Dominoes had apparently been a big hit. Judging from the pictures, the pastries she'd baked at home looked flakey and delicious. She rarely gave her father anything sugary, but he looked elated to be eating something that tasted like Miami.

Taylor promised to provide some balance to the massive sugar high, and they'd gone on a walk along the creek. As she watched the video she sent of her and her father strolling around the pond, Raquel made a note to tell her about the corn tin for the ducks for next time.

Next time.

The prospect of another day like this filled Raquel with a rush of warmth and excitement and terror. She wanted there to be a next time. She wanted there to be an everyday like this.

Oh, shit.

Raquel put the phone down and closed her eyes. Her heart thumping, her body tingling, perspiration starting at her temple. As if diagnosing the worst possible outcome, Raquel dropped her head in her hands.

I'm in love.

CHAPTER 41

HAVING GOTTEN stuck in a very long and awkward meeting with her department chair and one of the deans, Raquel arrived home nearly two hours later than expected. She hadn't stopped to check the cameras as she raced out of the building and toward the parking lot, but she called Taylor immediately to make sure they were okay.

When she walked in the front door, it was nearly sunset. Taylor was sitting on the couch a few steps from her father's hallway with her computer in her lap and an earbud in one ear. She looked up at Raquel and beamed.

"Honey! You're home," she said before closing her laptop and plucked out the headphone.

Raquel couldn't help grinning. "I think I'm supposed to say that." She hung her coat and purse on the rack by the door. "I'm so sorry I'm late."

Taylor strode toward her. "You're just in time for dinner."

Raquel cupped Taylor's face with both hands and kissed her. "I feel like I've been gone for a week," she said after easing out of their kiss and pressing her forehead against Taylor's.

"We missed you."

Raquel grinned. "I don't know. It looks like you two had quite the day without me."

Taylor chuckled. "Don't be jealous of our love affair, Raquel Miguel."

"Oh, God. Don't call me that. It's awful."

Taylor tipped her head to the side and scrunched her face as if to say *eek*.

"Why don't you go say goodnight to your dad? He wanted dinner early and then said he was ready for bed after he took his meds."

Raquel nodded. "He's usually in bed at this time."

"Even after he definitely didn't have a two-hour nap during a *Caso Cerrado* marathon?"

"He loves his naps." She didn't explain that as he reached the later stages of dementia, he'd spend even more time sleeping.

"Not as much as he loves trying to hustle me at dominos." She kissed her again and then turned toward the kitchen. "I'll go pull dinner out of the oven. Oh, and I have a little surprise for dessert."

Raquel found it impossible to take a deep breath while she watched Taylor walk away.

"What did you make?" She didn't let on that she knew about the pastries she'd had shipped, presumably overnight, from Miami.

Taylor smiled at her over her shoulder. "Oh, nothing much. A little baked pasta with roasted tomatoes, feta, fresh herbs." She shrugged "NBD."

Raquel's stomach soared like she was on a rollercoaster making a zero gravity turn; the thrill of flying with her feet still planted firmly on the floor.

When the feeling returned to her legs, she started for her dad's room. Tucked into bed, he was half dozing.

"I just wanted to say goodnight, *Papi*," Raquel whispered in Spanish.

"*Mi vida*." He reached out for her.

Raquel sat on the edge of his bed and took his hand in hers. "Did you have a nice day?"

"Oh, yes." His smile always made Raquel want to cry. It was so broad. So unburdened. It was weightless, without the anchors of his grief. "Luz came all the way from Santa Clara to see me. Can you believe it?"

Raquel blinked quickly, as if that might dry her tears before they formed. If they were still in Cuba, it would be a whole day affair to get from her aunt's house to theirs in Artemisa. But they hadn't been in Cuba in over forty years and Luz hadn't found the time to take the flight from Miami to Lockwood.

"I can't wait for *Raquelita* to get home from school. She's going to be so happy to see her *tia*. She loves my baby sister. Thick as thieves, those two." He laughed, as if recalling some specific bit of mischief, but Raquel didn't ask what it was. He had a hard time articulating things like that, and she didn't want to frustrate him after such a pleasant day.

Smiling, Raquel nodded. She and her aunt had been close. She'd been a blast of excitement when she arrived from Cuba. Raquel was a teenager then. It had been so cool to hang out with an adult who listened to rock music and let her drink beer.

She didn't understand the concept of growing apart then— couldn't imagine that her aunt would just drift away when her parents urged her to get a job and contribute to the household. When her father first got sick, she expected her to wander back to them, but it never happened. After a while, she stopped asking her to see him.

Leaning forward, Raquel kissed him on the cheek. "I love you, Papi."

He cupped her face, his watery eyes fixed on hers. "*Te quiero, mi vida.*"

Raquel let the words settle over her like a weighted blanket. She didn't care whether he knew exactly who she was at that moment. The love was what mattered, and the love was real.

CHAPTER 42

DISHES in the dishwasher and a bottle of pinot noir tucked under her arm, Taylor padded out of the kitchen and into the living room. Raquel was already waiting for her with a couple of wine glasses. When Raquel suggested they unwind after dinner with a drink, Taylor wasn't about to admit she was tired.

"You know, I could get used to this Mama Celeste, Betty Crocker, Sara Lee situation," Taylor said when she stood in front of Raquel to uncork the bottle.

Raquel looked up at her, burned honey eyes gleaming. "I'm not sure any of those are real people."

"Okay, then. Uncle Ben. His face is on the box. He has to be a real dude."

Chuckling, Raquel held up one glass for her to fill and then the other. "I think you're much better than any of that processed stuff. Where'd you learn to cook like that?"

Taylor tried not to let out an old man groan when she plopped onto the couch and accepted the glass of wine. "TikTok."

Raquel tipped her glass to clink with Taylor's. "No."

"Yep." Taylor took a sip, tasting the cherry and clove, letting it coat her tongue. "You should really lift your self-imposed ban on new social medias. It's very educational. I've found great books, learned to cook, became briefly obsessed with organizing all my feminine hygiene products. It's amazing."

"*Educational.*" Raquel sipped her wine. "So was Friendster."

"What the hell is that?"

Raquel waved her away as if to say it wasn't worth explaining.

Taylor took another sip of her drink. Every second she spent with Raquel recharged her faster than caffeine.

"How was your day?" Raquel set her glass on the coffee table and tucked her leg under herself to face Taylor. "How was it really?"

"Why are you looking at me like I'm harboring state secrets, Raquel?" She set her glass down too. "I told you it was really nice. Ramon is better at dominos, but I kicked his ass at coloring inside the lines. He was honestly super easy to hang out with, and I even got some work done when he was resting. And..." Taylor hesitated. "I've never considered myself the housewife type, but I kind of enjoyed making dinner and waiting for my husband to come home."

Raquel laughed, her throat bobbing as she brightened in a way Taylor hadn't seen in days. "Is that so?" With a quick tug, she pulled Taylor toward her.

"Yeah. Sue me, okay?"

"I can't say I've ever role-played this scenario." Raquel's breath, sweet and warm from the wine, landed on her mouth just before her lips did.

Taylor straddled Raquel's hips as she slid onto her lap. "Is that a thumb's up or down?" She ran her palms down Raquel's shoulders, feeling the silky material of her blouse. "Because if you're into it, you can put that suit jacket back on."

Raquel's smile morphed into something much hungrier. "Are you serious?"

Biting her bottom lip, Taylor played coy. She hadn't intended on bringing out one of her surprises tonight, but without knowing how long she was going to stay, it made little sense to wait. "I don't know. Are *you* serious?"

Raquel's eyes darkened as they searched her. "Aren't you tired?" There was a lilt to her words, the rising pitch of hope.

Taylor leaned in closer, her lips brushing against Raquel's mouth. "I will never be too tired for you," she promised in a slow whisper.

Craning her head, Raquel captured her in another kiss. This one was hotter and more desperate. Parting her lips, Taylor slipped her tongue inside Raquel's mouth like it belonged to her.

Her desire sprang to life immediately. It crested in waves and pulled low in her belly with destabilizing suddenness.

Raquel's hands were strong and purposeful as they slid under the back of her shirt. Her mouth searing as she ran her teeth over the sensitive skin of Taylor's neck. "What did you have in mind?"

Taylor tangled her fingers in the back of Raquel's hair and pulled. Raquel's lips curved with dangerous delight while she fixed her in a scorching stare.

Leaning forward, Taylor kept her fist in Raquel's hair as she ran the very tip of her tongue along the shell of her ear. "I'll meet you upstairs in ten minutes, Mrs. Alonso."

Raquel gasped something Taylor took for *yes*.

To be on the safe side, Raquel waited fifteen minutes before knocking on the bedroom door. While she waited, she freshened up in the guest bathroom and did her best to look professorial. She wasn't sure what Taylor wanted out of the fantasy, but she meant to give her whatever it was. Raquel couldn't think of a single thing she wouldn't do for her.

With the makeup she had buried at the bottom of her purse, Raquel applied black eyeliner and nude lipstick. She ran her fingers through her recently cut, straight bob until she liked the way it landed below her jaw.

In the mirror, she practiced how she'd stroll into the bedroom. Both hands in her trouser pockets. Just one. Suit jacket open. Jacket closed. They all looked like she was trying too hard.

Deciding to just go with the flow, Raquel strode across the hall to her bedroom. She'd never knocked on her own door, and she didn't count on the odd little rush it would give her.

When her second knock went unanswered, Raquel opened the door a crack and peeked in. Candles were lit on both nightstands and music was playing so softly, she hadn't heard it through the door. It was the kind of slow, bass-heavy tune that was conducive to deliberate and seductive hip swinging. What she didn't see was Taylor.

Easing into the room, Raquel lingered by the door she closed behind her. It was hard to see anything but the bed and the candles casting shadows on the wall.

The sound of the bathroom door creaking open called her attention to her left. As soon as she saw Taylor, she had to resist the urge to gasp.

Dressed in black thigh-high tights, a minuscule black garment Raquel guessed was a thong, a lacy garter and matching low-cut bra, Taylor was literally stunning. Her beautiful brown hair fell in long waves past her shoulders. Leaning in the doorway, Taylor looked like some exotic perfume model.

"Wow," Raquel breathed. A lifetime of learning words, and she couldn't think of a single one. Even a doctorate couldn't prepare her to be articulate in a situation like this.

Tossing her hair back, Taylor stretched one of her arms above her head as she held onto the door frame with her fingertips, her lips parted and eyes dreamy.

Parched, Raquel drank up every inch of her form. Taylor in the flesh was much better than any fantasy she could have ever imagined.

Sauntering toward her, Taylor emerged from the bathroom like an ancient muse. She was Peitho. She was Aphrodite. A Greek goddess personifying seduction and persuasion and sex.

"You look incredible," Raquel whispered when Taylor neared.

She slung her arms around Raquel's neck. "I wanted to show you how much I missed you."

Taylor's lips were too soft to resist. Raquel dove into them. As she kissed her, she dropped her hands down her back, feeling the smooth swell exposed by the tiny thong.

Taylor smiled into their kiss. "Do you really like it?"

Raquel squeezed her butt in overt approval. "I love it."

"Good." She pushed Raquel back a fraction, breaking their embrace before taking her by the hand. "Because it's only the beginning."

With a spin, Raquel landed at the foot of her bed. As she sat on the edge, she watched Taylor sway to the music.

Leaning back on the hands splayed on the mattress behind her, Raquel was lulled into a lusty haze as she watched every slow movement, every languid roll of her hips, every undulation.

Taylor neared, dancing slowly until she slipped between Raquel's legs. Her hands were warm when they crept beneath Raquel's suit jacket; confident as she coaxed it off, elegant when she carried it to the closet.

Convinced Taylor just wanted her to watch her walk away, Raquel let her attention linger over the sliver of back visible beneath her long hair before her focus dropped to the rest of her body.

When Taylor turned around with a wooden hanger in hand, she was openly pleased to catch Raquel staring at her ass.

"Hanging up clothes has never looked so good," Raquel said when Taylor started back toward the bed.

Taylor slipped between her legs again, but this time she bent down to whisper in her ear. "You've had such a long day. All I want to do is help ease your load." Her words were a python slithering their serpentine curves around Raquel's neck, down her chest, and coiling in her belly.

Closing her eyes, Raquel ran her open palms up the back of Taylor's legs. The stockings were soft against her touch. The straps were taut and stretched where they hugged the sides of her ass.

Unable to help herself, Raquel squeezed her, digging her nails into the firm flesh. The little moan that tumbled out of Taylor's lips floated over Raquel's increasingly tender skin.

Taylor's fingers found the top buttons of Raquel's blouse. She pulled apart the material like revealing what lay beneath was a sacred rite.

Raquel watched her until she couldn't stand it anymore. She yanked Taylor's leg forward, prompting her to kneel on the bed with one knee.

"Kiss me," Raquel demanded, her words a breathy rumble.

Taylor complied, her mouth hot and urgent on hers as she slipped one hand into Raquel's hair and the other one in her bra.

Raquel moaned into their kiss, her sensitive nipple stiffening between Taylor's deft fingers. Taylor's quick rhythm matched the increased speed of her tongue. Her desire rose with every flick, every swipe until perspiration misted the small of her back, until her core throbbed, desperate for Taylor's touch.

Gripping Taylor's hips with both hands, she broke their kiss. Ravenous, she bit into Taylor's neck, pulling her down to her mouth and devouring her.

"This is supposed to be about you," Taylor groaned when Raquel's lips dripped down her chest.

"And this is what I want," she replied before pulling down one side of Taylor's bra.

Taylor pulled her head flush against her chest, tangled her fingers in Raquel's hair, and groaned as Raquel licked and teased.

When she was sure Taylor was close to begging for more, she pulled her leg up so that instead of kneeling on it, she set her foot flat on the bed.

Raquel leaned back for a moment, needing to admire Taylor; to appreciate her effort. With her leg propped up, Taylor's inner thigh was exposed.

"Push it to one side," Raquel demanded. Her gaze drifted up Taylor's body to meet her eyes.

Taylor moistened her lips and pulled her hand out of Raquel's hair. Raquel watched Taylor's hand as it floated over her belly. "Push what to one side?"

"You know what I want."

Raquel's mouth went dry when Taylor's fingertips danced over her underwear. With a grin, Taylor shoved the material to one side.

"Is this what you want?" Taylor's voice dripped with the same arousal glistening on her body.

Raquel nodded, her body pulsing with unmet desire.

"Then take it. It's yours. I'm yours."

Raquel lunged. Wrapping her arm around Taylor's thigh, she tucked her shoulder under it.

As soon as she covered Taylor with her mouth, Raquel moaned. The taste of her filled her mouth like the most exquisite delicacy. She couldn't get enough.

Deep as she could get it, Raquel plunged her tongue inside of Taylor, wanting to taste more of her, to consume every drop of her soaking wet arousal.

Taylor's rhythmic breaths turned to panting as she pressed hard into Raquel's mouth, riding her tongue as best she could while still standing.

When Raquel couldn't hold off any longer, she ran her tongue up the length of her before circling her lips and tongue around Taylor's hard clit.

"That feels so good," Taylor moaned before cursing.

The seductive words were as effective as if she'd reached into her pants and touched her.

Raquel moved in a slow, steady rhythm, moaning against Taylor as she trembled and cursed and said the most delightfully filthy things.

When Taylor's body stiffened and she held her breath, Raquel launched a more targeted attack.

Knowing Taylor was close, Raquel slipped a finger inside of her, teasing her entrance just in time to feel her clench around her, a gush soaking her fingers as Taylor made a sudden fist in Raquel's hair and cried.

Raquel didn't stop until Taylor pulled her head away.

"Trying to kill me?" Taylor panted, looking down at Raquel with a smirk before climbing on top of her.

Straddling her hips, Taylor leaned forward and kissed Raquel. "God, I taste so good on you."

Raquel ran her hands over Taylor's body. "How long are you going to keep this on?" She tried not to sound hopeful.

"As long as you want me to," she promised.

Biting her bottom lip, Raquel let her imagination run wild.

CHAPTER 43

SATURDAY DISAPPEARED in a whirl of pleasant weather and walks in the sun. Sunday moved even faster; the space between breakfast and Taylor's roasted chicken dinner vanishing in a blink.

Raquel spent the first part of the work week debating whether she'd fallen into a coma. Whether perhaps she was in some kind of stasis, living a dream far too good to be true. Between classes, she checked on the cameras at home. Not out of anxiety or worry, but because watching Taylor and her father together was the single most beautiful thing she'd ever seen.

Taylor was gentle and sweet, finding ways around her father's occasional resistance instead of being frustrated by it.

When he didn't want to take his medication, Taylor didn't push. Instead, she sat next to him at the kitchen table, a handful of vitamins in front of her. She'd complained about having to take them until, at some point, she got *him* to convince *her* to take them. He'd promised to take his if she took hers.

On the rare occasion Taylor couldn't get her charm to work, she simply let things go before his frustration grew. When she'd try again a while later, she'd use a different approach, but she was always so calm, so gentle.

The way Taylor had folded into their lives, weaved herself into the fabric of their days, was more than Raquel could've ever hoped for.

As she texted with Taylor and ate the lunch she'd made for her, an idea started to form. A way to show her gratitude.

When she arrived home late that afternoon, she told a very tiny lie about completing her office hours from home. Upstairs, she prepared a little surprise.

After another shockingly good dinner sourced on TikTok, Raquel put her father to bed while Taylor stretched out on the couch.

Raquel left his room to find Taylor scrolling on her phone, her head propped up on the armrest and one leg thrown haphazardly over the backrest.

Taylor looked up from the screen as Raquel sauntered toward her, but Raquel didn't give her the chance to speak before she leaned over the back of the couch, her lips hovering over Taylor's ear.

"Meet me upstairs in a few minutes," she whispered a sultry promise before kissing her cheek.

Taylor's dark brown eyes widened, and she dropped her phone on her chest, as if her brain couldn't process her words and keep a grip at the same time.

Raquel forced her expression to remain neutral, giving nothing away before she turned and let Taylor watch her walk away.

In the large master bathroom, Raquel filled the clawfoot tub with steaming hot water. Like an ancient witch brewing a potion, she emptied a jar of luxurious bath milk. The scent of dried rose petals, buttermilk, and shea butter filled the room as it mixed with the water. The dried, dark red petals floated to the surface. To increase the calming and relaxing purpose of the bath, she added a few drops of lavender and eucalyptus essential oils.

As the bath filled, Raquel lit the white, lavender-scented candles she'd arranged at each corner of the double sinks. Then she lit the tall ones she'd put in hurricane vases near the glass shower.

She moved the little teak stool she used to prop her foot up in the shower and placed it next to the tub. Then she flipped off the light to check her work. Either Taylor was going to feel relaxed or like she was attending an extraordinarily fragrant seance.

When the bathroom door creaked open, Raquel ran her palms over her trousers, suddenly nervous; suddenly unsure of how her gesture would be received; suddenly worried it was silly and childish.

Taylor's gaze swept over the candlelit room. Her dimples appeared one at a time. "What's all this?"

Raquel moistened her lips, her nerves making her mouth dry and her throat scratchy. "Just... a thank you, I suppose."

Taking slow steps, Raquel crossed the room and met Taylor at the door.

Without another word, Raquel unbuttoned Taylor's flannel shirt and slid it off her shoulders. Her jeans fell next, followed by her bra and underwear.

Without an ounce of self-consciousness, Taylor stood naked in front of her. Instinctively, Taylor picked her hair up in a messy bun.

Resisting every urge to look at her with desire, Raquel led her toward the tub.

As Taylor eased slowly into the water, she let out a little sigh before resting her head on the edge of the tub. Positioning the stool between her legs, Raquel sat behind Taylor.

Dipping her hands into the hot water, slick with all the moisturizers in the milk bath, Raquel ran her thumbs up the middle of Taylor's neck. She pressed, moving in a swooping motion along her spine.

Taylor responded with an appreciative moan. Raquel continued to move in tight circles across Taylor's shoulders.

Beneath her fingers, Taylor relaxed, sighing and gasping appreciatively as Raquel massaged her neck and upper back.

"I really don't know what I did to deserve this." Taylor's voice was heavy and distant between her sighs.

"Are you kidding?" Raquel chuckled. "I don't even have words for everything you've done."

"It was that turkey and avocado sandwich I made you, wasn't it?"

Raquel rolled her eyes. "Yeah. That was it."

Taylor slipped away from her touch and turned in the tub. Her eyes gleamed in the flickering candlelight as she held Raquel in her gaze.

"Will you get in with me?"

"This is meant to be for you. About you unwinding—"

"If I relax any further, I might fall asleep and I don't want to waste any time with you." She flashed a lethal dimple. "Come on." She pulled herself to the edge of the tub, her pretty face inches from Raquel's lips. "I promise not to seduce you."

Raquel sighed her amusement. Unable to resist Taylor's puppy dog eyes, she stood.

"Wait," she called before Raquel had undone more than a couple of buttons.

She raised a brow, waiting for Taylor to continue.

"Take it off slowly," she added, her head resting on the edge of the tub and her attention fixed on Raquel's body.

"And here I thought you weren't interested in seduction."

"I'm not." She grinned. "Strictly speaking, I think this is voyeurism."

"Now who is being precise with language?"

Unable to deny her, Raquel took her time removing her clothes; allowed Taylor's gaze to linger over each part of her body before she revealed the next, moving slowest over her deadly curves.

She didn't hurry to get in the water, letting Taylor's attention rake over her as she stepped in, loving how she couldn't resist staring at her thighs.

Raquel intended to sit across from her. There was plenty of space for them both, but Taylor took her hand and pulled her in. As if engaged in a dance, she spun Raquel around so her back was resting against Taylor's chest.

Holding her from behind, Taylor wrapped her arms around her, her skin hot from the bath and fragrant with roses and lavender. Her embrace pulled Raquel into another dimension as she nestled herself against Taylor and fell headlong into her.

"This feels so nice," Taylor whispered, resting her chin on Raquel's neck. Her fingertips danced along Raquel's forearm. "Thank you for this." She kissed the side of Raquel's neck, sending a small seismic wave pulsing over her skin.

"It's me who's supposed to be thanking you." She took a deep breath, letting the heat of the bath penetrate her muscles and the softness of Taylor's touch soothe her.

"For what? Hanging out with a cool dude all day?" Taylor's words were feather soft against Raquel's skin. Her fingers were gentle as they traced her wrist bone, her palm, her knuckles.

Lulled into something of a meditative state, Raquel broke open a fraction. "I'm not really used to this," she confessed, her voice skipping over the small ripples in the fragrant water. "I almost don't know how to receive it all." She closed her eyes, short of divulging that she'd never been taken care of like this.

She wanted to keep talking. To explain just how much Taylor's actions had meant to her. That they'd meant everything. That even if she left, and she never saw her again, she would always love this act of kindness. This boon of generosity. That she would always love her for it.

Taylor held her tighter. "Thank you for trusting me to be here. For letting me help." She dropped both hands beneath the surface of the water and slid them over Raquel's belly.

Raquel placed her arms over Taylor's and intertwined their fingers. She was weightless in the water; floating under the surface and out of her body.

Her lips ached to keep talking; to purge the whole truth, but it got caught on the lump in her throat. She didn't know what scared her. After everything they'd showed each other, telling Taylor that she loved her seemed like stating the obvious.

"Can I tell you something kinda lame?"

Raquel stroked Taylor's hand under the water, feeling so close to her. So connected. "You can tell me anything."

"I've never really felt comfortable showing this side of myself."

"What do you mean?"

"We all know what people expect from us, right? And I'm the fun girl. The light and breezy girl people don't usually get serious about."

"What about Robbie?"

Taylor shrugged, sending little waves over the water. "I did get the closest with her. It was all good until we moved in together. Then the romance just died. It's like I can't be both. I can't be adventure and nurture, you know? If you fall for one, you don't want the other."

Raquel spun around, splashing a little water over the edge. Taylor's eyes were filled with something she'd never seen before: uncertainty and doubt.

"You're perfect." Raquel held her gaze when she said it, so Taylor would understand just how much she meant it. "I love… all the things about you. Your spirit. Your kindness. Your sweetness. Your joy."

Snaking her arms around her waist, Taylor pulled her in, sending more water to the tiled floor. When she kissed her, Raquel breathed into her everything she was still too scared to say.

CHAPTER 44

RAQUEL STIRRED in bed before Taylor woke. Before her alarm clock rang. Before her father's monitors chirped. Even the sky was still sleepy, blanketed in soft pink and hazy blue and pale gold.

Next to her, Taylor was sleeping on her back, one arm above her head and the other at her side. Her hair was a dark river splayed out over the white pillowcase.

The sight of her careless beauty was a silk-wrapped fist slamming into Raquel's chest.

From the moment they reconnected, they'd been shrouded in goodbye. It hung over them all the time, charging every exchange; making it feel special, not to be taken for granted, but tingeing it with a little gray in the process.

Without any time to waste, Raquel leaned over to where Taylor's T-shirt had scrunched up around her ribs. Her skin still carried the feint scent of rose from last night's bath.

Raquel closed her eyes, inhaling her fragrance before kissing the constellation of freckles scattered on her side. Taylor didn't have many blemishes on her skin, and Raquel especially loved the smattering of tiny marks.

She pressed lips further down Taylor's torso, pushing down the duvet to follow the curve of her body until she reached her hip bone.

Taylor's breathing grew shallow, but she didn't move. She kept still while Raquel continued to lavish her body with gentle, loving attention.

Raquel was working her way across Taylor's belly when Taylor's fingers slid into her hair, scraping her nails over her scalp as she smoothed it back.

Raquel glanced up to find Taylor looking down at her, sleepy brown eyes full of curiosity and affection.

"Well, good morning." Taylor's voice was raspy and soft as it floated down to her.

"Good morning," Raquel whispered, continuing her trek down Taylor's body.

Parting her legs, she skimmed over the thin fabric of her underwear and drifted between her thighs.

Taylor sighed her appreciation, running her fingers through Raquel's hair encouragingly. Raquel's eyes closed at her touch, the sensation on her scalp mixing with the softness against her lips.

"You feel so good," Taylor murmured, her fingers growing more insistent as they tangled and pulled.

Drunk on Taylor, Raquel continued along the inside of her thigh and over her other hip. Thirsty for more, she slithered down her leg, tasting the side of her knee, her calf, her ankle, the top of her foot.

Her return trip up the other side of Taylor's body lacked the same restraint she'd started with. She wanted to go slow, to show her she felt something other than passion, something that burned even hotter than lust, but she was losing focus.

Taylor squirmed beneath her, her restraint waning and her hips digging into the mattress.

Raquel grinned. Grazing her teeth over Taylor's ribs, she watched Taylor's expression as she stifled a groan.

When she couldn't stand it anymore, Taylor reached down and pulled Raquel into a deep, lingering kiss.

Taylor's mouth was hot and insistent as she pulled her in. Her legs hooked around Raquel, holding her in place as she kissed her.

Pulling away suddenly, Taylor grinned. "My turn," she said before flipping Raquel onto her back and climbing on top of her in a single motion.

Taylor pushed Raquel's hair out of her face, her eyes brightening as she looked down at her. "I could really get used to waking up like this." She smiled. "It beats my neighbor's occasional five a.m. *Zumba* sessions."

At the prospect of spending every day with Taylor, Raquel's heart soared. She could easily imagine it; easily let herself wish for it.

"Me too," Raquel agreed, her entire chest throbbing with her quickening pulse, a wild bird fluttering colorful wings against its cage. The truth burned her lips, desperate to break free.

"Who needs breakfast when I have you?" Taylor whispered, her mouth igniting Raquel's neck where she placed a languid kiss.

"I'm not sure how much nutritional value you'll find," she whispered, her focus on the sensation of Taylor's mouth over her collarbone.

"Nutritional value is overrated." Taylor pushed up Raquel's nightshirt, exposing her fully nude body underneath.

The morning glowed through the sheer window shades. The light illuminated Taylor, revealing the wonder in her eyes. She always looked at her like she'd never seen her before, like she couldn't see the places that could be slimmer, tighter, firmer, higher.

"You're so perfect." Taylor sunk her face between her breasts, kissing the tender space at the center of her chest.

"You don't have to say that." Raquel held her breath when Taylor's mouth found her nipple, kissing it softly as she followed the curve down to her belly.

"I say what I mean, Raquel." Her tone was stern and out of place with the softness of her touch as she brushed her lips over Raquel's navel.

Raquel closed her eyes, relishing the softness of Taylor's lips on the inside of her thigh; the light flutter of her tongue as she blazed a scorching trail toward her center.

"I don't know how I'll ever go back to sleeping without you," Taylor confessed before she kissed her higher, dangerously close to where she'd started aching for her.

Raquel's eyes snapped open in time for the ever-looming dark clouds to gather above her bed.

The inescapable farewell was derailed by the shrill buzz of Raquel's alarm clock.

"No," Taylor cried out like she'd been shot and dropped her head onto Raquel's pelvis. "I was just getting to the good part."

Raquel couldn't help but chuckle as she stretched her arm and turned off the irritating noise. "It'll still be there when I get home, I promise."

"One kiss?" Taylor looked up at her with pleading eyes. "So quick."

Raquel pretended to be stern. "One."

Taylor dove between her thighs like she was jumping headfirst into a swimming pool. Raquel would have made a joke about it, but Taylor's mouth was on her like she meant to swallow her whole.

"That's more than one," Raquel groaned as Taylor's tongue moved in slow circles.

"It's a French kiss," she moaned into her.

Raquel's eyes slipped closed, letting the minutes pass as Taylor did the most incredible things with her mouth. She reached down, tangling her fingers in Taylor's hair, knowing she should push her away, but pulling her closer instead.

When the monitor in her dad's room crackled, Taylor stopped. She didn't whine, which impressed Raquel, but she wore her disappointment on her face.

Raquel cupped her face and guided her up to her mouth. She kissed her, tasting herself on her lips, a thrill that could never get old.

"It'll still be there later," Raquel repeated before sliding out from under her.

Taylor remained kneeling on the bed.

"Is that an invitation?"

Raquel pulled on a pair of pajama pants she'd discarded on the floor overnight. With Taylor no longer on top of her, the room was suddenly cold. "An invitation?"

Taylor wiggled her eyebrows. "A *to be continued?*"

Moistening her lips, Raquel flashed her a momentary grin. "Maybe," she replied as if she wouldn't be counting the hours before she was back with her again, and slipped out to the cold hallway and downstairs to get her father out of bed.

CHAPTER 45

RAMON WAS NAPPING, mouth open and fully snoring, when Taylor saw an opportunity. After over two weeks together, she'd gotten to know his routine well. There was no way he was going to wake up before three. She had plenty of time to sanitize the special deliveries she'd brought with her from New York without being spotted.

While he snoozed, Taylor stood in the kitchen, letting the silicone toys boil away on the stove like queer alchemy.

As she waited, Taylor thought about how she'd approach Raquel tonight. When they'd talked about this, she got the sense that Raquel had a particular fantasy; a role she wanted Taylor to play.

Having used a strap-on a handful of times, Taylor wasn't a rookie, but she didn't feel super experienced. She wanted so much to fulfill Raquel's every desire, to show her she could be everything she needed.

If she'd learned anything about Raquel in the last couple of weeks, it was how little she lived her life for herself. How little she had left for herself at the end of the day.

Ramon was Raquel's priority. His needs were always met first and without question.

Her responsibilities to her students were always satisfied before her own, too. Before she slept or rested or ate, she made sure she'd taken care of them.

Tired as Raquel was, she didn't let it show when they got on their video calls at the end of her long day. Talking to Taylor until midnight most nights, and waking up near dawn to take care of her father, there was no time for Raquel in between. Nothing but the tiniest of stolen moments.

Even the divorce hadn't been for Raquel. She'd agreed with Max that they hadn't gotten the chance to experience things after marrying so young, but Taylor got the sense that Raquel wouldn't have initiated the separation. That she valued the stability of their partnership more than she did with passion and adventure.

Taylor had never known anyone like her. Never known someone so generous, so giving, so capable of deep love. It stirred something Taylor had never felt before, a fierce desire to take care of Raquel. To show up for her the way she showed up for everyone else.

If Taylor hadn't been sure she loved Raquel before she left New York, she would've been convinced of it the first day they spent together in Vermont. Seeing her in her element. The person behind the sultry, serious persona was so sweet, so thoughtful, so giving. There was no guarding her heart.

Thinking about going back to New York made Taylor's stomach churn. She didn't want to leave Raquel, didn't want to negotiate a long distance relationship, especially when they didn't really have to. There was no reason she couldn't move to Vermont. No reason except that Raquel hadn't mentioned anything beyond this trip.

Taylor understood her hesitation, but she wished Raquel saw how much she wanted to be there. How being with her felt more like home than she'd ever experienced. How she'd never felt such deep and wonderfully complex feelings for anyone in her life.

Her phone on the counter vibrated, indicating her sanitizing timer was up. With the toys bundled in a clean towel, Taylor tiptoed through the living room and up the stairs without waking Ramon.

She left the door to Raquel's bedroom open so she could keep an ear on Ramon and tried on her outfit while wearing the strap-on. A black muscle tee and gray joggers.

"You look ridiculous," she said to her reflection in the framed mirror above the dresser.

Deciding she needed an expert, she picked up her phone.

Taylor: *Can you text me when you're free? I need help.*

She added the eggplant emoji to give her a hint and waited for a response. It took less than a minute.

Alexis: *Girl, what?!*

Taylor: *I need to consult the master, okay? Can you video chat sometime in the next two hours?*

When Alexis called her during her break a few minutes later, she was dressed in dark blue scrubs and sitting in Heart Stopper while parked in the hospital's garage.

"First of all," Alexis started like she was laying out a treatment plan, "we're gonna need to do something about that hair."

Taylor touched her messy bun. "What's wrong with it?"

"Nothing, but I think slicking it back fits what you're going for."

Taylor laughed. "So I should look like you, basically."

She shrugged. "You called to ask for my advice, right? This is what I'd do. If you don't want to commit to an undercut, you can at least get a shit-ton of product in there."

With a sigh, Taylor agreed. She had a lot more hair than Alexis, but she followed her instructions until she was left with a bun so tight it felt weird to blink.

"How do you wear your hair like this every day without giving yourself a headache?" Taylor joked as she checked herself out in the mirror. The sleek look didn't look terrible, but it was incredibly uncomfortable.

"Dedication." She chuckled. "Is that what you're going to wear?" She pointed at Taylor's clothes.

"This is what she mentioned."

Alexis nodded while assessing her outfit before offering her diagnosis. "Can you open the sleeves up more? Do you have a sports bra?"

Taylor found a pair of scissors in the bathroom and widened the armholes on the muscle tee until they all but exposed her entire sides. After showing Alexis her options, she selected a solid black sports bra that revealed the least amount of cleavage. It had been a toss-up between bra and no bra, but they'd agreed the black garment under the tee looked best.

"Alright, let's see the strap." Alexis' eyes darted to the side. "Break's almost over and I need to get coffee."

Taylor winced. "I feel stupid wearing it," she confessed.

Alexis shook her head. "You gotta own that thing, bitch! You're wearing it, it's not wearing you. If you can't rock it with confidence, you're not going to have any fun doing this. And if you're not having fun, what's the point?"

With a deep breath, Taylor nodded and slid the black harness on.

"Do you have boxer briefs?" Alexis asked as she evaluated her get up without making any jokes. Taylor imagined this was her clinical expression. It gave away nothing.

"No, but I have boy shorts."

"I'd cut a hole in them for your friend." She pointed at the skin-toned toy protruding beneath Taylor's pelvis. "But I don't like the straps and shit visible. And if the outfit is part of her kink, I'd tuck that bad boy in and wear it when she gets home."

"What do you call it?" Taylor looked at herself in the mirror. In just the tee and strap-on, it looked so vulgar.

"What do you mean?"

"*Dildo* is… not sexy," Taylor said. "What do you call it when you're, you know… when you're having sex?"

"I mean, when I use one, I get super into it." Alexis leaned back in her seat. "I see it as an extension of myself. So I call it whatever feels right in the moment. Don't overthink this, dude. You're gonna be fine. Just remember, you don't need to use your hips as much as you think you do. Keep them straight and thrust lightly."

Taylor wasn't too proud to make note of all of Alexis' strap-on tips. She even decided she'd tuck the little bottle of lube in her pocket so she wouldn't be fumbling for it later. Next time, she'd get condoms for easy clean up too.

By the time they got off the phone, Taylor was ready to seduce the hell out of Raquel.

CHAPTER 46

THE MOMENT RAQUEL started the bedtime routine with Ramon, Taylor flew up the stairs to change out of her jeans. Thinking about anything other than this during dinner had been nearly impossible. It hadn't helped that the day was on the warmer side and Raquel had decided to wear a pencil skirt and blazer combo. Her kryptonite.

Standing in the bedroom, Taylor positioned the toy in her underwear the way Alexis had instructed, but no matter how she maneuvered it, it still looked like she was trying to hide a huge boner in her gray sweatpants. Trying and failing.

Giving herself a final look in the mirror, Taylor laughed. She looked like Alexis' carbon copy, but with less swag. She glanced down at her package and was grateful that her anatomy didn't give away how turned on she was or she'd be constantly embarrassed.

She pulled down the black muscle tee and tried to remember how she normally walked while she made her way back downstairs. The straps she was hiding under her underwear were tight around her butt and pulled when she walked, but she tried to give less haggard cowboy and more smooth operator.

Since Raquel was still with her dad when she returned, Taylor started washing up the kitchen. She distracted herself long enough to forget about the seven inches of silicone pressed to her thigh.

"I thought you went upstairs," Raquel said from behind her.

Taylor closed the dishwasher door and turned around, grateful the kitchen island was covering the lower half of her body. Judging by the hungry look in Raquel's eyes, she'd guessed what she had planned, but she didn't want to confirm it. Not yet.

Taking her time to provide a response, Taylor dried her hands with a kitchen towel. "I was."

Raquel moistened her lips, her gaze dripping over Taylor's body in open approval. "What's this?"

Taylor's eyes pooled with feigned innocence. "What's what?"

Raquel sauntered toward her, her expression ravenous.

The kitchen counter cut into Taylor's lower back as she leaned against it. She watched as Raquel's gaze feasted on her, running over every inch of her body.

Raquel closed in, pinning Taylor against the counter. "Is this the reason for the new hairstyle?" She ran her palm over Taylor's abdomen, stopping short of her waistline.

"Is *what* the reason?" Taylor craned her head to meet Raquel's lips, but Raquel didn't kiss her. She hovered over her lips instead. Her breath was warm and sweet from the spoonful of chocolate mousse she'd indulged in after dinner.

With a sudden jerk, Raquel reached down and grabbed the toy through her pants. The roughness of her touch sent a thrilling jolt through Taylor's unprepared body, making her gasp as if she'd felt Raquel's hand on her flesh.

"If only you were always this excited to see me." Raquel's lips brushing her cheek, combined with her insistent touch, were enough to send a tidal wave of desire surging through her.

"I am always this excited," Taylor whispered. "You just can't see it."

Raquel pressed her mouth to Taylor's jaw, sighing before slipping her hand inside of Taylor's sweats. "I like seeing it," she said against the shell of her ear.

Taylor's eyes rolled into the back of her head as the base of the toy pressed into her in a sensual rhythm. The rhythm of Raquel's moving hand.

"This should not be turning me on this much." Taylor strained her imagination, willed herself to feel Raquel's elegant fingers wrapped around her, sliding over her.

"Are you wet?" The whispered words scorched Taylor's skin and sunk into her tense jaw muscles.

Taylor swallowed hard, the admission tumbling out of her in a groan. "Soaked."

With her lips on Taylor's neck, Raquel slid her fingertips in through the side of the harness strap. When she discovered the evidence of Taylor's arousal, a pained groan rumbled in her chest.

At the slightest touch, Taylor's hips rolled forward, hungrily seeking more.

"Soaked *and* hard," Raquel mused as she coated her fingers in Taylor's arousal.

Biting down on her own bottom lip, Taylor kept from moaning out loud. The kitchen was far from the rest of the house, but she didn't want to test how far.

"Don't make a sound," Raquel whispered before kissing her hard, her fingers plunging into her.

Taylor produced something of a whimper while trying to return Raquel's kiss, but she was overwhelmed by Raquel's quickly working fingers. Raquel pulled away from the kiss, but her fingers didn't lose their speed.

"Don't make a sound," she warned again with such authority that Taylor was sure Raquel missed her calling as a high-end dominatrix. "Stop me if you get close," she whispered against her ear. "I want you about to come."

Taylor nodded feebly, her jaws clenched to keep her moan from escaping. She was already pulled so tight, she didn't know how long she could hold back the snap.

When Raquel dropped to her knees in her glasses and her skirt and her fiery dark eyes, Taylor knew she wouldn't last long.

Helpless, she watched Raquel pull her gray sweats halfway down her thighs. When Raquel collected Taylor's arousal and painted the tip of the toy with it. Taylor's knees weakened. When she looked up at her with a dangerous expression before she slowly licked Taylor off of the strap-on, she nearly fainted.

The combination of Raquel's show and her skilled fingers working under the harness was overwhelming. Watching Raquel sent her rushing to the edge, but she couldn't stop.

"God, baby. You're killing me." Reaching down, she tangled her fingers in Raquel's glossy hair and yanked her away. "Close," she choked out, breathless, heart pounding, thighs trembling.

Raquel withdrew her fingers, her gaze fixed on Taylor as she tasted the fruits of her labor and groaned.

Drawing her up and into her arms, Taylor kissed Raquel hard, tasting herself on her tongue. She pressed into her, pulling at her clothes, desperate to feel all of her.

Taylor growled before leading her out of the kitchen.

KISSING her like she meant to consume her, Raquel pushed Taylor into the bedroom. Until she walked in on Taylor in the kitchen, she hadn't realized just how much she wanted to play this game.

Taylor's hands were everywhere, her mouth hot and hard over her lips, her jaw, her neck, her throat. Instead of shoving her onto the bed like Raquel expected, Taylor took her to the armchair near the closed window.

"Is from behind okay?" Taylor whispered against her ear, her soft tone inconsistent with her firm touch.

"Start slow." Raquel's response was just as quiet. "Ease in."

Yanking her blouse over her head, Taylor left Raquel in a bra and pencil skirt. Judging by the expression on her face, it was exactly what she wanted.

With her hands on Raquel's hips, Taylor spun her around and over the chair. When Taylor bent her over, she couldn't help but moan as she gripped the back of the chair. Another hard jerk and Taylor had shoved the skirt up over her hips.

Raquel bit her bottom lip to keep from moaning. They'd never had sex quite like this before, but it was absolutely intoxicating. Taylor's confidence was as exciting as her touch.

"Put your leg up," Taylor demanded, her voice harsh and dark and thrilling.

Raquel complied, leaving one foot on the floor and propping her knee up on the armrest. Not being able to see what Taylor was doing added to the heat drenching her skin.

"You look so fucking good," Taylor groaned, and then her hands were on her, grabbing her ass, smacking it.

Raquel cursed, her desire collecting into a single throbbing point between her parted thighs.

When Taylor pulled down her underwear, she didn't take them off. She left them there, stretched over Raquel's thighs and cutting into her, making the moment all that much filthier.

She heard Taylor drop to her knees behind her a second before she felt her tongue glide over her. Taylor's moans as she tasted her arousal alone would have been enough to send her over the edge, but combined with her tongue invading every inch of her, it was almost too much to take.

Gripping the back of the armchair like she was holding on to driftwood in the middle of the ocean, Raquel had to concentrate to keep her orgasm at bay.

Mercifully, Taylor retreated before she had to beg her to stop. The pop of a cap Raquel guessed was lube sounded just before Taylor slid a finger slowly inside of her, and then another. Every part of Raquel ached for more.

"Are you ready for me?"

Raquel didn't care that she was pleading or that her breath was ragged when she said, "Please. I need you inside of me." It was worth it to hear Taylor's cursing in response.

Taylor's fingers slid out and something significantly larger pressed against her opening. Raquel reminded herself to relax, to unclench her tight muscles.

Instead of pushing into her immediately, Taylor teased her. Running the length of her, she gathered her arousal and spread it everywhere. Each taunting pass brought Raquel closer and closer to begging for it.

When Taylor finally slid inside, she'd teased her so long that she slipped in without resistance.

Dropping her head, Raquel cursed. If she wasn't already in love with Taylor, she would have fallen right then. Taylor moved so slowly, so focused on how Raquel stretched and adjusted and moved. So in tune with her. So connected. It was like Taylor could feel what she was feeling, like she knew exactly when to push and when to withdraw.

As soon as Raquel was ready, Taylor gripped her hips and thrust completely inside of her until she felt her flush against the back of her thighs.

"You feel incredible," Taylor said in such a shaky, faraway voice that Raquel almost believed she could feel it.

The illusion was a crush of desire, testing the strength of her trembling thighs. Pushing back against her, Raquel met each move with her own until she was setting the pace.

Raquel curved her back, opening herself up a little more, letting Taylor just that much further in. Perspiration gathered in a thick film over her skin and her knees threatened to give, but Raquel didn't slow down. She meant to give Taylor something unforgettable to take with her, something worth coming back for.

"I want to see you." Taylor's voice was barely above a husky whisper. "I want to kiss you."

The transition to the bed and the shedding of her clothes was as messy as it was fast. When Raquel landed on her back, naked and legs spread apart, desperate for Taylor's return, Taylor didn't let her get far after stuffing a pillow under her ass.

Standing at the foot of the bed, still dressed, Taylor grabbed

Raquel's legs and threw them over her chest. From her sweatpants, Taylor produced a sleek, black toy.

"What is that?" Raquel asked.

Taylor, her face flushed, smirked. "Do you trust me?"

Raquel nodded just as Taylor slid into her again, filling her.

"Use it like a vibrator," Taylor instructed, handing her the toy before taking hold of her thighs with both hands and thrusting deep into her.

Guessing where the hole in the toy went, Raquel positioned it over her clit and turned it on.

"Holy shit," Raquel groaned before an undefinable sensation pulsed over her.

Her eyes slammed shut and her back arched off the bed. With a strangled moan, she tried to hold herself together, but it was impossible. Taylor was angled perfectly inside her while the toy mimicked the sensation of Taylor going down on her. It was too much. She rushed to a powerful climax she could barely hold at bay.

Bending forward, Taylor pressed her chest against Raquel's before she whispered against her ear. "Tell me if I get carried away. I don't want to hurt you."

"Didn't I tell you I would give you anything you wanted?" Raquel drenched her words in dark promises.

Taylor's arms trembled as if holding herself up became infinitely more difficult under the weight of her rhetorical question.

Raquel moistened her lips before digging her nails into the back of Taylor's neck. She was ready to go in for the kill.

In response, Taylor cursed. Pleasure and pain mixing to produce a perfect gasp.

Raquel dug her nails in further, signaling just how hard she'd allow Taylor to go. "Fuck me exactly how you want to fuck me."

Moved nearly to tears, Taylor dropped her forehead onto Raquel's shoulder. For a moment, Raquel expected her to thank her or pass out or actually cry. But she regrouped instead. She looked down at Raquel, her dark eyes blazing with a ferocity she'd never imagined possible.

Then, Taylor kissed her like she owned every inch of her mouth. Taylor was gone before Raquel could wrap her arms around her.

She leaned back again, her brow furrowed and her bottom lip caught between her teeth. Opening Raquel's legs further apart, she gripped the backs of Raquel's knees, her hamstrings stretching as Taylor plunged deep and hard and unrestrained.

Moaning and cursing like she was the one who was about to come, Taylor filled her ears with exquisitely dirty talk.

Raquel lost herself to the unexpected thrill of being dominated. Overwhelmed by having nearly all her senses stimulated at once.

"I'm so close," Raquel managed, her body trembling hard with impending release.

"Me too," Taylor moaned.

Raquel wasn't sure if she was serious, but it was enough for her to lose her grip on her composure. Thrashing, she bucked her hips against Taylor and let go. The orgasm didn't so much happen as it thundered through her. Clasping her hand over her mouth, Raquel had never wanted to release such a guttural cry. It was like something deep and ancient had taken over her body. Something previously untouched had cracked open and rushed out of her.

Aftershocks pulled and pulsed as Raquel eased out of the most intense sensation she'd ever experienced.

Gently dropping her legs, Taylor stayed inside of her as she leaned over.

Raquel cupped her face and pulled her down to her lips. Their sweat mingled as they kissed.

"Fuck. I love you," Taylor confessed breathlessly before she pulled out of Raquel a centimeter at a time.

Raquel was so sensitive that even the slightest movement inside of her robbed her of her voice; made it impossible for her to respond until too many seconds had gone by. Before she had an opportunity to understand Taylor's words and process them, her chance to return the sentiment slipped away. In her haze, she wasn't even sure she'd heard Taylor right.

Taylor's face was still dressed in rapture, her eyes closed and her eyebrows drawn together. She gave no indication that she'd realized what she'd said. No hint that she'd meant it.

Closing her eyes, Raquel felt every single touch of Taylor's lips as she placed light kisses over her chest, her torso, her inner thigh.

When Raquel realized where she was going, she reached down to stop her. "The lube," was all she managed from her dry, raw throat.

"I don't care."

Raquel was still recovering, her body still shuddering and twitching. She didn't think she could handle another second of Taylor's attention. But then she felt her lips grazing softly over her, pressing so lightly against her.

Taylor lavished her with the tenderest touch, easing the aching soreness. Raquel had never done drugs, but she imagined this is what it would feel like; the absolute hijacking of her brain and tingling euphoria on every inch of her body.

When she could open her eyes again, Raquel looked at the woman moving gently between her legs. "Come here."

As soon as Taylor was halfway up her body, Raquel dug her fingers into her sports bra and yanked it off along with her shirt.

"Take off your pants," Raquel instructed, needing more than anything to feel Taylor's naked body completely against hers.

Taylor slipped off the bed and stood to remove the rest of her clothes.

Raquel sat up and shuffled to sit on the end of the bed. She didn't trust her legs to hold her, so she didn't even try to stand.

Before Taylor could remove the strap-on, Raquel took over. She unfastened it slowly, loving the way Taylor's fingers felt in her hair as she kissed all the places the straps had bitten into Taylor's skin.

"You had it on too tight." Raquel pulled off the strap-on and tossed it on the foot of the bed.

Taylor grinned before collapsing onto the bed next to her. "You didn't seem to be complaining a minute ago."

Ignoring her, Raquel kissed the side of Taylor's thigh, running her mouth over her curves. All Taylor needed was a light touch to turn from her side to her back.

"Did you really come?" Raquel asked as she slid between Taylor's parted thighs.

"I was close," she replied softly, as if just knowing Raquel was about to put her mouth on her was enough to drive her crazy. "You looked so fucking incredible. I've never seen you like that."

Raquel grazed Taylor's inner thigh with her lips and then the tip of her tongue. "We've come a long way from magic wands."

Taylor chuckled. "I knew you'd love it."

She pressed a kiss on Taylor's pelvis and then started the trek down Taylor's freshly shaven skin. "It's not nearly as good as watching your head wedged between my thighs."

Taylor moaned a curse before making a fist in the sheets. "It's definitely not as good as feeling you tighten around my tongue."

Raquel ran the tips of her fingers along Taylor's opening and nearly gasped at how shockingly wet she was.

At the slight contact, Taylor cursed, her hips lifting off the mattress. Raquel bit down on her lip. She loved how aroused Taylor always was, how ready. She was sure it wouldn't stay this way forever. At some point, the thrill of being with her was going to have to wane. But today was obviously not that day.

The moment Raquel circled her lips around Taylor, she started to moan.

CHAPTER 47

BUTTERNUT SQUASH SOUP simmered away on the stove while Ramon took his regular afternoon nap. Taylor closed her laptop after submitting a transcript to her supervisor for review. She still had paid time off left, and her boss wasn't rushing her back to work, but she had such long swaths of unused time while Ramon slept. She made use of it by working part-time.

She didn't have enough time to start a new project before Raquel came home, so she found herself perusing the massive bookshelves framing the fireplace.

Near the top, she spotted a familiar leather-bound book. Four of them lined up in chronological order. Dark blue with gold lettering embossed on the spine. She stretched up to reach the one marked *1993*, presumably Raquel's senior year.

Apart from the year, Taylor's yearbooks were identical to the ones on Raquel's shelf. The same austere cover with *Our Lady of Solitude Catholic High School* emblazoned on the front cover.

Taylor took the yearbook with her and plopped on the couch. The first place she found teenage Raquel was playing volleyball. In shockingly tiny black shorts for a Catholic school, Raquel had been immortalized in a moment of raw athleticism. Flying at least a foot above the net, Raquel looked like an Amazon as she spiked the white ball to the opposing team.

Love bloomed like an orb in her chest; glowing and radiating and expanding against her ribs and heart and stomach. It inflated until it was almost too big to fit inside of her.

Taylor traced Raquel's muscled thighs, her flexed calves, her exposed biceps. She laughed at the caption. *Raquel Miguel gives the enemy no quarter.*

That name really is terrible, she thought with a grin. *Raquel Lopez sounds way better than Miguel or Alonso.*

Flipping through the portraits of girls with crimped waves, questionably teased volume, and feathered bangs, she found Raquel.

In her senior portrait, Raquel's brown hair was long and her waves voluminous and crunchy. The black-and-white picture made her expression seem sterner than it was, like she was challenging the person behind the camera to a duel.

Taylor collapsed onto her side like a felled tree. Clutching the yearbook to her chest, she imagined what life would have been like if they'd gone to school together. If they'd known each other a lifetime ago.

She pictured herself with a wavy side-pony, three different color scrunchies in her hair. Visualizing the halls of Solitude in her plaid skirt and white Oxford shirt, she saw herself waiting for Raquel to get out of volleyball practice. Maybe they would hang out with friends or do homework together or make out in the back of somebody's Mustang.

Her stomach fluttered and her skin warmed at the thought of her. Being in her house, in her life, seeing her every day… Taylor had no idea how she was going to go back to being apart.

She'd fallen so hard and so fast, she hadn't noticed the drop. She'd just woken up one day with a lightness in her heart and an inability to think about anything other than Raquel.

Memories from the night before invaded her heart-shaped thoughts. She hadn't meant for the L-bomb to break free from her arsenal and drop on Raquel. The sex had been so shattering; it had trampled the gate and let the truth escape.

No part of Taylor regretted saying it, but she worried that it was too soon for Raquel. Although given that Raquel hadn't had any reaction, she wasn't even sure Raquel had heard her.

Curled up on the couch, Taylor let herself drift away. Let herself indulge in thoughts of Raquel. Let herself pretend that goodbye wasn't stalking them like a hungry jungle cat.

When Raquel came home a little before sunset, Taylor was almost finished preparing the crab meat she was going to arrange on top of the soup like she saw in the picture attached to the online recipe. Ramon was sitting at the kitchen table snapping peas for tomorrow's dinner.

As soon as Raquel walked into the kitchen, Ramon's face brightened. "*Raquelita.*" He extended his arms.

Raquel and Taylor froze. He usually recognized Raquel, but he didn't always call her by name. Especially not at night. As best Taylor could tell, Raquel was no older than a teenager in his mind, and sometimes she was far younger than that.

"How was school?" he asked in Spanish.

Raquel's honey eyes welled up with glistening emotion. She leaned down and embraced her dad before caressing his cheek. The way she looked at him was pure adoration. Complete devotion.

"It was good, *Papi*. How was your day?"

"Oh, very nice. Do you know my friend? I'm showing her how to cook. We've had such a long day. The trip to Santa Clara is always such a hassle."

"Was it?" Raquel's attention drifted to Taylor, who was washing her hands.

"Ramon and I spent a while talking about my trip to Cuba," she explained, though she left out the part when she realized that showing him the pictures she took had been a mistake. When Ramon talked about Cuba, he envisioned a place that hadn't existed for decades. She should've known better than to confuse him with photos. She'd tell

Raquel about it later, but there was no reason to ruin the fledgling joy now.

Dinner was full of delightful conversations about old times Taylor wished she'd experienced firsthand. Raquel did most of the talking, but Ramon obviously enjoyed reminiscing. He'd laughed so hard, he'd nearly choked on his soup.

Every second filled Taylor with a sense of belonging she'd never known… never knew she wanted. It was like a coiled muscle in her chest relaxed for the first time. She didn't want to be anywhere but there. Didn't want to see anything but Raquel making her father laugh. Didn't want to taste anything but the sweetness of their presence.

After the chia seed and coconut pudding dessert that was much better in theory than it was in practice, Ramon gave Taylor a hug before shuffling off with Raquel.

When the kitchen was clean, and Raquel's lunch packed up for the next day, Taylor opened the bottle of red they'd been slowly drinking all week. She poured two modest glasses and started for the living room.

Before she reached the couch, Raquel emerged from Ramon's room.

"Perfect timing." Taylor handed Raquel one of the glasses.

Raquel accepted the glass before curling her arm around Taylor's waist. Her kiss was soft and warm and enveloped Taylor's entire being in affection. They'd never talked about PDA in front of Ramon, but they both instinctively avoided anything more than a kiss on the cheek or a hug.

"What's that doing out here?" Raquel aimed her gaze at the year-book on the end of the couch before sitting at the other end.

Taylor snuggled next to her. Something about being close to Raquel made it easier to breathe.

"I was doing a little light reading." Taylor took a sip of her wine before setting it down on the coffee table. "I can't believe Sister Gloria looked exactly the same. You think she was born eighty and terrifying? Like, can you imagine her as a little girl? She was probably pulling grenade pins with her teeth during the Franco-Prussian War."

When Raquel didn't laugh, Taylor turned to face her. "What's wrong? Something happen at work?"

Something was swimming in Raquel's soft, brown eyes like an unseen monster lurking beneath dark waves, threatening to break the surface and snap its jaws around its prey.

An icy, acidic pit opened at the mouth of Taylor's stomach. Had she heard her confession last night? Had she spent all day brooding on it? Been practicing the best way to let her down gently?

Taylor choked down the threatening nausea while she waited for Raquel to form the words. The words that would break her unprotected heart.

"I'm sorry." Raquel averted her gaze before forcing it back to Taylor. "You've been so amazing." She rested her glass on her thigh and ran her thumb over the stem. "I'm sorry it's been almost three weeks and you haven't seen anything but the inside of this house. You've been so cooped up. You have to be pretty desperate if you're searching the bookshelves for entertainment."

"Oh sweet Jesus." Taylor clutched her chest and keeled over into Raquel's lap as she let the spike in adrenaline work its way out of her system. "You scared the shit out of me."

"Why?"

Taylor shot up, her body still buzzing from the near hit to the chest. "Because it sounded like you wanted to end things, Raquel." Her nerves manifested in a mildly unhinged laugh.

Raquel furrowed her brow. "Why would I be breaking up with you?"

"I don't know." Taylor reached for her wine instead of taking a guess.

"Why don't you go out somewhere? Maybe tomorrow night you can go into town and have a nice meal, take in the sights. Or if you prefer to take a day trip this weekend. Whatever you want, I can—"

"Raquel." Taylor cupped her face to stop her. "I've been all around the world. I've seen the most incredible things." She smiled, running her thumb over Raquel's cheek. "There is nowhere I want to be more than here. With you. With your dad."

"You're going to tire of it." Raquel's voice was low and the hand she placed over Taylor's soft. "This might not be so bad in small bites." Her eyes glistened with emotion. "But this is my life. This is my every day. Every month. Every year. It's never going to be African sand dunes or parasailing over the coast or hiking in Denali."

Taylor put both glasses on the coffee table and focused all of her attention on Raquel. On her trembling lips and glistening eyes. "I know what I'm doing, Raquel. I've spent my entire life doing exactly what I want. Going where I want. Living life on my terms." Emotion bubbled up in her chest. "And that's not going to change any time soon. I want to be here. I want to be with you, and I'm choosing you with eyes wide open. *All* of you."

Raquel's eyes grew larger, her cheeks flushing with color that dripped down her neck. She parted her lips, but instead of speaking, she leaned in and captured Taylor in a deep, lingering kiss.

Raquel didn't confess her feelings, but as she led her upstairs, Taylor was sure she felt them in her kiss, her touch.

CHAPTER 48

"You're cheating again, Ramon." Taylor gave him a long look while suppressing her amusement. The object of the game was to play the best game possible with whatever hand chance dealt.

Ramon pretended not to hear her. He continued to look at each overturned domino tile before selecting the ones he wanted.

Taylor cradled her chin in her hand and propped her elbow on the kitchen table. "I thought we were friends, but this is how you treat me? Even after I ordered you *pastelitos* again? You'd think overnight shipping would earn a little respect."

He started whistling a tune as he lined up his ten tiles on the wooden holder.

"Oh, now you have nothing to say? Very convenient." She leaned in, a smile on her lips. "You're not going to swindle me out of my winnings, Ramon." She glanced at her pile of M&M's, their bargaining chips, the pile that had shrunk significantly since they'd started playing. Ramon was having a very clear day, and he apparently meant to use it to his advantage.

A knock at the door startled Taylor out of her playful teasing. Expecting the delivery guy with Pastry King delights ready to bake in the oven, she hurried toward the door.

"Don't go looking at my tiles," she warned over her shoulder, knowing he was going to peek as soon as she was out of the kitchen.

She was still smiling when she looked through the peephole to make sure it was the delivery driver before opening the door. Her mood dissolved as soon as she saw two women wearing scrubs under their coats standing on the porch.

Taylor's stomach sank, and for a fraction of a second, she considered not opening the door. Considered pretending she hadn't heard it. She and Ramon could've been out on one of their daily walks. They didn't have to be home. It's not like there was a car in the driveway or a ton of lights on.

She yanked open the door before she could talk herself out of it.

The women on the front step smiled. Taylor had never seen Nadia before, but she knew instinctively she was the woman with the dark curls standing in front of the younger woman.

"Hello, my name is Nadia Uribe. I wasn't able to get a hold of Raquel, but I came right here from my doctor's appointment. I'm Ramon's—"

"Hi, yeah." Taylor stepped away to stop blocking the doorway.

Ramon shuffled in behind her and shouted his greetings to Nadia. He didn't know her name, but he was obviously excited to see her.

Nadia's delight at seeing Ramon beamed from her eyes. Warmed by their reunion, Taylor stepped aside and let the women into the house.

"Raquel is teaching for another twenty minutes." Taylor closed the door against the crisp fall morning. "I'll call her as soon as she's out."

Taylor introduced herself to the young aide Nadia had brought along to help while she gave Ramon a very thorough once-over. After Nadia was satisfied he'd been well cared for in her absence, she asked Taylor about his sleeping, his eating, his digestion, and his clarity in a way that was a touch gentler than the Spanish Inquisition.

When Taylor told her about the new routine she'd crafted—and how many brain-stimulating activities she'd incorporated into his day —Nadia nodded with obvious approval.

Ramon invited Nadia into the kitchen and toward the dominos

scattered on the table. Nadia moved through the house with complete and enviable authority. It was obvious she belonged here, and that Ramon was thrilled to see her.

The moment she knew Raquel was done with her class, she called.

"What's wrong?" Raquel said instead of hello.

"Don't worry. Everything is okay." Taylor stood in the living room, her eye on Ramon in the kitchen. Intellectually, she understood that he was safe in Nadia's care, but she was struggling to adapt to the sudden change in their dynamic. "Nadia is here."

"I was about to return her call, but I'm still in the building."

In the background, Taylor heard shuffling and the low murmur of distant conversations.

"She got the all clear to return to work from her doctor and she came right over. She has another nurse from the agency with her until she can do the more physical stuff on her own."

There was a long silence on the other end. It matched the hollow feeling in Taylor's chest. The queasiness in her belly.

"I suppose that means you're relieved of duty." Raquel's tone was flat and emotionless.

Taylor didn't know how to interpret it. Was Raquel as shocked and destabilized by Nadia's sudden presence as she was? She wanted more than anything to know what Raquel was thinking, for her to just speak openly and plainly for once.

"Did you get Raquel on the phone?" After leaving her assistant sitting with Ramon, Nadia barreled toward her. "Do you mind if I talk to her a minute?"

Nadia was taking her phone before Taylor processed her request.

Disoriented, Taylor drifted toward the kitchen like a boat unmoored. With Nadia back, would Raquel expect her to leave tonight? Tomorrow? After the weekend?

CHAPTER 49

DAZED, Raquel sat in her office staring at her computer screen, unable to get her brain to focus on work. She knew this moment was coming, knew that Nadia would be back. And she very much wanted her back.

What she didn't want was for Taylor to leave. There was no way around that fact, so she just accepted it. The last three weeks had been the happiest Raquel could remember. Apart from her father thriving, Raquel loved how intrinsically intertwined the three of them had become. The ritual of meals and walks and coming home to her. Of kissing her goodbye and opening the little notes she slipped into her lunch bag.

Raquel pressed her palm to her chest. She reminded herself that they weren't breaking up. That Taylor was just going back home after a temporary arrangement, but they'd continue to talk to each other every day. There was no reason they couldn't pick up where they left off before this unexpected time together. It wasn't the end.

A pit opened in Raquel's stomach, sending a sickly chill over her skin. The thought of missing Taylor left her empty. She didn't want to miss her. Didn't want to sleep without her. Didn't want to say goodbye.

Dread was pricking the backs of her eyes when a knock at her door startled her out of her misery. Collecting herself, Raquel cleared her throat and sat up straighter in her chair.

"Come in," she called loud enough to be heard through the solid wood.

The door creaked open, revealing a sight that took Raquel a second to process. She hadn't expected Taylor in her doorway, so her brain couldn't place her where it had never seen her before.

"Hi," Taylor said when she poked her head in the doorway.

"Hey." Raquel shot to her feet. "What are you doing here?"

Dressed in a thin, faded gray sweatshirt and jeans, Taylor looked like one of her students. "Sorry. I—"

"No, don't be sorry." Raquel crossed her office in a few long strides. "I'm so glad you're here, I just wasn't expecting you." She pulled Taylor in and closed the door behind her.

Taylor flung her arms around Raquel's neck, locking her in her dark gaze. "Hi," she said again before pulling Raquel down into a kiss.

"Hi," Raquel whispered against her lips. "I missed you."

Despite it only having been a few hours since she left the house, Taylor didn't laugh at her sincere declaration. Instead, she held her tighter and sighed. "I've missed you too."

They lingered near the door, unable to let each other go, until Taylor spoke again. "Sorry for just dropping in on you. I felt kind of in the way at home."

At home. The way she said it lifted Raquel's darkening mood. She liked how it sounded.

"Nadia is kind of a juggernaut." Raquel smirked, understanding the feeling of being displaced.

"Your dad absolutely adores her." Taylor's voice was drenched in melancholy.

Raquel chuckled. "Don't be jealous. He adores you too."

Taylor replied in something of a pout Raquel couldn't help but kiss. The bond Taylor had established with her dad meant more to her than she could ever put into words. In her last few years of dating, she'd merely hoped for someone who understood and accepted that Raquel couldn't show up to a relationship empty-handed, but she never imagined someone wanting to be part of her life. To do more than tolerate her situation. To see her father as a person rather than a burden. It was too good to be true.

"So..." Taylor tucked Raquel's hair behind her ears, jiggling her glasses. "I suppose I'm free for a date this afternoon." She bit her bottom lip in the suggestive way that instantly turned Raquel's thoughts from sweet to devious.

Raquel held her closer, her lips hovering over hers like moths to a flame, dazzled by a beauty worth burning for. "I still have a class to teach this afternoon, Miss Lopez."

Taylor's bright brown eyes ignited with the familiar devilish glint she got every time Raquel called her *Miss Lopez*.

"But Professor, I really need your help." Her voice, low and husky, warmed Raquel's skin before sinking into her chest.

Unable to resist temptation, Raquel closed the gap. With Taylor's lips on hers, Raquel found herself pressed against the front of her desk.

Taylor pushed Raquel's thighs apart with her hips and forced herself between them. Behind Raquel, her pen holder fell over, spilling its contents all over her desk as Taylor pushed her further back.

"I have a class to teach, Miss Lopez," Raquel whispered, while Taylor's mouth found the sensitive part of her neck with her inexorable mouth.

Taylor moaned, her palms sliding down Raquel's back.

Raquel let her linger a moment longer before she pulled away.

Whining, Taylor took a step back; the hunger in her eyes roaring and unsatisfied. If Raquel was sure no one would darken her doorstep for an hour, she'd give Taylor what she wanted—what she wanted too.

"Can I come with you?" Taylor started cleaning up the mess on the desk.

Raquel hopped off the desk and straightened her clothes. "While I teach?"

She wiggled her eyebrows. "I thought we'd established I liked to watch."

"And do you think you can keep the leering to a minimum?"

Taylor gasped. "Leering, Raquel? Really?"

Raquel tipped her head to the side and waited for her to promise to behave.

"I promise to only think about history while you're teaching." She pulled her in and kissed her again.

Slipping her hand in Taylor's, she started for Edward's office, proud to make the introduction. "Let's go before I do something unbecoming of an academic professional. And I want to introduce you to a dear friend before class starts."

CHAPTER 50

NADIA DECIDED to be a superstar and offer to stay through dinner to give Raquel and Taylor a chance to step out and unwind. Despite Taylor's lingering jealousy and how quickly Ramon had dumped her for Nadia, she had to agree they had a lovely connection.

The cool afternoon had turned into a cold evening when they emerged from the house dressed in coats and gloves.

"God, I love this weather. Doesn't it make you so happy we left Florida?" Taylor stood by the passenger door, waiting for Raquel to unlock it. "I feel like no matter what you're wearing underneath, you look so cute and put together as long as you've got a nice coat."

"It's all fun and games until you have to break out the snow blower," she replied with a smirk.

"Don't worry, I'm excellent at clearing snow." Taylor slid into her seat.

Raquel shot her a glance while she turned on the car and cranked up the heat. "You've cleared snow? For your apartment building?"

Taylor flashed her a dimple. "Okay, fine. Theoretically, I'd be excellent at it. And snow blowers look cool as shit." She didn't say that she hoped to be there in the winter, but left the inference lingering in the warming car.

"I'm sure you'd be great at anything you put your mind to," Raquel said before slipping her hand in Taylor's denim-covered lap.

"Oh, God. Don't say it that way. You sound like my elementary school report card." She laughed.

Raquel chuckled before turning onto the street that would lead them through the college campus and out to Main Street. As they passed red brick buildings with smoke coming out of chimneys and colonials with white siding and black shutters framed with maples starting to turn yellow, Taylor relaxed into her seat. She breathed in the moment, let it seep into her muscles and marrow.

Out the window, the terrain changed from spaced out homes to a quaint downtown. The Church Street led to the white church with the storybook steeple where the bus dropped her off a thousand years ago. The strip of low-rise red brick buildings with business names stamped onto awnings. Dreamy things like a bookstore, a cycle shop, a record store, and a place to buy outdoorsy gear.

As they drove on the sparsely populated street, Raquel told her about a tea house opened in 1880 by a pair of sapphic queens living their gay dreams. She loved listening to Raquel talk about the history of things. She always knew the most interesting details.

Raquel parallel parked in the first empty spot they found. "I'm sorry it's a bit of a walk and I'm sure it's nowhere near as good as what you're used to in New York, but—"

Before they got out of the car, Taylor put her hand on Raquel's arm. "It's going to be amazing." She reached over and pulled her into a kiss.

Taylor smiled into their kiss when she realized for the first time that Raquel was nervous.

"What?" Raquel asked when she pulled back.

Illuminated by the dome light, Raquel looked more human than usual. More beautiful than when she was an unattainable fantasy.

"Nothing," Taylor said, trapped in her gaze.

Raquel's eyes narrowed, as if she could divine the truth if she tried to read her face a little harder.

"Have we ever been on a real date?" Taylor asked, instead of pointing out that Raquel was nervous.

Raquel's lip twitched into a momentary smile. "We've been on plenty of dates, haven't we?"

"I don't know... a dinner date? In person? Like an adorably real couple?"

Raquel cupped her face before kissing her again. "If this is the first, then I do hope it is the first of many."

They took their time walking to their destination.

"Are you afraid of running into your students?" Taylor noticed that almost everyone they crossed was barely old enough to vote.

Raquel hooked her arm in Taylor's like a booming declaration. "It's bound to happen. It's a very small town and they recognize me more often than I recognize them."

Taylor laughed. "Oh my God. If I'd seen you strolling around town with a woman, I think I would have dropped dead."

At the end of the block, Taylor stopped at the corner building; a real estate agency with half a dozen printouts advertising rental listings taped to the windows.

"Is this for the whole house?" Taylor pointed to a three-bedroom farmhouse in another town. It wasn't upgraded or new, but it was a whole house on a giant lot. "Get out. I pay more than that for a half a shoebox. How far away is that?"

"Fifteen minutes or so. It's right up the state road. Landlords are competing for college student money. It keeps the prices on rentals low."

Taylor waited for Raquel to say more. To broach the subject of her moving to Vermont, but she continued to peruse the listings silently instead.

"This must be so cute during the holidays," Taylor said when they started walking again.

Raquel nodded. "Lights and garlands and wreaths and bows as far as the eye can see. Santa even comes down Main Street on a sled pulled by Clydesdales. It almost always snows on Christmas, so it's very dramatic."

Taylor breathed in a lungful of the cold night air as she pictured it. "I can't imagine what it must be like to grow up in a place like this. Not like Miami or New York." She gripped Raquel's arm more tightly. "All these traditions that everyone shares. It makes it feel like a real home. Not a place to visit or somewhere overrun with tourists. It's just so authentically itself."

"Every place has its own vibration. Isn't that what you told me about your travels?" Raquel slowed her pace to a lazy stroll.

"It's true. And you know, I used to think traveling was about soaking up all these experiences, but I don't know. Lately I've been wondering if it's about not wanting to sit still. Like I've kinda been searching for something without realizing it. Like my life has been an unwitting pilgrimage." She sighed. "I don't know. That sounds stupid."

"It's not stupid. I felt kind of like that when I finally moved away from Miami. Before I found this little town, it was like I'd been stuck playing a role in someone else's movie. I was the supporting character to my parents and then Max, and it's not that I was unhappy, but I didn't have anything of my own. I had never had a home of my choosing. A life I got to pick. Not until I landed in Lockwood."

"And you still feel that way? Even when you didn't expect to be taking care of your dad here when you planned out your new life?"

"I wouldn't change a thing."

Taylor laid down a more aggressive hint. "Nothing? You wouldn't change anything?"

Raquel stopped short of walking into the Indian restaurant named *Desilicious* and held her in her gaze. Taylor could feel her holding back; knew so certainly that she wanted to say more.

Ask me to stay, she screamed in her head, but all Raquel did was kiss her cheek and lead her into the restaurant.

CHAPTER 51

DINNER HAD NOT GONE like Raquel expected. When they'd left the house, they'd been excited, almost giddy, but it didn't take long for the looming goodbye to blanket them in a thick, gray fog.

Taylor hadn't said a word during the drive back home. She'd just stared out the window, looking small and so unlike herself.

After checking in on her dad, who was happily snoring, Raquel chatted with Nadia for a while. Taylor stayed with them for a few minutes, just long enough to be polite, before excusing herself and disappearing.

When Raquel locked the front door behind Nadia and joined Taylor upstairs, she wasn't sure what she'd find. Would she be packing already? Would she have already booked her ticket home? The possibility made the spicy chicken korma churn in her stomach.

Holding her breath, Raquel peeked through her open bedroom door as she reached the top of the stairs. Taylor was stretched out across the foot of the bed and staring into her phone. She wasn't packing, which was a small comfort, but she hadn't changed out of her jeans and sweater either. The acidic pit in Raquel's stomach widened far enough to swallow dinosaurs.

Unsure of what to say, Raquel went to the bathroom to start

removing her makeup. She was finished and on to brushing her teeth when Taylor slipped in behind her.

The sensation of Taylor wrapping her arms around her waist and resting her cheek on her shoulder snapped the vice tightening her chest. Raquel rinsed her mouth and tossed the toothbrush in the holder.

"I don't want to go," Taylor said so softly, her words barely reached Raquel.

Closing her eyes, Raquel clasped her arms around Taylor's arms. She stopped worrying about the implications, the future, the risks, the fear that her life would be too much for Taylor. That one day she would realize that and leave her heartbroken.

Wrestling away the doubt, Raquel spun in her arms. Holding Taylor in her gaze, she leaped. "I don't want you to leave."

The cloud that had followed them home lifted from Taylor, her eyes brightening. "Yeah?"

Raquel nodded.

"You want me to stay a few more days?"

Running her fingers through Taylor's soft hair, Raquel smiled. "I want you to stay as long as you like."

Taylor searched her face, digging for more. "A week?"

"Sure."

"A month?"

"As long as you want."

"Well…" Taylor grinned. "What if I don't want to go back to New York at all?"

Raquel's hammering heart neared the point of combustion. She didn't try to stop her smile from widening. "Then we'll need to work on converting the attic to your office right away."

Taylor threw her arms around Raquel's neck. "Yeah? Just like that?"

"Or we could wait until your lease is up in the city. Make careful plans. Take our time."

"Or I could put Robbie out of her misery and ask her if she wants to break the lease." Taylor laughed, her excitement scaring away Raquel's fears. "We have like six months left, so even with the penalty, it's cheaper than her pretending to live there. She's basically paying a shit ton of money for a closet in the Bronx when she's really living in Jersey City."

"How much is the penalty?"

"If Robbie and I split it, it comes out to a month's rent each. Plus, we lose our deposit. I'm sure Bellamy will be more than happy to take that hit not to have to commute to the city a few times a month to make use of the apartment. It's been time for us to move on. I know Robbie's been holding on as my roommate for my benefit more than hers."

Raquel would be more than happy to pay Taylor's penalty for her and help her move. "And Philip?"

Taylor's shoulders dropped. "My little guy. I'm going to miss him like crazy, but I can't take him away from his soulmate."

"You're probably the least selfish person I've ever met." Love bloomed hard in Raquel's chest.

"Nah. It's just the right thing to do." She shrugged. "Anyone would do the same thing."

Raquel disagreed, but she let it go.

"So... are we really doing this, or is this just wishful thinking because we're sad that I'm leaving?"

Raquel leaned against the vanity and pulled Taylor in close. "I want you to stay, but only if you want to. And there is no rush. I don't want you to make an impulsive decision you later regret. I don't want to move too fast. Living together is a lot, and if you're not ready, I completely understand. This isn't a particularly exciting place to live, and with my dad and everything..."

The more Raquel heard herself speak, the more confident she was that Taylor would decline. That she wouldn't want to trade her freedom for a quiet life in a rural college town where they were limited by Raquel's responsibilities.

Taylor held her gaze as if there was so much she wanted to say, like her words failed to capture her emotions. Raquel knew that feeling so well.

"I've always had this restlessness in me." The emotion in Taylor's voice instantly made Raquel well up. "And I think it took me less than a day here to realize you're the home I've been looking for."

If Raquel hadn't been resting her weight against the counter, her legs might have failed her when her knees weakened. There was no skirting around it anymore. No reason not to name the thing surging in her chest.

"I love you," Raquel whispered and watched the confession change Taylor's expression like bright paint on a brand-new canvas. "I think I've loved you since before we left Miami."

"I can't even remember a time I didn't love you. This feeling is so big, it's gone back in time and colored my memories."

Propelled by the enormity of their declarations, Raquel closed the gap and kissed Taylor like she'd never tasted her before. Like they'd been kissing all their lives. Like they'd never known anyone else.

ONE YEAR LATER

TAYLOR'S second Christmas in Lockwood was as magical as her first. Raquel hadn't been exaggerating when she said the town went all out for the holidays. Even Mother Nature had gotten in on the fun and blanketed the town with just enough snow to give the landscape a wholesome postcard aesthetic.

Driving her used pickup truck, Taylor pulled up to the converted barn, decked out for Christmas, at the end of Main Street. She parked next to the mound of snow that had been plowed out of the lot. She wasn't meeting Raquel for an early lunch for another hour yet, but she had a few things to set up before her arrival.

Using the back door, Taylor made her third trip into the tea house in half as many hours. Getting the entire place to themselves had been much easier than Taylor expected. They were the tea house's most loyal and regular customers. As soon as she told the owner what she planned to do, she agreed to let Taylor use the space before the lunch rush. She agreed there was no better way to honor the original founders of the place than to have two ladies get engaged in the dining room.

In the kitchen, the locally sourced, farm-to-table fare was being prepared. The fresh ginger being grated for the golden beet and carrot bisque hit her first, followed by the heavenly scent of roasting black garlic potatoes.

The dining room honored the original tea house. With its rich wood paneling and scattered round tables and handcrafted wooden chairs, the space radiated warmth. The focal point was a massive stone fireplace that had no trouble heating the entire room.

Taylor made tiny adjustments to the dozens of ruffled white peony-like Camellia flowers she'd arranged in a bunch of small vases around the fireplace. The stark white flowers were surrounded with mason jars full of fairy lights. Taylor hoped it would add to the ethereal vibe she was trying to create.

She stared at the pillars of cream-colored candles she'd scattered around the fireplace and decided that while it was close to being too much, it wasn't quite there.

Pulling out her portable speaker, Taylor cued up the playlist she'd been curating for weeks; acoustic guitar versions of some of Raquel's favorite songs.

A raw and unexpectedly moving version of Eternal Flame had just started when someone from the kitchen shouted that Raquel had pulled into the lot.

A pang of anxiety and excitement and naked terror rocked Taylor's stomach. Rubbing her sweating palms down the front of her jeans, Taylor tried to keep calm. They'd talked about getting married before. It's not like she was springing it on her. She was surprising her, but it would be a welcomed surprise. She hoped.

Reminding herself to breathe instead of pant, Taylor rushed to the front door and prepared to greet Raquel. In her pocket, she felt for the modest solitaire engagement ring she'd purchased a month ago. The one she was hoping Raquel would love.

Taylor shook out her hands and hopped in placed to work out the nerves replicating faster than she could absorb. A sudden panic made her empty stomach churn.

What if she says no? What if she thinks this is too soon? Or what if, when faced with the prospect of getting married again, when it's real instead of just dreamy conversations in bed, she realizes she doesn't want to risk it? Maybe she doesn't want things to change?

Taylor's thoughts were a runaway train heading straight for the side of a mountain.

When Raquel walked through the front door, Taylor nearly puked from the pent-up terror squeezing her guts.

Behind her wide-rimmed black glasses, Raquel's gaze darted around the room. In an instant, she noticed they were the only ones there. It probably only took another second to clock the flowers and candles and music that now felt like too much.

I should have done something simple at home. This was such a mistake. Oh, God. Why did I plan this like this?

"What's going on?" Raquel furrowed her brow, but her cheeks were turning pink and her lips were twitching into a hesitant smile.

Okay, okay. A smile. She's not running away screaming.

"Nothing's going on." Taylor's voice was too shaky to sell the lie. "Kat is making the most delicious lunch."

"Okay," Raquel replied with open suspicion before leaning in and giving Taylor a quick kiss.

The contact with Raquel's lips helped settle Taylor's extreme nerves.

"And lunch is just for us?" Raquel's eyes gave away that she'd probably put together exactly what Taylor had up her sleeve.

With Taylor Swift's *Lover* floating toward them from behind a bouquet of white flowers, they started toward the table nearest the fireplace. The one adorned with flowers and candles.

Before they sat, Taylor interlaced her fingers with Raquel's and tried to talk around the heart hammering in her throat.

"I don't know how many people's lives are changed in an airport, much less LaGuardia."

Taylor's nervous laugh was met with Raquel's widening smile. In an effort to comfort her, Raquel took both of Taylor's quivering hands in hers.

"But that's what happened." Taylor heaved a steadying breath as her stomach tightened. "The moment I saw you sitting in that airport bar, I knew somewhere deep in my soul my life would never be the same. Every day since has only confirmed my suspicion that it was no accident we ran into each other. That we had a chance to meet again, or maybe meet for the first time. From that first conversation over arguably the worst and most overpriced food I've ever eaten."

Taylor laughed to counteract the emotion blurring her vision.

"It was pretty horrific," Raquel agreed, her voice trembling.

"Every moment we have spent together since that first day has been my favorite. I could never have imagined finding someone like you. Someone who is so loving and kind and devoted and strong and smart, and I would be so lucky to spend the rest of my life with you."

Taylor let go of Raquel's hand to retrieve the ring in her pocket. She held it in front of Raquel, whose eyes had gone wide.

"I've spent so long looking for adventure that I didn't realize life itself is the greatest unknown. It has so many different stages and impossible to predict turns, and that's what I want to experience with you. I want to take every leap with you. Every plunge." She swallowed hard before holding Raquel's watery gaze in hers. "Will you marry me?"

Raquel cried and laughed and pulled Taylor into a shaky kiss.

"You have brought so much beauty into my life. You have been a source of light I never imagined existed. There hasn't been a day since we met that you haven't made me laugh. You are joy and love and—" Raquel's expression broke into raw emotion. Taylor cupped her face, holding her close. "Taylor, there is nothing I'd rather do than spend the rest of my life with you. To make you feel special and loved."

Relief poured out of Taylor, leaving her a teary, unsteady mess. "I love you so much."

Raquel wrapped herself around Taylor and kissed her deeply. Kissed her until the staff popped their heads in from the kitchen and started clapping for them. Kissed her until the cork flew off the bottle and they toasted to the rest of their lives.

READY FOR THE MORE? Sign up to my newsletter to get the bonus epilogue and attend the wedding! https://www.jjarias.com/

WEDDING INVITE!

Did you miss your invitation to the wedding? It's not too late! Click the link or go to www.jjarias.com and sign up to my mailing list to attend!

ABOUT THE AUTHOR

I am an independent author writing about fictional lesbians of all varieties. I am a Scorpio woman (I know, I know, but I'm a nice one I PROMISE) happily married to a uniquely wonderful Cancer lady. Together we have several fur babies of the feline and canine varieties.

Printed in Great Britain
by Amazon

25468421R00169